LOVE, LIES & MUSIC 2:

The Next Verse!

Midnight Storm

Copyright © 2024 by Midnight Storm

All rights reserved. No part of this publication may be reproduced, distributed, or transmitted in any form or by any means, including photocopying, recording, or other electronic or mechanical methods, without the prior written permission of the publisher, except in the case of brief quotations embodied in critical reviews and certain other noncommercial uses permitted by copyright law. For permission requests, email the publisher:

Attention: Permissions Coordinator
Welcome To The Storm Publishing!
info@midnightstorm.net
www.midnightstorm.net

Ordering Information:
Quantity sales. Special discounts available on quantity purchases by corporations, associations, and others. For details, contact the publisher at the email address above.

Library of Congress Control Number: 2024916390

Orders by U.S. trade bookstores and wholesalers.

ISBN: 979-8-9914117-1-4

Book Cover Design: KL Harris of Gifft Grafix
First Printed Edition: October 2024
Printed in the United States of America

In a world of love, lies, and betrayal,
can three hearts find love through music?

JUNIPER, LORENZO, AND KAI JAE

Dedication

This book is dedicated to my dear Aunt Patrica "Pat" Bolar, my second mom. Your absence is deeply felt, and you are missed more than words can express. Thank you for the unwavering strength, wisdom, and guidance you shared with me. Your light continues to inspire and guide us from above.

Table of Contents

CHAPTER 1: KAI JAE 1

CHAPTER 2: JUNIPER 15

CHAPTER 3: LORENZO 21

CHAPTER 4: KAI JAE 36

CHAPTER 5: LORENZO 45

CHAPTER 6: KAI JAE 52

CHAPTER 7: KAI JAE 62

CHAPTER 8: JUNIPER 68

CHAPTER 9: KAI JAE 77

CHAPTER 10: JUNIPER 82

CHAPTER 11: KAI JAE 90

CHAPTER 12: LORENZO 97

CHAPTER 13: JUNIPER 109

CHAPTER 14: LORENZO 113

CHAPTER 15: JUNIPER 117

CHAPTER 16: JUNIPER 131

CHAPTER 17: LORENZO 136

CHAPTER 18: KAI JAE 153

CHAPTER 19: JUNIPER 159

CHAPTER 20: KAI JAE 168

CHAPTER 21: KAI JAE 177

CHAPTER 22: JUNIPER 189

CHAPTER 23: KAI JAE 196

CHAPTER 24: JUNIPER 202

CHAPTER 25: LORENZO 212

CHAPTER 26: KAI JAE 218

CHAPTER 27: JUNIPER 225

CHAPTER 28: KAI JAE 233

CHAPTER 29: JUNIPER 240

CHAPTER 30: KAI JAE 243

CHAPTER 31: JUNIPER 259

LOVE, LIES & MUSIC 3: COMING FALL 2025

CHAPTER 1: LACI 264

CHAPTER 2: SPEX 269

CHAPTER 3: KAI JAE 277

ACKNOWLEDGMENTS 286

ABOUT THE AUTHOR 288

Chapter 1

KAI JAE

"Kiss me right here, baby," I said to DJ Spex, a celebrity DJ and radio announcer for Slim Shady Radio on Sirius XM. In fact, he was one of the hottest DJs in L.A. and the Inland Empire. With his two million Instagram followers and one million TikTok fans, he had the social media power to make any music career soar. Not only that, but he had a freaky sex drive and a love for role-playing, and I was more than happy to oblige.

I climbed off of my weekend lover and gobbled up a few marijuana gummies while he caught his breath. I grabbed a bottled water from the mini-fridge and stood in front of him. He watched me chug the entire sixteen ounces without stopping. We had just finished a wild round of hot, steamy, amazing sex, and I needed that fresh H_2O to get ready for our next round. Dressing up as a black kitty-cat and purring for him was fun, but it was also exhausting.

I think he enjoyed my Halle Berry Catwoman rendition. I did what he asked and wore it for him while allowing him to tame my kitty. We had rented the presidential suite at the Omni in Riverside, California for the weekend. Spex had agreed to host my show for free, so I had to show him how much I appreciated it.

The man was tall, about six-one, not small in stature. Rather, he was 240 pounds of pure muscle wrapped in milk chocolate, silky skin. His six-pack abs were sculpted to perfection, like a work of art that hinted at the power beneath his smooth exterior. His mesmerizing brown eyes always held a glint of bad boy, and I loved the way his beard and mustache were meticulously trimmed, framing his chiseled jawline with precision. He was always impeccably groomed, and his clothes fit like they were tailor-made to accentuate his athletic build and undeniable swag. Every time Spex walked into a room, he owned it, exuding a magnetic confidence and leaving in his wake a scented trail of his signature cologne that lingered in the air. His style was on point, effortlessly blending casual cool with sophisticated elegance. The way he carried himself, with that easy swagger and a grin that could melt hearts, made him the center of attention wherever he went. His laughter was deep and infectious, his smile dazzling and genuine, capable of illuminating even the darkest room.

When Spex spoke, his deep, smooth voice commanded attention, leaving everyone hanging on every word. He had a natural charisma and charm that was simply irresistible, a perfect blend of confidence and approachability. Whether he was cracking a joke, sharing a story, or simply engaging in conversation, he did it all with a flair that was uniquely his own.

"You ready for Round Two, pretty, pretty?" Spex asked, sitting on the bed, and stroking his hard dick.

"Always ready for you, baby," I said, purring and crawling back to him like the black kitty he craved for.

"C'mon, babe. Go drink from the bowl on the floor for Daddy," Spex said, pointing to the pink and blue dish I'd brought with me.

I crawled to the bowl I'd placed alcoholic lemon drops in earlier, feeling the anticipation build in my chest as Spex instructed me. The MALINERO feather tickler whip lightly stung my ass as I obediently lapped up alcohol from the bowl, the sensations mixing with the thrill of submission. Spex's dominance over me fueled a fire within, igniting my desire for more.

As Spex approached me, whip in hand, I groaned with pleasure when his light spanks sent stinging shivers down my spine. His touch was both gentle and commanding, a mixture that sent me into a frenzy of desire.

I felt his hot breath against my skin as he knelt behind me, his tongue tracing delicious patterns along my pussy, sending waves of pleasure through me. The sensation of his tongue against my skin, combined with the alcohol swirling in my system, hurled me to the edge of ecstasy.

When he stopped, I wasted no time in straddling his face. I loved feeling the wetness between my thighs drip onto his waiting mouth, and I gasped as he greedily lapped at me just like I had lapped from the bowl, his tongue driving me wild with pleasure.

With my hands pressed against the walls for support, I surrendered to the delicious sensations coursing through me, moaning with absolute pleasure as Spex expertly brought me to the brink of release. The bondage toys and the feather tickler whip only added an extra layer of excitement, intensifying the pleasure to new heights.

As Spex flipped me onto the floor and thrust himself inside me, I welcomed him eagerly, my body responding to his every movement with a desperate hunger. I arched my back and dug my nails into the soft carpet as he drove into me with a relentless need that mirrored my own.

In a wild frenzy of passion, I felt the pressure building deep within me, ready to explode. When it finally did, I released a torrent of pleasure, squirting and gushing over him in a primal display of raw desire. The room filled with the intoxicating aroma of our intimacy, a reminder of the intense connection we shared in those moments of blissful abandon. The lovemaking rounds repeated for the remainder of the night, until we were both exhausted and high on the gummies and the intensity of our passion.

When it came to the bedroom, Spex was the best I'd ever had. The way he caressed me while we sexed each other was intoxicating. Every touch, every kiss, was electrifying. He knew exactly how to make my body sing. He had a way of making me lose control, of pushing me to the edge, then pulling me back just when I thought I couldn't take any more.

He loved to make me scream and beg for him to stop, his eyes glowing with desire as he watched me orgasm. The way he took charge, the way he made me feel completely possessed, was unlike anything I'd ever experienced. He thrived on my pleasure, on my cries of ecstasy, on the way my body responded to his every touch. I loved riding him reverse cowgirl, feeling his hard dick fill me up as I bounced up and down. His hands gripped my hips, guiding me, controlling me, while driving me wild. The sight of him beneath me, with those dark, alluring eyes half-closed in pleasure, was enough to send even more shivers down my spine. I loved the way he moaned my name, the way his hands roamed my body, the way he made me feel like the most desired woman in the world.

One night, he tied me up in the sex swing, suspending my body in the air and leaving me completely at his mercy. He teased me with the vibrating rabbit, sending waves of pleasure through me. He took his time to let the intensity build up inside me, bringing me closer and closer to the edge until I had to beg him to stop. When he finally entered me, it was like an explosion of pleasure, every nerve in my body igniting with bliss. He loved to push me to my limits, to see how far he could take me, and I loved every second of it. With Spex, I felt alive, desired, even worshiped. He knew my body better than anyone ever had, and he took pleasure in making me lose control. Every touch, every kiss, every thrust was a symphony of pleasure, and I couldn't get enough.

Things had been going well for me on the music scene. I was excited to be working with MUSIC4LIFE Records, managed by a dope-ass producer name Lorenzo Ryan. As an R&B artist, competing with other females in the industry was no easy feat, so I always had to be on my A game. That meant doing whatever I needed to do to get a spin or two.

A smash here and there helped my new single, "Give it to Me," chart on the top 100 at Number 8. It was written by Juniper Alexander, Lorenzo's girl, and I was thrilled to show up on the same chart with artists like Cardi B and Drake.

My chance encounter with Spex happened one morning at a studio session with Lorenzo. Just as I arrived, ready to dive into the day's work, the famed DJ walked in. His confident demeanor and effortless charm immediately commanded attention. I recognized him instantly, having seen his popularity explode on social media. He moved through the room with a natural ease, exuding a charm that was impossible to ignore. As he greeted everyone with that trademark warm smile and firm handshake, I couldn't help but be drawn to him. It was as if he had a spotlight on him wherever he went, and it was easy to see why so many people were captivated by his online persona. His reputation preceded him, and seeing him in person, I understood why he had such a massive following.

We exchanged introductions, and I was struck by how approachable and down-to-earth he was, despite his fame. His voice was smooth and engaging, and his laughter resonated through the studio, setting a positive tone for the day. Spex wasn't just a social media star;

he was a presence, someone who could effortlessly command a room and make everyone feel at ease. That morning marked the beginning of an unforgettable connection, one that went far beyond the digital world.

As the session wrapped up, Spex offered to walk me to my car. "Yo, Ren, I'm heading out too. Mind if I walk your artist to her car?" he asked, his tone polite and genuine.

Lorenzo made it a rule to see everyone off safely, no matter their gender, and he answered, "Thanks, man. I need to talk to T for a few anyway. I'll catch up with you later, Kai."

As we made our way out of the studio, Spex's attention remained on his phone. Even in the elevator, his focus didn't waver until we reached the basement floor of the parking lot, where he finally placed his phone in his pocket.

"This you?" he inquired, gesturing toward my black Mercedes Benz 2024 GLB 250, dazzling with its red interior and panoramic roof.

"Yup, this me," I confirmed, with some pride evident in my voice. "A little somethin'-somethin' I bought myself upon moving to the City of Angels."

"Nice ride. Where are you from, by the way?" Spex inquired, his curiosity piqued.

"Not one to beat around the bush, huh?" I teased. "I'm from Detroit, born and raised, 8 Mile Road."

"Ah, a Detroiter," Spex remarked, seemingly even more interested. "What's life like in Detroit?"

"Shit, survival mode. Why you think I moved here?"

"Hmm. I'd like the rundown on why, so how about we swap numbers?" he suggested, reaching for my phone with a smile.

Also eager to continue our conversation beyond the parking lot, I allowed him to key his digits into my phone.

"I'll text you my number, so add me," I said as he watched me get into my car. A few seconds later, just before I drove off, I sent the promised text.

Later that evening, I received a message: "Yo, pretty, how are you?"

I smiled when I saw it, amused by his choice of words. "You sure you meant to text *me*? I think Pretty may be the name of your babe," I teased.

"Naw, I'm single…but *you* can be my babe," he replied, adding a laughing emoji.

Chuckling to myself, I tapped out my response, which I punctuated with a winking emoji of my own: "Smooth talker, huh?"

In the course of our text conversation, we learned a lot about each other. Spex shared fascinating stories about his passion for music, recounting his adventures traveling the world as a DJ. His experiences seemed to unfold like vibrant scenes in my mind, each tale adding depth to his personality. In return, I found myself opening up about my career aspirations and my own deep connection to music. It was refreshing to connect on such a meaningful level, revealing more about ourselves with each message and creating a bond that felt both natural and exciting.

Four months later, we were sexing like wild rabbits. We had rules: it was always no strings attached and a professional relationship in the music streets. Those rules ironically gave us a lot of freedom, allowed us to be as freaky as we wanted with each other without judgment. From day one, Spex had brought the freaky side out of me. I loved everything he did to my body, the way he made my head swim. I'd never dabbled in bondage before we met, but it wasn't long before I was really into it. After he introduced me to it, I found myself buying all kinds of freaky clothes and toys. I was Spex's little freak, and he was mine.

One night, after a particularly intense session, I lay beside him, our bodies glistening with sweat. "You know, you're spoiling me," I said, tracing a finger along his chiseled chest. "No one else will ever measure up to this."

He chuckled, pulling me closer. "Good. I like knowing you're all mine when we're together."

I sighed happily as I rested my head on his shoulder. "How do you keep up with it all?"

"With what? With you?"

"No, silly!" I said, playfully smacking his bicep. "With the fame, the fans, the constant demand…"

Spex shrugged, and I noticed a mischievous glint in his eye. "I have my ways. Plus, having someone like you to unwind with helps a lot."

I smiled as a surge of affection came over me for the complex, driven man. Our arrangement might have been unconventional, but it worked for us. I appreciated the freedom it gave me to focus on my own music career without the complications of a traditional commitment. It was all of the benefits with none of the handcuffs, except for the ones we actually enjoyed using in the bedroom.

As I lay there, my mind drifted to the upcoming weeks. With my single climbing the charts and more studio sessions lined up with Lorenzo, my schedule was about to get even more hectic. But for that moment, I was exactly where I wanted to be—wrapped up in the arms of the man who made everything else fade away.

The next day, I awoke early. I had a meeting with Lorenzo to discuss my next steps and potential collaborations, so I left Spex sleeping soundly in the bed. As I got ready for the day, I couldn't help but feel a sense of excitement. My career was on the rise, but I knew I had to remain focused and determined if I was going to keep up that momentum.

I slipped into a sleek black dress that hugged my curves, knowing it would make a statement at the meeting. After a quick glance in the mirror, I smiled, satisfied with my reflection. I grabbed my keys and left quietly, so as not to wake my sleeping lover.

The drive to the studio was smooth, with surprisingly light L.A. traffic. As I pulled into the parking lot, I spotted Lorenzo's car. I took a deep breath, gathered my thoughts, and headed inside.

Lorenzo greeted me with a warm smile as soon as I walked into the studio. "Kai, look at you glowing, girl! Something good must have happened last night."

I chuckled and gave him a little shrug and a playful wink. "Let's just say I had a great time…unwinding."

Lorenzo shook his head and laughed. "Whatever keeps you happy and focused, I guess. Ready to get down to business?"

"Absolutely," I replied as I took a seat across from him. "What's on the agenda?"

"We've got a few things to go over," Lorenzo said, sliding a folder toward me. "First, I want to talk about your next single. We need something that will keep your momentum going."

I opened the folder and skimmed the list of song options he had compiled. Each track had potential, but one in particular caught my eye. "What about this one?" I asked, pointing to "Freak Like Me."

Lorenzo raised an eyebrow. "Hmm. Definitely a bold choice. It's got that edgy vibe that suits you, but are you sure you want to go that route?"

I nodded, feeling a surge of confidence. "Absolutely. I want to push boundaries and show people a side of me they haven't seen before."

Lorenzo chuckled. "I see you, ma. Fair enough. We'll start working on it right away. I'll contact Monique. She's a beast with vocal production."

As we continued to discuss logistics, my phone buzzed with a text from Spex. "Miss me already?" the message read, followed by a heart emoji.

I couldn't help but smile as I quickly typed out a response: "Always. Just getting started on some new music. Can't wait to share it with you."

By the time our meeting wrapped up, I felt energized and ready to tackle whatever came next. Lorenzo lined up a few high-profile collaborations, and we planned a mini tour to promote my current single. Things were moving fast, but I was ready for the ride.

Later that night, I met Spex at a trendy L.A. bar. The place was buzzing with energy, filled with the city elite.

Spex spotted me as soon as I walked in, his eyes lighting up with appreciation. "Damn, girl, you clean up nice," he said before pulling me in for a kiss.

"Kissing me in public? This is new. And you don't look so bad yourself," I replied, running my fingers through his neatly trimmed beard. "Ready to celebrate?"

"Hell, yeah!" he said before leading me to a private VIP area. "Tonight's all about you, Kai. You deserve it."

We spent the evening sipping cocktails and dancing. The chemistry between us was undeniable. The VIP section he reserved was just for the two of us. It felt good to let loose and enjoy the moment together. We had something special, and we both knew it, even if it was unconventional. While dancing, Spex continually grabbed my ass, making me wet. I wanted him so badly. I felt his hardness on my stomach, and I wanted it all between my legs. Spex planted juicy, delicious kisses all over my neck, my face, and my lips.

The music pounded through the speakers, making the floor vibrate beneath us. We were lost in our own world. Every touch from Spex sent a jolt of electricity through me. I could feel the heat rising between us, a physical tension that promised more.

"I can't take it anymore," I whispered into his ear, my breath hot against his skin. "Let's get out of here."

He grinned, with a naughty sparkle in his eyes. "I was hoping you'd say that."

We quickly made our way through the crowd, his hand firmly gripping mine. When we finally burst through the doors and into the cool night air, the electricity of the city cast a glow around us. Spex ordered an Uber Black, and soon, a sleek, luxurious black car pulled up, its polished exterior reflecting the city lights. The interior of the vehicle was just as impressive, with plush leather seats and a sophisticated ambiance that spoke of elegance. A bottle of chilled wine awaited us, adding a touch of indulgence to our evening. The ride to his place was a blur of tongue-kissing and whispered sexual talk.

Once we dreamily climbed out of the car and inside the building, we were unable to keep our hands off each other. The passion between us was electric, each collision of his fingers against me sending shivers down my spine. He knew exactly how to get me wet with just the touch of his hands on my ass.

"I wanna kiss all over your soft body," he announced.

"So, show me," I challenged, pulling him down for another kiss.

Spex took his time, exploring every inch of me with his hands and mouth. The sensation was nearly too much to bear, but I didn't want it to end. I arched my back, pressing myself closer to him, needing to feel every part of him.

Finally, he positioned himself above me, and I felt him enter me, filling me completely. We moved together, our bodies in perfect sync. It was intense, raw, and everything I had ever wanted. The world outside ceased to exist; it was just the two of us, lost in our own ecstasy.

"You wanna be my prisoner tonight?" he asked, pulling the pink, fluffy handcuffs from the drawer as a playful grin spreading across his face.

"Yeah, I've been a bad girl, Officer," I replied, biting my lip as I met his gaze.

Spex gently snapped the naughty cuffs around my wrists, and the soft fur brushed against my skin. He moved closer, till his lips found mine again in a slow, teasing kiss. Light and neon from the cityscape flickered through the window, casting a soft glow and dancing shadows across the room. His hands roamed my body, sending another tidal wave of electric shivers through me.

I moaned, a mix of protest and desire, as his kisses trailed down my neck. "Stop," I whimpered, but my body betrayed me, bending toward him, craving more. His small bites on my inner thighs drove me wild, a perfect blend of pleasure and pain. His fingers slipped inside me, expertly teasing, making me yearn for more.

My back arched off the bed, my body trembling as he skillfully brought me closer and closer to the edge. Each movement was deliberate, pushing me further until I couldn't hold back anymore. I cried out, overwhelmed by the sensations storming through my mind and body, and I squirted all over his face.

He looked up, his eyes dark with desire, and licked his lips. "Damn, you taste so good," he murmured, "but we aren't done yet."

Next, he released the cuffs from the bedframe but kept them on my wrists as he guided me upward. His hands moved over my body, exploring and caressing, as he whispered dirty promises in my ear. The sounds of the city outside seemed to fade away, leaving lost in our own world once again. He positioned me at the edge of the bed with my knees on the floor, my hands still bound. His fingers traced down my back, sending me into shivers. The anticipation was electric, every nerve ending on fire.

"Ready for more, bad girl?" he asked, his voice low and commanding.

"Yes, Officer," I breathed, my heart racing.

With a wicked grin, he entered me slowly. The sensation was as intense as it was overwhelming. He moved with a steady rhythm, each thrust deep and powerful. My senses were alight, every touch sending waves of pleasure through me. His hand reached around and instinctively found my most sensitive spot once more, and I lost myself in the ecstasy. We moved together, a perfect dance of give and take, until I was crying out his name, my body consumed by another mind-blowing orgasm.

Afterward, we lay breathless together, exhausted and content.

He kissed my forehead softly. "I'm going to let you go on a warning," he teased, releasing the handcuffs.

I smiled, snuggling closer. "Thank you," I replied, warmed by a deep sense of satisfaction and connection.

"Ya know," Spex said, tracing circles on my skin, "I've been thinking."

"About what?" I asked as I sat up and arched a curious brow at him.

"About us, what we have. I know we agreed it would just be sex, but… Well, damn it, Kai, you've got me hooked."

I looked into his eyes, surprised by his words. "Spex, you mean a lot to me, too, but you know how crazy my life is right now. I don't want to mess this up by complicating things."

He sighed and nodded. "I get it. I just… I don't want to lose what we have. I mean, girl, your deep throat game is *on*," he said, then laughed.

"Fuck you, Spex," I said before I playfully hit him in the chest. "We won't lose it," I promised, leaning in to kiss him softly. "We'll figure it out together."

The days that followed were a whirlwind of studio sessions, promotional events, and late-night rendezvous with Spex. Our connection grew stronger with each tryst, and, despite the chaos of our lives, we found solace in one another.

Chapter 2

JUNIPER

Life had taken me on a journey filled with twists and turns, highs, and lows, but through it all, I finally found my way to a place of happiness and contentment. It was a feeling I never thought possible, especially after enduring the nightmare that was DaMarco. The scars on my palms served as a constant reminder of the chaos he'd brought into my life. I still felt the sting of his betrayal, the horror of the moment he tried to mow me down with his car when he caught me with my boss. That desperate act was fueled by jealousy and rage, and even though the wounds it left me with appeared to heal on the outside, I feared they would forever ache within.

Amidst all that darkness, though, there was a little, precious beacon of light named Kaylee. Despite DaMarco's initial denial, a DNA test proved what I knew all along: She was his daughter. His little Kaybae brought joy and laughter into our lives with her infectious smile.

DaMarco's bitterness about my engagement to Lorenzo was no secret. He convinced himself that Pharral, formerly his best friend, was only distant from him because of me. It wasn't my fault, but he was unable to see past his own ego to understand the complexities of friendship. Still, I refused to let his toxic energy dampen my spirits. I moved beyond his narcissism and chose to focus instead on building a life filled with love and positivity.

He was a monster in many ways, but I couldn't deny that DaMarco was a wonderful father to Kaylee. Despite his flaws, he loved her fiercely. For that, I'd always be grateful. As for the rest of his drama, though, I had better things to do than dwell on the past. With Lorenzo by my side and our future bright with promise, I was ready to leave the shadows behind and embrace the happiness I truly deserved.

Tas gave birth to twins a month early, and the babies were doing well. Mama and I spent most of the nights over at her and Pharral's place. Kacia came over in the daytime, because she had her own business to tend to. She and Philly were trying to have kids of their own and had opted to try in vitro fertilization. Their two miscarriages had been hard on them, but being with her new niece and nephew gave her a beam of hope. Philly suggested adoption, but my stubborn sister was persistent when it came to having her own biological child. I really couldn't blame her.

Bailey had a terrible case of colic and cried constantly, but Pharral Jr. was always at peace. Our presence there brought balance and gave Tas time to heal and rest. The stress and exhaustion of popping two human beings out of her body and her exhaustion was palpable, but so was the love and dedication we all shared for those tiny, new members of our family. Each of us found a role to play in the delicate dance of nurturing and support.

Kaylee, with her boundless energy and curiosity, was a natural with the babies. She sat by their cribs for endless hours, singing softly or telling them stories in her sweet, high-pitched voice. Watching her interact with them filled me with a profound sense of gratitude. Despite everything, our family was growing stronger, united by love and the promise of new beginnings.

Evenings at Tas and Pharral's place were filled with quiet moments of togetherness. We sat around the kitchen table, sharing stories and laughter, the babies' soft coos and cries punctuating our conversations. These moments were precious, a reminder of the importance of family and the strength we found in each other.

In the backdrop of my family bliss, I was also very excited that I had a few more artists to write for. When "Give It to Me" made it to the top eight, I was ecstatic. Then, when I received my first ASCAP royalty check in the astonishing amount of $20,000, I was even happier. I still kept my secret account, like Mama told me to, even when I was with Lorenzo. If nothing else, my relationship with DaMarco taught me that I could never really know what might happen. Lorenzo and I never talked about money; I had mine, and he had his. I knew it would be something to talk about once we were married, but for the time being, I still owned my place, the one I'd bought from the Browns when they retired and moved to San Bernardino. I even had the plant his wife had given me for Kaylee, and it had grown to over three feet tall and looked beautiful on my back porch.

A recent remodel had added 800 square feet to my home, and I found myself spending more time experimenting with new recipes and enjoying the upgraded space. The gourmet kitchen was everything I had hoped for and more. I loved the way the sunlight streamed in through the windows, illuminating the flecked white granite countertops and making the whole room feel warm and inviting.

My master bedroom and bath went through equally spectacular transformations. My boudoir now offered a serene, luxurious feel with new layout and furnishings. The hardwood floor gave it a timeless elegance, and I had chosen a soothing color palette that created a perfect retreat at the end of a long day. The bathroom, with more modern fixtures and spacious design, felt like a private spa.

Even though it was a process of remodeling was challenging, especially when I came to dealing with permits and contractors, the end result was worth every bit of effort. My home was now more spacious and accommodating, and that truly enhanced my daily living experience. It felt good to have invested in something that not only increased the value of my home by over $80,000 but also brought me so much personal satisfaction.

When Dalvin, my brother, and Lorenzo took off on their boys' weekends, I often took the opportunity to relax and recharge. Sometimes, I hosted friends for dinner in my new kitchen or spent quiet evenings with a good book in my cozy master bedroom. Other times, I took drives out to see Tas or Mama to hang out with the family.

Thinking about the future, I knew there would be more projects and improvements to tackle, but for the time being, I was content and comfortable. My home felt like a true reflection of my hard work and dedication as a songwriter and soon-to-be entertainment law attorney. Every corner of the house held a piece of my journey, from the late-night writing sessions in the kitchen to the moments of inspiration in my serene master bedroom.

The kitchen, with its two stainless steel double-ovens and state-of-the-art Bosch appliances, was more than just a place to cook; it was a creative space where melodies and lyrics often came to life amidst the aroma of fresh coffee. The countertops bore witness to countless hours of brainstorming and refining my craft. The solid hardwood floor echoed with the sounds of my pacing footsteps as I pieced together the perfect lines for a new song.

Lorenzo and I enjoyed a strong relationship, something I hadn't experienced in years. Our connection was deep and genuine, and I wanted to make sure it lasted. He was definitely my soulmate, the one who understood and supported me through all my creative endeavors. His presence brought a sense of stability and love that I had longed for.

We spent countless evenings in the master bedroom, discussing our dreams and aspirations, finding solace in each other's company. It was our sanctuary, the place where we could escape the pressures of the outside world and just be ourselves. The love and understanding we shared were the foundations of my strength, fueling my ambition and inspiring my creativity.

As I looked around my home, I felt a profound sense of pride and accomplishment. The remodel had not only increased the value of the house but also made it a true haven where I could nurture my passions and build a future with Lorenzo. Every detail, every choice, every effort put into making this house a home had been worth it.

Now, though, I faced a new dilemma. DaMarco had been blowing up my phone, begging to take Kaylee to Chicago for a week to visit his parents. They'd been spoiling her to the core since the very moment they found out they had a granddaughter. It certainly was a tempting offer, and Chicago in the summer sounded amazing. However, the timing was challenging.

The weekend DaMarco planned to take Kaylee was also Daddy's birthday. Every year, we honored his memory by placing flowers on his grave. I knew Kaylee never met Daddy, but the tradition was important to me. It was not just about remembering him but about keeping his memory alive for Kaylee and making sure she understood where her roots came from.

As I weighed the options, I couldn't shake the feeling that missing that ritual would be like letting go of something significant and important. I wanted Kaylee to experience the love and history of our family, even if she never knew Daddy personally. I was torn between giving her a wonderful opportunity to bond with her grandparents and preserving a cherished family tradition.

I knew I had to make a decision soon, and it wasn't one I could make lightly. I wanted to do what was best for Kaylee while also honoring the memories that mattered so much to me.

***

DaMarco had recently brought up a new request: He wanted to know if Steven, my boss, could give his brother Javier a job. Javier and his wife, Akemi, were looking to moving back to California from Atlanta. They weren't used to the weather there and missed the family and the hustle and bustle.

I told DaMarco I would pass Javier's résumé to Steven, but I made it clear that I would not push the issue further. I remembered Javier being nice to me when we finally met, and he had come down for Kaylee's christening. He was genuinely kind and supportive, so I did want to help in some small way. That said, I needed DaMarco to understand that I could make no promises. Passing the résumé along was the extent of my involvement; the decision would ultimately be up to Steven and the hiring process. Honestly, he was lucky I even did that. I had to maintain a positive relationship with DaMarco for Kaylee's sake, so that was important to me.

Chapter 3

LORENZO

I couldn't believe I was managing Kai Jae, one of the newest sensations to hit the music scene. Juniper's "Give It to Me," while originally intended for her, was eventually sung by Kai Jae, and skyrocketed to Number 8 on the Billboard Top 100. That phenomenal success marked my new protégé as one of the hottest rising stars. She was easy on the eyes, too, standing at 5'4," a fit 130 pounds, with mocha-brown skin and natural curves in all the right places. Her medium-length hair framed her almond-shaped, black eyes, and her contagious smile drew people to her. When Mr. Mac from MUSIC4LIFE Records asked me to manage Kai Jae and serve as her main producer, I was flattered, and I wasn't about to mess it up. Once he told me her contract was signed, I knew I had to bring my A game. That meant getting Juniper onboard to start writing.

I had met Juniper a few years earlier, when I started managing her as one of my artists. That first year was tough. First, I lost Erin, my daughter's mother, in a car accident after she survived a stab wound to the bowels. Juniper was there for me through all that. Over time, our relationship grew organically, and that led to me putting a ring on it. We planned to marry within the year, but our wedding date kept getting pushed back due to our music commitments and her decision to pursue a law degree. She was just a few months away from taking the bar exam, so wedding planning wasn't a priority. Her boss, Steven Harrison, had encouraged her to go after an entertainment law degree, and I was incredibly proud of her. She had initiative, drive, and determination, and that was impressive, especially after everything she'd gone through with DaMarco, the father of her daughter. Kaylee, now 3, and my daughter Symone, now 4, already got along like sisters. Of course, I still hadn't shared with anyone that Symone wasn't biologically mine.

I remembered the day like it was yesterday. Symone had a medical issue, and the pediatrician took blood from me in the hopes of a necessary transfusion. It wasn't a match, but that didn't change anything; she was my daughter in every way that mattered. Erin's parents were great grandparents to Symone and even embraced Kaylee as their granddaughter too.

As I readied myself for a Zoom meeting with Kai Jae and the team, I grabbed a quick bite to eat. Juniper was at her sister Tas's place, helping with the twins, so we agreed I would fill her in on the details later.

As the Zoom call began, familiar faces started to fill the screen one by one. T-Rock, my steadfast engineer, was the first one to sign in. His was a comforting presence, a reminder of the years we had spent working together, navigating the highs and lows of the music industry. His loyalty was always solid, especially during my tumultuous times with Erin's parents.

The next to join us was Kai Jae, her beauty radiating through the screen. "Hi, Mr. Ryan," she greeted softly.

"Mister? C'mon, Kai. Didn't I tell you to call me Lorenzo or Ren?"

"Sorry…Lorenzo," she replied with a smile that could light up a room.

As the rest of the team logged on, I felt a sense of anticipation. It was an important meeting, and I needed to ensure that we had a solid plan to keep Kai Jae's momentum going. We were there to discuss her six-month promotional plan, a critical period to help her maintain her rising star status.

"All right, team," I began, before I took a deep breath, "we need to map out the next six months for Kai Jae. We want to do more than maintain her current status, to push her even higher on the charts. We've got the talent and the hit single. Now, we need the strategy."

T-Rock nodded, his face serious. "We should capitalize on the success of 'Give It to Me.' It's doing great, but we need to keep it fresh in people's minds. I suggest a series of remixes and acoustic versions."

Kai Jae's eyes lit up. "Ooh, I love that idea, T-Rock. I've always wanted to do some acoustic songs. It would really show a different side of my voice."

"Great," I said, making a note. "We'll set up some recording sessions for those. What about live performances? Any upcoming opportunities?" Sam, our tour manager, chimed in, "There's a music festival in Atlanta in two months. It's a big deal, lots of exposure. We could use that as a springboard for a small tour."

"Perfect!" I said. "Let's get her on that lineup. Also, let's see if we can book some late-night TV performances. Those always help boost visibility."

Kai Jae nodded enthusiastically. "I'm ready for whatever it takes."

"Social media will be crucial," said Maria, our social media strategist. "We need to keep engaging with fans, posting regularly, offering behind-the-scenes content and live Q&A sessions. People want to feel connected to you, Kai."

"Absolutely," I agreed. "Maria, can you draft a content calendar for the next three months? We'll review it and adjust as needed."

"On it," Maria replied, already typing away. "Oh, and let's schedule a photoshoot," she added. "A fresh set of stylish photos will boost her social media presence and give us more content to share."

Kai Jae's smile grew even wider. "I'm really excited about that! I love getting creative with my style."

"Also, let's not forget about collaborations," T-Rock added. "We should identify a few artists who align with Kai's style and reach out for potential features. Always a great way to tap into new fan bases."

"Good point," I said. "I'll reach out to some contacts and see who's interested."

As we continued to hash out the plan, I felt a surge of excitement. It was exactly the kind of work I loved: strategic, creative, and collaborative. A big plus was that with an artist like Kai Jae, the possibilities were endless.

"All right, team," I said, prepared to wrap it up, "Looks like we've got a solid plan, here, plenty to work on. Let's execute it flawlessly and make these next six months incredible for Kai Jae."

"Thanks, everyone," Kai Jae said, her smile reflecting her gratitude. "I'm really excited about all of this. Let's make it happen."

As we signed off, I couldn't help but feel a sense of pride. Kai Jae was a star in the making, and I was determined to help her shine as brightly as possible. With the right strategy and the right team, I knew we could take her to the top.

After the meeting, I checked on the girls. Juniper and I were still living in separate places, but we spent most of our time between the two homes. She didn't mind Symone calling her Mommy, but we made sure we often showed Symone pictures of Erin and talked about her. She was too young to fully understand, but for the time being, the little girl was content with having two mommies, and that was fine by me.

As I walked down the hall, I thought about the whirlwind of the past few years. Managing rising stars like Kai Jae, juggling personal tragedies, and building a new life with Juniper had been a challenge. Still, those happy moments, seeing the girls playing together, made it all worth it. Symone giggled as she played with her dolls, and Kaylee babbled away in toddler talk, trying to keep up.

I picked up Symone and spun her around, loving the sound of her laughter filling the room.

"Daddy, higher!" she squealed.

Kaylee looked up at me with big eyes. "Me too, Daddy Ren."

I chuckled and scooped her up, too, then spun both girls gently. Being with them like that, the weight of the world lifted, replaced by pure, unfiltered joy.

A short while later, just as I was about to work on some music in my home studio, my phone buzzed with a text from Juniper: "How did the meeting go?"

I texted back, "Great. I'll fill you in when you get home. How are the twins?"

"Exhausting but adorable. Tas is hanging in there. Be home soon. Love you."

"Love you too," I replied, a smile tugging at my lips.

As I put my phone down, I felt a sense of peace wash over me. Despite the chaos and challenges, I had a wonderful partner, two beautiful daughters, and a promising career. Kai Jae's success was just beginning, and I knew there were great things ahead for all of us.

After I fixed the girls something to eat, I helped them get dressed, then set them up for a session of *Hooked on Phonics*. Preparing Symone and Kaylee to learn high-frequency words and basic reading skills before kindergarten was important to us. We wanted to give them the best start possible, so we did all we could to ensure they were ready for school.

"All right, girls," I said, as I sat down with the workbook and flashcards, "let's start with some sounds today."

Symone, with her bright, curious eyes, looked up at me. "Daddy, can we do the animal sounds too?"

"Of course, sweetie," I replied, smiling. "We'll do both."

Kaylee, always eager to follow her big sister's lead, clapped her hands. "Yay! I like the lion best."

We began with the basics, going through the alphabet sounds, then moved on to simple words. The girls were quick learners, and I found joy in their progress. It was moments like those that reminded me of the importance of balance, of nurturing their young minds while chasing my own dreams.

"What's this word?" I asked, pointing to c-a-t.

"Cat!" they both shouted in unison.

"Very good," I said, then gave them each a high-five. "You're both doing so well."

We continued our session, mixing animal sounds in here and there to keep it fun and engaging. I watched them mimic the roars and howls, as their laughter filled the room. It was a simple yet profound reminder of why I worked so hard. Everything I did was for them, for my family that I so dearly loved.

After our lesson, I decided to take the girls to the park. The sun was shining, and it was a perfect day to let them run around and expend some energy. As we walked, Symone held my left hand, while Kaylee held my right, both chattering away.

When we arrived, they immediately ran toward the swings. I pushed them gently, their giggles blending with the rustling of leaves and the distant sounds of other children playing. I took a moment to appreciate the simple joy of being present, of being there for my daughters in every way that mattered.

My phone buzzed in my pocket, pulling me momentarily out of the blissful bubble. It was another text from Juniper, to check in on us. After I responded and put my phone away, I felt another wave of gratitude. Juniper was my rock, my partner in everything. Her dedication to her career and our family was beautiful, and I admired her strength every day. We were a team, supporting each other through every challenge and celebrating every success.

"Daddy, higher!" Symone called out, bringing me back to the present.

"All right, here we go!" I said as I gave the swing another gentle push.

As the afternoon faded into evening, we made our way back home, tired but happy. I prepared dinner while the little ones played with their toys, their imaginations running wild. We were so happy they were finally getting used to always being around each other. Juniper would be home soon, and I looked forward to hearing about her day and sharing mine with her.

Later, after our daughters were snugly tucked into bed at Juniper's place, she and I sat on the couch, soothed by the comfortable silence between us. She leaned her head on my shoulder, and I wrapped my arm around her.

"How's Tas doing?" I asked.

"She's good, tired but happy. Mama has them babies spoiled, even worse than our girls."

"That's what grandparents do," I said with a shrug.

I got up to take a shower, and Juniper went to wash the dinner dishes. After drying off, I stepped out of the bathroom and dressed in my Nike basketball shorts and a comfortable T-shirt. Juniper headed into the bathroom but left the door open. I couldn't help but notice the nakedness of her body as she undressed, because her skin was beautiful. She practically glowed like the goddess she was.

Her breasts were high and perky, and her round, chocolate nipples were hard, likely from the light breeze and the mist of the shower. Gazing at her instantly hardened me. We had made a commitment to each other that we would not have sex until our wedding night, but while I had agreed, I desperately longed to walk into that bathroom and lick her glorious body all over. The temptation was almost too much, but all I could do was helplessly watch as she stepped into the shower. I was unable to peel my eyes away as she sponged herself, from her neck to her feet. She looked radiant; her brown skin covered in bubbles that slid down her curves. I was so jealous of that sponge and those bubbles.

The sight was almost too much to bear. I clenched my fists, trying to distract myself by focusing on the sound of the water. Juniper was a vision of beauty and strength, but my love for her was deepened by our shared commitment and the promises we had made to each other. It was a hard fight to control my carnal desires, but I took a deep breath and turned away to give her the privacy she deserved. I busied myself by tidying up the living room, making sure the toys were put away and everything was in its place.

A few minutes later, my bride-to-be emerged from the bathroom, wrapped in a towel. Her hair was damp, her skin silky and glowing from the warmth of the shower. She smiled at me, with a knowing look in her eyes. She sensed the struggle I was going through, and it was clear she felt it too. "Thank you for helping with the girls," she said, her voice soft and tender.

"Of course," I replied, in a tone huskier than I intended. "Anything for them…and you."

Together, we walked to the couch and sat down. I pulled her close, savoring the warmth of her body next to mine. We remained there for a while, enjoying the quiet and the intimacy of the moment. Words were not necessary, but she felt compelled to speak first.

"Ren," she whispered, looking up at me with those deep, soulful eyes, "I know it's hard, but it will be worth it. I promise."

"I know," I said before kissing her on the lips. "I believe that too." I said it to convince myself as much as I was trying to convince her.

Once again, we were immersed in silence, just holding each other, our hearts beating in sync. The anticipation of our wedding night loomed over us, a promise of what was to come. For now, though, it was enough to just be together, to love one another, and to share those delicious moments of quiet intimacy.

The hours ticked away, and the night grew deeper. When we finally headed to bed, Juniper put on her satin pajamas and slipped under the covers. I joined her and instantly wrapped my arms around her. While I held her, I felt the rise and fall of her breath as she drifted off to sleep. I closed my eyes, letting the calm wash over me. *Tomorrow is another day, to be filled with its own challenges and joys,* I thought, *but tonight, I've got everything I need, right here in my arms.*

***

The next morning, after a restless night, I awoke early to find Juniper reviewing her law books, still determined as ever to pass that bar exam with flying colors. I admired her dedication, her focus, even as I struggled with my own thoughts. The dreams of Erin's death had returned, haunting me once again.

I quietly left the room and went to check on Symone and Kaylee. They were both still fast asleep. Their innocent faces, soft and peaceful, were a stark contrast to the turmoil in my mind. I leaned against the doorframe for a moment, watching them breathe steadily, and reminded myself that I had to keep going for them.

Determined to push forward, I headed to the studio for a session with Kai Jae. Music had always been my refuge, and on that day, I needed it more than ever. As I drove, my thoughts kept drifting back to the dream that had invaded my sleep. I kept seeing that SUV, the one that struck the vehicle when Erin's aunt traveled to the hospital to pick her up. The impact, the sound of metal crashing, the helplessness I felt: It all replayed in vivid detail, leaving me feeling hollow and raw. The reminiscent nightmare always started the same way, with a smiling Erin, relieved to be leaving the hospital after her surgery. She looked fragile but hopeful. In my hazy imagination, Erin's aunt's car came into view, and Erin climbed into the passenger seat and waved at me through the window. Then, out of nowhere, an SUV ran a red light and smashed into their car. The screams, the blood, the chaos felt so real each and every time, horrifically playing on repeat. Erin tried to speak to me, to tell me she was sorry. Every time, I awoke drenched in sweat, my heart pounding, feeling the loss all over again.

With that dark pain swimming in my head, I parked at the studio and sat in the car for a moment, trying to shake off the remnants of the nightmare. Erin's death was something I still struggled with every day. No matter how much time passed, the aching agony of that loss was always there, lurking just beneath the surface.

Kai Jae was always on time, so she was already there, warming up her voice. Her presence was like a beacon of positivity amidst the chaos. She greeted me with a bright smile that momentarily eased my worries. T-Rock was already on the mixing board as well, ready to do his thing.

"Morning, Ren! Ready to make some magic?" the talented singer asked, her enthusiasm infectious.

"Absolutely. Let's make this a great session," I replied, forcing a smile.

We dove into the work, and for a while, I lost myself in the music. Kai Jae's voice soared through the studio, filling the space with powerful energy. We were working on a new track, something soulful that highlighted her incredible range.

Just as we were getting into the groove, the door swung open, and DJ Spex strolled in. He was a well-known radio announcer, adored by many, and his signature look—dark sunglasses and a fitted cap—was instantly recognizable.

"Spex! What brings you here?" I asked, genuinely surprised to see him.

"I heard you're working with the new sensation, and I had to see for myself," he said, wearing a grin. "Mind if I sit in?"

Kai Jae's eyes lit up at the sight of him. She had mentioned before how much she admired his work, and I knew she'd always wanted to meet him.

"Of course, man. Grab a seat," I said, gesturing to a chair in the corner.

As Kai Jae sung, Spex nodded along, clearly impressed. When the track ended, he stood and applauded. "Kai, you've got something special," he said. "Lorenzo, my dude, you've got an eye for talent."

"Thanks, Spex," I replied, feeling a surge of pride. "Kai's the real deal."

Spex turned to Kai Jae. "How would you feel about me DJing for you in the future?"

Kai Jae's face lit up. "What!? I'd love that! It would be an honor."

We spent the rest of the session brainstorming and playing around with different sounds. Spex's input was invaluable, and, by the end of the day, we had the foundation for yet another potential hit.

After the session, I sat in the control room, watching Kai Jae listen to the playback. She was understandably thrilled with the results, her smile wide and genuine. Seeing her happiness reminded me why I did what I did, why I kept pushing forward in spite of my own internal pain.

I left the studio feeling a bit lighter, though the weight of Erin's loss still pressed on me. As I drove home, I resolved to keep moving forward, to cherish the moments of joy and love that life still offered. Erin's death was part of my past and would always be part of who I was, but it didn't have to define my future.

At home, I found my beautiful Juniper waiting for me, her law books set aside. She greeted me with a warm embrace. She knew me well and always sensed when I needed a little extra tender loving care. We didn't need words; our connection was strong enough to convey everything we felt. Her presence was soothing, a reminder that I wasn't alone on my journey, no matter how difficult things were sometimes.

On the couch, she nestled close to me, her warmth providing a sense of peace.

I took a deep breath and decided it was time to share what had been haunting me. "Juniper," I began, my voice heavy with emotion, "I've been having those dreams again…about Erin."

She looked up at me, her eyes filled with concern and understanding. "Do you want to talk about it?" she asked gently.

I nodded, took another deep breath to steady myself, and continued, "In the dreams, it's always the same. I see the SUV crashing into her aunt's car. I hear the screams, feel the chaos. It's like I'm reliving that day over and over again."

"I'm sorry. That must be awful," she sweetly consoled.

"It is, but… Well, there's something else. I-I can't stop blaming myself for her death."

Juniper held my hand, her grip firm and reassuring. "Why, Ren? Why would you blame yourself?"

I swallowed hard in an effort to gulp down the guilt that weighed so heavily on my chest. "Because *I* asked her to pick up the check from my house that day. It's my fault she was there, Juniper. I can't shake the feeling that if I had just handled it myself, she'd still be alive."

"Lorenzo, you gave her money. Maybe they saw her getting the check and wanted it. The police deemed it a random act of violence, right?" Tears welled in Juniper's eyes as she spoke, her own pain visible. "Oh, Ren," she whispered, "you mustn't blame yourself for any of it. You couldn't have known what would happen."

"It's hard not to," I said, my voice breaking. "Every time I think about that day, every detail is vivid in my head. *I* made the choice that put her in harm's way. I know it doesn't make sense to keep torturing myself, but it feels like I'm carrying this immense weight, a burden of guilt and remorse that I can't escape."

She squeezed my hand more tightly, and her eyes never left mine. "You're doing the best you can, and that's all anyone can ask of you. It's okay to have bad days, to feel the pain, but remember that you're not alone. I'm here with you, every step of the way. I always will be, Ren."

Her words were a balm to my aching heart. "Thank you," I said, my voice barely above a whisper. "I don't know what I would do without you."

"You'll never have to find out. We're in this together," she reassured, her voice strong and solid. "We'll get through it, one day at a time."

I pulled her closer, grateful for the heart she had. "I want to be the best I can for you and the girls. Erin will always be part of me, but I need to find a way to live in the present, to build a future with you."

"And you will," Juniper softly said. "We'll find a way to honor her memory without letting it overshadow our lives. It's a journey, and I'll be here for all of it."

As we sat there, wrapped in each other's arms, I felt a glimmer of hope. Talking about Erin, sharing my struggles, brought a sense of relief. I was so grateful Juniper was understanding and willing to listen. It didn't erase the pain, but knowing I had someone to share it with made it more bearable. Erin's memory would remain with me, but it didn't have to define my future.

Changing the subject, I asked, "Are you ready for the bar?"

"Uh, no," she said with a cute chuckle. "Who knew wanting to be an entertainment attorney comes with so much entertainment?" she said. She laughed when the words spilled out, but there was an edge to it, a hint of the stress she was carrying, and I could see the strain in her eyes.

"What's been the hardest part," I asked gently.

Juniper sighed, leaning back against the couch. "Honestly, it's everything, but music law is really kicking my tail. The sheer volume of material I need to know is overwhelming. Understanding contracts, licensing, royalties, nondisclosure agreements, copyright issues. It's a lot to keep straight. I thought my experience working in the field would give me a leg up, but the exam covers so many theoretical aspects that I don't deal with day to day." She paused and ran a hand through her hair. "Then there's the pressure. I know how much is riding on this, not just for my career but for us. I need to be able to handle our legal issues, to protect us and our business."

"You'll get it done," I said.

She sighed. "I hope. It's just… Well, every time I sit down to study, I get this gnawing feeling that it's too much, that I'm just not cut out for it."

I squeezed her hand, trying to offer some comfort. "You are more than capable, Juniper. Look at everything you've accomplished so far. You're one of the smartest, most determined people I know. If anyone can do this, it's you."

She gave me a small smile, but I could see the doubt lingering in her eyes. "I appreciate that, Ren, but it's not just about being smart or determined. It's about endurance, about keeping up this relentless pace. Some days, I just want to give up, to throw in the towel. Sometimes, it just feels like it's too hard."

I nodded. "I understand your frustration, but you don't give up. You never have. That's just not you. It's one of the things I love most about you. You've faced so many challenges, but you come out stronger every time. This is just another hurdle, and I have no doubt you'll clear it."

Juniper sighed again, but a bit of the tension seemed to ease from her shoulders. "Thank you. It helps to hear that, especially on days when I feel overwhelmed. I just need to remember to take it one step at a time, to not let the fear of failure paralyze me."

"Ma, you've got this," I said firmly, "and I'm here for you, whatever you need. Like you said, we'll get through this together, just like everything else."

She leaned into me and rested her head on my shoulder. "I know we will. It's just hard to see the light at the end of the tunnel sometimes."

"We'll find it," I assured her. "One day at a time, just like you said."

We sat in silence for a while, holding each other close, drawing strength from our shared bond, a bond I hoped would never break.

Chapter 4

KAI JAE

It was my third week in Los Angeles, and I was starting to settle into the pace of the city. Despite the excitement and opportunities available in the City of Angels, I couldn't help but occasionally long for some of what I'd left behind in Detroit. Memories of the vibrant neighborhoods, the sense of community, and the cultural richness lingered in my mind. Of course, Detroit also held difficult memories and challenges that I needed to leave behind. The demons that haunted me were still there, so in that way, being in L.A. offered a fresh start, a chance to grow beyond those past struggles. As I navigated my new chapter, I was fueled forward by a mix of nostalgia for Detroit's positives and a determination to overcome its negatives in pursuit of a brighter future.

My brother Erick still lived in Michigan, and I'd promised that I'd help him join me in Los Angeles once my career took off. For the time being, I was willing to cover his rent and send him money until he found a new job. He had majored in business management and had successfully managed a real estate company before the pandemic forced a layoff. He was talented and willing to work, but things had been tough for him lately in Detroit.

Erick and I had both grown up in the foster care system, the proverbial School of Hard Knocks. Survival mode was all we knew. He was really my half-brother, two years older than me, and we shared the same mother but had different dads. Our mother passed away from a drug overdose, and since no relatives were willing to take us in, not even our deadbeat dads or our grandmother, we became wards of the state. Thankfully, we were placed with the same foster parents, which provided some stability during those tough years.

After we aged out of foster care, Erick attended Morehouse College and graduated, then eventually moved back to Detroit. I managed to secure a job, but life threw me into situations I could never have anticipated. I found myself doing things I didn't want to do, just to make ends meet. It was a tough time, but I held on to hope and continued to pursue my passion for music.

Little did I know that those challenging moments would lead me toward an unexpected opportunity, a record deal. It felt like a dream come true when I finally signed. My music showing up on the charts was far beyond anything I could have imagined.

Through it all, Erick was there, always showing his support. He knew the struggles I'd faced but never judged me for my past mistakes. We'd only really had each other, and once I was in a position to give back, I was determined to take care of him, just as he had taken care of me when we were younger.

Our journey from foster care to our stations in adult life represented a rollercoaster of highs and lows, but Erick's belief in me never wavered. He was a city boy through and through, and as much as he tried to stay out the streets, he had been forced to rough up many men in the past to protect me. They said they loved me, especially the one I had truly given my heart to.

No one knew about my past or my brother, and I wanted to keep it that way. In my opinion, the less people knew about the former me, the better. I didn't want bloggers, social media users, or anyone else digging up my history or prying into how I got to where I was. My journey from foster care to music success was a deeply personal story, one I was not ready to share with the world.

Every time a new project or achievement came up, I found myself treading carefully, making sure my past stayed buried, where it belonged. I'd worked too hard to build a reputation and a life for myself, and I wasn't about to let any perceived reputation undermine that. I wanted everyone to focus on what I'd become and what I'd accomplished, not on the struggles I'd faced or the hurdles I'd had to overcome.

Finally, I was making a life for myself, a real name for myself, and I want to protect that. The people who mattered to me knew the truth, and that was enough. I'd fought too hard, and I would not let anyone tear down the walls I'd built to safeguard my future.

***

The week was shaping up to be a marathon. I had to fly to New York for an interview on *The Breakfast Club*, and my schedule was already booked solid. Meetings were starting to pile up, and I could feel the pressure mounting.

The Breakfast Club interview was a big deal, and I wanted to make sure I was prepared for every question and every topic that might come up. The syndicated radio show aired in over ninety radio markets, including Chicago, Houston, Atlanta, and Miami, so it would definitely gain me some exposure. It was an opportunity to reach a wider audience and share my story, but that also meant I had to be on top of my game. The last thing I needed was to let my nerves get the best of me.

On top of that, I was nearly overwhelmed by endless meetings and professional commitments. It felt like I was constantly running from one place to the next, with barely a moment to catch my breath. Each appointment or meeting was important, but juggling it all was becoming difficult. I did my best to stay focused and organized, because I didn't want to let anything slip through the cracks.

Despite the craziness, though, I was determined to push through. I constantly reminded myself why I was doing all of it, why I was enduring the hard work, the long hours, and the relentless hustle. *It will all lead to something greater,* I told myself, time and time again. It was a lot to manage, but I was ready to rise to the challenge and make the most of every opportunity that came my way.

After I arrived in New York and checked into my hotel, I decided to grab a bite to eat downstairs. My radio interview was scheduled for the next morning at 8 a.m. After that, I had to catch a flight to Detroit. The schedule was tight, and I had to stay sharp.

After dinner, I retreated to my room and took a long, hot shower to help me unwind. I took a little time to pamper myself, then dried off and called Spex to update him on my arrival.

"Hey, Spex," I said when he picked up. "Just wanted to let you know I made it to New York. Got a bit of time to go over some things before the interview?"

"Hey," Spex replied. "Glad you made it safely. Sure, let's run through a few things. First off, remember to keep your answers concise and to the point. They might try to dig into personal stuff, so steer the conversation toward your achievements and current projects. When they ask about your past, try to keep it brief and redirect to how you've grown and what you're doing now."

"Got it," I said. "Anything specific I should focus on?"

"Definitely," Spex said. "Emphasize your current work and the positive impact you're making. Remember… If they try to press on anything uncomfortable, just pivot back to your successes and future goals."

"Okay, that makes sense," I said, feeling emboldened and a little more confident with his wise guidance. "What about, uh…unexpected questions?"

"Just stay calm and take a moment to think before you respond," Spex advised. "If you're unsure, it's okay to ask for a moment to gather your thoughts. No matter what, always bring it back to your core message, what you want people to remember about you."

"Thanks, Spex. I appreciate it. I feel more prepared now," I said. "I'll follow up with you after the interview, okay?"

"Sure thing. Good luck, Kai. You'll do great," he assured me before he hung up.

After I got off the phone, I turned on my HBO app to watch a movie. *Fifty Shades of Gray* was showing. The film instantly reminded me of the life I was getting accustomed to. It also brought back erotic memories of the night Spex had fully introduced me to a world I didn't even know I would enjoy.

It all started when he texted an invitation to his place. I had just finished working with Juniper, putting the final touches on, "Freak Like Me." I hopped in my car and drove over to see Spex.

As soon as I walked in, my ears were smacked with the sound of slow, instrumental music, a soft but melodic beat. The dim lighting and the faint scent of incense filled the air, creating an atmosphere of anticipation. My heart raced with excitement as I laid eyes on the array of sex toys and tools spread out before me: dildos, chains, whips, handcuffs, restraints, ties, nipple clamps, masks, blindfolds, whips, and

Try-Angle sex cushions. The sight of his bondage wall sent a thrill down my spine, and I felt my arousal building with every passing moment.

Spex approached me slowly, his eyes dark with desire. Without a word, he began to undress me, his touch sending shivers through me and pimpling my skin with goosebumps all over. His hands caressed every inch of my body, igniting a fire within me that I couldn't ignore.

His dominance was intoxicating, sending waves of pleasure coursing through my veins. As Spex's tongue traced patterns across my skin, igniting every nerve ending with a fiery intensity, I felt heat building deep within me. He clamped my hands to the wall, leaving only my legs free. The chains held me in place, heightening my sense of vulnerability and surrender.

When he positioned himself between my legs, his ten-inch, hard dick pressing against me, I gasped at the sensation of being filled so completely. As he began to thrust into me with primal urgency, the sound of skin slapping against skin filled the room, mingling with my moans of pleasure and the creak of the chains.

Each powerful thrust drove me to the edge of ecstasy, pushing me closer and closer to a release that promised to be explosive. My body arched against the chains, my nails digging into the rough surface of the wall as I gave in to the pleasure that consumed me.

Spex's movements were relentless, his grip on my hips firm and solid as he claimed me as his own. With each thrust, I felt myself teetering on the edge of oblivion, completely lost in the raw passion of the moment. His dominance was a force to be reckoned with, a magnetic pull that drew me deeper into a world of forbidden desires.

As he continued to drive into me with a fierce intensity, I surrendered to the overwhelming pleasure that coursed through me, embracing the sweet agony of being utterly and completely under his control. In that moment, with the chains binding me and his passion consuming me, I knew I was his, body and soul, and I wouldn't have had it any other way. Each touch, each whisper of sensual promises, caused me to surrender to him completely. The pleasure and pain mingled in a heady mixture that left me craving more. I was his, all his, a prisoner of my own passion and his, lost in a world of ecstasy that I had never known existed.

As I cried out, "Green, baby, Green!" the safe word became my lifeline.

Spex quickly unclamped me from the chains, released me from the intense sensation that had left my vajayjay sore and sensitive.

When we finished, we meticulously cleaned and sanitized everything in the room, erasing any and all evidence of our passionate encounter. The secrecy of his sex room was paramount, a hidden world that only we shared, and we were determined to keep it that way.

The intimacy we shared, both in pleasure and in setting boundaries, only deepened our connection. The trust we had built allowed us to explore our desires freely, safe in the knowledge that we would always respect each other's limits.

Our private world, filled with passion and secrecy, was a place where we could be completely ourselves, without judgment. As we locked the door behind us, leaving the outside world unaware of our hidden sanctuary, I felt a sense of closeness and understanding that only we could fully grasp. As the night unfolded, with each new experience and sensation, I knew it was only the beginning of a journey into pleasure unlike anything I had ever known.

The memory of that night, of being embraced by darkness and desire, would forever be etched in my mind as the moment I truly discovered the depths of my own cravings. I had my own world of *Fifty Shades* with Spex, and there were no gray areas about it.

***

The next morning, after my interview on *The Breakfast Club*, I was leaving the hotel elevator when I unexpectedly ran into a familiar face.

"Yo, pretty!" Spex called out, his face bright but his mouth curling into a big smirk. "I came to surprise you and see how things went."

I was genuinely delighted to see him. "Spex! I didn't expect you to come here. The interview went well, I think. It was intense, but I felt ready…thanks to you."

We made our way to my room, and I couldn't help but admire the view of my visitor, as well as the cityscape from the window. The hotel was perched high above the street, offering an incredible panorama of New York. The floor-to-ceiling windows framed the skyline like a living masterpiece, with skyscrapers shimmering in the sunlight. The Empire State Building stood tall among them, its spire reaching for the sky, while the other towering structures created a dramatic, dynamic horizon.

The room was modern and stylish, with a sleek design that let the view take center stage. The bed was positioned to face the windows, allowing for an uninterrupted view of the city. A plush armchair sat in the corner, perfect for soaking in the scene, and a desk by the window offered a front-row seat to the city lights as they began to twinkle with the onset of dusk.

As soon as we stepped inside, the atmosphere shifted. My yellow tank top, adorned with a Chanel brooch, was almost instantly discarded onto the floor, adding a splash of color against the neutral carpet.

Spex threw his bag on the chair in the corner with a decisive thud, and we moved toward the bed. He was hard as a rock, and I felt his monstrous dick poking my legs as he kissed me with enthusiasm, lying on top of me. His mouth on my neck only made me wetter; I wanted him inside me. Spex slowly pulled off my black, lacy bra, exposing my hard, erect nipples. Each of his licks made my desire for him more urgent. He removed my panties and, without making me wait any longer, slid his hard dick inside me.

"Damn, baby, you're tight," he said, as if he had never felt me before.

His hands grabbed mine, pinning them above my head as he made love to me with minimum force. Each movement spun me into a mix of pleas and screams. My voice became hoarse from calling out his name in an intense blend of pleasure and pain.

"Glad I hopped on that flight?" he asked between heavy breaths.

My thoughts were too scattered for me to answer him, for I was consumed by the urgent need to reach my peak. His firm thrusts drove me closer and closer, a symphony of moans escaping my lips in accord with his own. Our bodies moved in sync until the orgasm hit us like a crashing wave, drowning us in shared ecstasy.

After we finished, I ran my nails down his damp back, feeling the shivers of pleasure ripple through his body. The gleam of sweat on his skin served as a testament to the passion we shared, each scratch leaving a mark of our sexual encounter. I fell asleep in his arms and decided Detroit would have to wait another day.

Chapter 5

LORENZO

After wrapping up a successful studio session, I headed home, my excitement growing with each step. Spex was set to DJ Kai Jae's party, and given his impressive résumé and extensive experience, I knew it would be an unforgettable event. When I walked through the front door, the house greeted me with a serene ambiance, the soft hum of the living room TV blending seamlessly with the comforting sounds of home.

Juniper had gone to the library for some peace and quiet to study more for the bar exam. We were both grateful her mother had volunteered to come over to help with our daughters. Symone and Kaylee were playing in their room, their giggles providing a heartwarming soundtrack.

Juniper's mom greeted me with a warm smile as I walked in. "Hi, Lorenzo. How was your day?" she politely asked.

"Hey, Mrs. Alexander. It was good, busy as usual," I replied, trying to sound upbeat despite all the things I had on my plate.

"I'm glad to hear it. The girls have been great. I just got them settled down for some quiet playtime."

"Thanks so much for watching them. We really appreciate it," I said sincerely. Mrs. Alexander had always loved Symone unconditionally and treated her like her own granddaughter, even though they were not biologically related in any way.

"It's no trouble at all. I enjoy spending time with my granddaughters. I should get going now though. Can you let June know I'll call her tomorrow?"

"Will do. Thanks again."

I walked her to her car, then watched her get in and head out of the driveway, I checked my mail and sifted through the usual bills, advertisements, and junk, but one envelope caught my eye, with a return address from a law firm I didn't recognize.

Back inside the house, I tore the envelope open and pulled out the letter inside it. My heart dropped as I scanned the document, which announced that someone by the name of Shamar Collins was requesting a paternity test for Symone. I stood there frozen, with the letter trembling in my hands. I knew Erin had cheated on me, and I knew Symone was not really mine, but I'd never been told who her biological father was. My mind raced, jumping to the worst conclusions: *Is this some sort of cruel joke? A mistake maybe? Why now?*

I paced the living room, the weight of the situation bearing down on me. I had always been prepared to raise Symone as my own, regardless of her biological sperm donor, but now, this Shamar was coming out of nowhere, demanding a paternity test. I felt a surge of anger and confusion. *Who is this man, anyway, and how did he get my information?*

I grabbed my phone and called Juniper, but the call went straight to voicemail. I left a message, struggling to steady my voice: "Hey, babe, it's me. I, uh… I need to talk to you as soon as possible. Please call me. Something's comes up, something serious about Symone. Call me back when you get this."

I hung up and sat on the couch, staring at the letter. I knew I couldn't just wait. I had to do something, so I decided to call the law firm for some answers.

The phone rang a few times before a receptionist picked up. "Law Offices of Marshall and Greene. How can I help you?"

"Hi. Uh, this is Lorenzo Ryan. I received a letter about a paternity test for my daughter, Symone. I need to speak to whoever's handling the case," I explained.

"Please hold for a moment, Mr. Ryan," she replied, very calmly and professionally.

As I sat on hold, listening to "Four Seasons of Vivaldi, Excerpt 1," my heart raced as if I had just run a marathon. The advertisement about the law firm breaking into the classical piece seemed endless, droning in my ear. Then, the hold music resumed, its upbeat melody of strings a stark contrast to the turmoil brewing inside me. Each passing second felt like an eternity as I waited for someone to address my concerns. I drummed my fingers nervously on the arm of the chair, my mind racing with a thousand questions and fears. *What if this Shamar is right? What will it mean for Symone? For us? For our family?*

Finally, after what felt like an eternity, a voice came back on the line. "Mr. Ryan, this is Attorney Thomas Greene. How can I assist you?"

I took a deep breath, again trying to steady my nerves. "Well, I received a letter stating that someone named Shamar Collins is requesting a paternity test for my daughter, Symone."

Mr. Greene's tone was professional but slightly guarded. "Mr. Ryan, I understand your concern. Shamar Collins has recently come forward, claiming to be Symone's biological father. He's requesting a paternity test to confirm his claim."

My blood ran cold. "Okay, but how did he get my information?"

"I'm not at liberty to disclose that, but Mr. Collins is certain she is his biological child. I'm glad you called, as we need to discuss the process for the paternity test and your legal options."

I clenched my fist, struggling to keep my voice from becoming hostile or defensive. "There must be a mistake. Symone is *my* daughter. I've raised her since she was born. I need to talk to my own attorney before we proceed with anything."

"Of course, Mr. Ryan. You have every right to seek legal counsel. Please have your attorney contact us at his or her earliest convenience. We're willing to cooperate fully to resolve this matter."

I ended the call and slumped back on the couch, overwhelmed. *How can this be happening?* I needed to protect Symone, but I felt powerless against the unexpected threat. Until I heard back from someone, all I could do was try to stay calm and reassure myself that we would get through it, no matter what it took.

As I sat there on the couch, lost in a whirlwind of thoughts, my phone buzzed with Juniper's call. I answered it quickly, my heart racing with anticipation. "Juniper? Oh, thank goodness you called back," I said, my voice tight with emotion. "I need you to come home as soon as possible. It's urgent."

There was a pause on the other end of the line before Juniper responded, her concern evident. "Is everything okay, Lorenzo? What's going on? You said it's something about Symone."

"I'll explain when you get here. Just please hurry," I replied, trying to keep my voice calm despite the turmoil inside. "I need you."

After what felt like forever, she finally pulled into the driveway. She rushed through the door, her expression a mix of worry and curiosity. "What's going on, Lorenzo? You're scaring me," she said, hurrying to sit beside me on the couch.

I took a deep breath and braced myself for the difficult conversation ahead. "Juniper, I have something to tell you, and it's not easy, something I should have told you a few years back."

Her brow furrowed in concern as she reached for my hand, giving it a reassuring squeeze. "You can tell me anything, Ren. What's up? Is Symone sick or something?"

"No, not this time," I said, meeting her gaze and feeling the weight of the words I was about to speak. "Remember a few years ago, when we thought she might have leukemia?" I asked, looking at Juniper.

"Yes, but she's okay, right? Are you telling me something else is wrong?" Juniper asked, her voice now shaky.

"No, no, nothing like that, but... Well, that day, I had to have some blood taken, in case she needed a transfusion or something, but..." I trailed off, unable to continue just yet.

"But what?" Juniper nervously coaxed.

"But it wasn't a match."

"Huh? A match to what?"

"Her blood type, Juniper. That day, I found out she is not biologically mine."

The words hung heavily in the air between us, as thick as maple syrup. The silence between us that was often comfortable now felt eerie, echoing with the magnitude of what I had just revealed. Juniper's eyes widened in shock, her hand trembling in mine. A lump formed in my throat, and the only sounds in the atmosphere were the voices of the girls who were still giggling, without a care in the world, none the wiser to the drama unfolding on our couch.

"Lorenzo, I-I don't know what to say," she whispered, choked with emotion. "I had no idea. I mean, if you're not her father, then who is?"

"I'm so sorry, Juniper," I said, my voice dripping with remorse. "I should have told you sooner, but I didn't know how. I wanted to protect Symone. Crazy thing is, I don't really know who this sperm donor is."

Tears welled in Juniper's eyes as she pulled away slightly, her expression a mix of hurt and betrayal. "Lorenzo, why didn't you tell me? We're supposed to be in this together. We're about to get married, damn it! This shit affects me too!"

I hung my head, shamed by the weight of her disappointment. "I know. I should have told you, should have trusted you to handle it. I'm sorry. I was just so scared of losing Symone. I didn't know how to face this."

After a moment, Juniper took a deep breath, visibly trying to calm herself. "We'll talk about that later. Right now, we need to focus on Symone."

I nodded, grateful for her understanding, even in the midst of her own pain. "You're right. Let's figure out what to do next."

Juniper took another deep breath, her resolve shining through. "I'll text Steven and let him know what's going on. Let me see the letter."

I handed the letter to her, my hands still shaking slightly as she took it from me. She scanned it with a furrowed brow, her face gradually growing more serious. The silence became even heavier when she wordlessly walked to my home office, letter still in hand. I followed her and watched her place it on the scanner and meticulously scan each page to my computer. Then, she swiftly attached the file to an email and sent it to Steven.

"First thing, tomorrow, I'll talk to him. My boss will know what legal steps we can take to protect Symone and navigate this situation," she said, her voice steady and firm.

I felt a surge of gratitude and relief, though the anxiety still concerned me. I squeezed her hand tightly, feeling the warmth of her strength and determination flow into me. "Thank you, babe. I can't lose my daughter. I just can't."

She looked at me, her eyes filled with compassion. "We won't let that happen. We'll do everything we can to keep her with us and to keep her safe. This is her home, and we are her family. She belongs here."

Her words, combined with her actions, gave me a renewed sense of hope. The fear of losing Symone lingered, but at least it was tempered with the reassurance that I wasn't alone in the battle.

Chapter 6

KAI JAE

As I wrapped up an evening recording session with Lorenzo, my phone buzzed with an urgent message from Spex: "Need to see you. Important." My heart skipped a beat, and a mix of worry and excitement flooded my thoughts. I knew I had to go, but I couldn't reveal the real reason. "Lorenzo, I'm really sorry, but I have to split," I said, trying to keep my voice calm as I hastily gathered my things.

Lorenzo looked up from the soundboard, his brows furrowed in surprise. "Everything good, Kai?"

"Yeah, it's just… Something came up, and I have to take care of it," I replied, carefully avoiding his gaze, and trying to sound casual. "I'll make up the session. Promise."

He nodded slowly, suspicion flickering in his eyes, but he didn't press further. "All right, Ma, but time is money, and money is time. Take care. We'll finish this later."

I gave him a quick, tense smile and hurried out the door. My heart pounded violently in my chest as I drove to Spex's place, and not for the normal sexual reasons. The secrecy of our affair only added to the urgency, and my mind raced with what might be wrong.

When I finally arrived, I found him pacing the living room, and a troubled expression was etched in his face. The sight of him looking so unsettled made my heart ache. He looked up, his eyes filled with unease and relief. The room was dimly lit, and our shadows only made the place seem more somber, matching his demeanor.

"Spex, what's wrong?" I asked. I crossed the room to get closer to him, my concern deepening with each step.

He took a deep breath and locked his gaze on mine. "Kai Jae, thanks for coming. I didn't know who else to turn to. I need your help."

"What's wrong?" I asked, rushing to his side.

"I have something to tell you," he said, looking at me worriedly.

"Okay, spill."

"Do you remember Monique, the vocal producer helping with your production on 'Freak Like Me?'" he asked.

"Yes. Why? What's up?" I asked, feeling a knot of anxiety tighten in my stomach.

"Um, Kai, she says she's pregnant…by me."

The room seemed to tilt. "What!?" I nearly shouted, my voice rising with a mix of shock and disbelief. "Are you fucking kidding me right now, Spex? What the fuck!? You've been fucking me *and* this bitch!?" I yelled.

"Yes, I'm serious. I mean, no, I'm not kidding. Shit, Kai, I wasn't sleeping with you both at the same time," he yelled back, still pacing.

"How the hell did this happen then?" I demanded, my anger

bubbling to the surface. "When the hell were you guys even together like that?"

"We hooked up a few times before you, and then... Well, things just got complicated," he admitted.

I instantly noticed the hesitation in his voice. "Complicated?" I echoed, in disbelief. "That's the understatement of the century, Spex! This is fucked up beyond belief! Just last week, you told me how much you supposedly care about me. Were you lying then, or are you lying now? Which is it!?" I yelled.

"I wasn't thinking, okay?" he snapped, his frustration matching mine. "I fucked up, and now I don't know what to do."

"Damn right, you fucked up," I shot back. "This affects everything—our work, our lives. How could you do this to me, Spex? I trusted you."

"I know, Kai. I know!" he yelled, pacing faster. "But yelling at me isn't gonna solve anything."

"Well, what do you expect me to do?" I countered, throwing my hands up. "Am I supposed to just sit back and act like everything's fine? For months, I've been giving you sex on the regular, doing every freaky-ass, shit thing you wanted me to do," I said. I pushed him into a corner between his kitchen pantry and the side-by-side Samsung stainless steel refrigerator. I heard a few things drop on the pantry floor, but we both just stood there, face to face.

Suddenly, he laughed. "Don't you think I've heard about you fucking other guys in the industry? People talk, Kai," he said, trying to do a reverse UNO on me. "You're no angel either."

"But am *I* knocked up?" I barked. "Also, for your information, you're the only nigga I've been sleeping with, no matter what kind of bullshit you've heard," I said.

Then, without another word, he captured my mouth in a kiss, and I kissed him back, hard. He picked me up and carried me into his room, where the aroma of his scented candle hit my nose. That flicker was the only thing illuminating the space. The bed wasn't made, but he dropped me on top of his messy sheets, pulled off my pants and panties, and rammed his hard dick inside me with a hard thrust, harder than ever before. Our moans were loud.

Next, Spex lifted my legs and wrapped them around his neck. "You're mine," he said, "and I'm going to enjoy every bit of your sexy ass. Come on."

He grabbed my hands and guided me into his back yard. As soon as we stepped foot in the grass, the automatic lights flickered on. His privacy fence, twelve feet tall, kept any Peeping Toms or neighborhood security cameras from watching us. The sounds of the waterfalls in his pool were soothing and relaxing. Spex led me to a nearby tree and pressed my back against the bark of the thick trunk. My breath hissed through my lips as the rough texture bit into my skin, causing me to moan. As his left hand squeezed my ass, he stuck two of his right fingers inside my wet pussy. He kissed and nibbled at my shoulder as his fingers played with my wetness.

"You're soaking for me. Why?" he asked, whispering in my ear. "Aren't you supposed to be mad at me?"

"I-I don't know," I said in a breathy moan.

His fingers circled my clit, slowly at first, but then he picked up speed. It caused my hips to convulse and thrust into his hand, forcing my ass to grind harder against his thick dick. Spex knew how to make me cum, and when he sank his teeth into my neck and shoulder I came hard, grinding my soaking wet pussy against his hand.

"Mmm. I like that," he urged before he kissed my lips. He turned me around quickly and began stroking his hard dick. "On your knees now," he demanded.

I did as he asked and got on my knees in front of him, then started slowly licking the tip of his hardness. Spex grabbed my hair roughly, enjoying every movement of my tongue. He then picked me up, spun me around, and pinned me to the tree again. He opened my legs wider and stuck his hard dick in me once again. I felt the sharp sting of his hand smacking against my ass cheek. I knew it would leave a mark, but I didn't care. I could only moan with delight as he slowly pushed his hard dick deeper inside me.

"I love how wet you are," he moaned in my ear.

"Please," I begged, "fuck me good."

Electricity seemed to jolt through my body as he pounded into my pussy that was gushing and spasming around his hardness. Spex then took his dick out of me and jacked off on my legs.

We stood there for a silent moment, just breathing hard on each other. The thought of Monique's possible pregnancy had been completely wiped out of my mind for those few minutes of ecstasy, but it swiftly returned, and I pushed Spex away and turned to go indoors.

He followed me back to his home and watched as I grabbed my clothes and started to dress myself.

"This pregnancy shit isn't' over," I said. "We'll deal with it later." I then pulled my keys out of my purse and left.

A whirlwind of emotions stormed through me on my drive home from Spex's place. Anger, confusion, and betrayal were all tangled inside me like a messy knot. I tried to focus on the road, but my mind kept replaying the scene in his back yard. *How could I let myself get swept away like that, even for a moment?*

The night air felt heavy when I inhaled it through my window after pulling into the parking lot of my high-rise apartment. I sat in my car for a while, trying to gather my thoughts. Truthfully, I had no idea how to react or what to do next. Any trust I had in Spex was shattered, and I couldn't shake the feeling of being used and betrayed.

As I stepped into my apartment building, I was greeted by the modern elegance of the lobby. The floor was polished marble, gleaming under the soft, ambient lighting. Tall, sleek columns stretched upward, and the walls were adorned with tasteful abstract art. Plush, contemporary furniture in neutral tones was arranged in cozy seating areas, inviting residents and their guests to relax and unwind. A large, decorative plant stood in the corner, adding a touch of Greenery to the sophisticated space.

When I reached the elevator doors, I ran into Maxwell. The security guard was a tall Caucasian with a broad build. He had short, sandy blond hair, always neatly trimmed, and his piercing blue eyes were both sharp and kind. His uniform was always impeccably neat, giving him an air of professionalism that I appreciated.

"Good evening, Miss," he greeted with a warm, familiar smile that softened his otherwise chiseled features. "Long day?"

I managed a tired smile in return. "You could say that. It's been one of those when everything just piles up, you know?"

Maxwell nodded sympathetically, with a hint of concern flickering in his eyes. "I hear you. Anything I can do to help?"

"Not unless you can make the next twenty-four hours disappear." It was a joke, but there was a hint of sincere longing in my tone.

He chuckled, his laughter revealing a small dimple on his left cheek. "If I had that kind of power, I think I'd be the one taking a break right now."

"True enough," I said, then sighed. "Thanks, Maxwell. It's just nice that someone noticed and asked."

"Anytime," he replied with a reassuring nod. "You take care now, and if there is anything I can do, you know where to find me."

"Thanks," I said again, giving him a genuine smile this time.

I stepped into the elevator and pressed the button for the fifth floor. I felt a little better after that brief exchange with a friendly soul. As the elevator ascended, I thought about how often Maxwell's simple kindnesses had brightened my day.

When I finally reached my apartment, I collapsed on the couch, overwhelmed, and exhausted. My phone buzzed with a text message, but I hesitated to look at it. When I finally checked, I saw that it was Lorenzo, checking to make sure I was okay. I stared at the screen for a moment before typing my response: "Yes, just some personal things. I'm fine."

Spex and I had set specific rules in the beginning. We had both agreed to keep it casual, just for fun and with no strings attached. However, the more time I spent with him, the more I realized I was catching feelings. I was mad at myself for having sex with him, but I had to admit that Spex knew how to please me. Every time we were together, it was as if he could read my mind, anticipate my needs. That was as terrifying as it was intoxicating. The boundaries we had established seemed to blur more with each encounter, and I couldn't help but wonder where it was all headed.

I sighed, set my phone on the side table, and closed my eyes for a moment, hoping to gather my thoughts. The lavish sofa cushions enveloped me, providing a small comfort amidst the turmoil of my emotions. My back ached and stung from the tree bark scratches, a reminder of the spontaneous adventure Spex and I had shared. I got up to take a shower, hoping the hot water would wash away some of the confusion I felt.

Just as I reached for the bathroom door, my phone rang, and the screen lit up with Erick's name. "Hello?" I said, then put it on speaker.

Immediately, his frantic voice filled the room. "Kai, someone broke into my apartment and tore it apart. They must have been looking for something, but I don't know what. Nothing was stolen."

I jumped up, adrenaline surging through me. "Erick, forget the apartment. Are *you* okay? Did you call the police?"

"Yes. They've already been here and taken a report, but Kai, I know it wasn't just a random break-in. They had to be looking for something specific. My whole place was ransacked."

My mind raced. "Stay put. I'll get to Detroit as soon as I can. Don't touch anything else until I get there."

I hung up and quickly began throwing clothes and toiletries into a bag, my head swarming with concern and determination. As I threw my essentials into the suitcase, I was smacked with the reality that I would have to handle it on my own. No one in my current life even knew I had a brother, and I had to protect him, at all costs.

The long flight from California to Michigan was a blur. I couldn't get the sound of Erick's frantic, panicked voice out of my head, and I wondered what was so important that someone would toss his place to find it.

Erick met me at the door, his face pale, and eyes wide with worry. "Kai, I don't know what's going on," he said, his voice trembling. "They didn't take anything, but they went through everything."

I hugged him tightly and glanced over his shoulder at his place behind him. The sight of the aftermath sent a chill down my spine. The police had come and gone, but the place looked like a warzone, with everything strewn everywhere. "We'll figure this out, Erick," I said. "Did the police find anything?"

He shook his head. "Nothing yet. They said it looks like a professional job, like someone who knew what they were doing."

As we stepped inside, the extent of the damage became clearer. Drawers were pulled out, furniture overturned, and papers scattered everywhere. As we started to clean up, my mind raced with questions: *Who was behind this? What were they looking for?*

Later that evening, after we managed to clean up most of the mess, Erick and I sat down to try and make sense of it all.

"You can't think of anything anyone might have been after?" I asked.

Erick frowned, and his brow wrinkled in deep thought. "I don't know, Kai. I don't have anything valuable, and I've really got no secrets to keep." He paused for a moment, looked at me seriously, and said, "But…" He trailed off, a look of realization dawning on his face.

"But what?" I pressed.

"A package came a few days ago, from someone named Victor."

I felt a jolt of recognition. "Victor? Erick, do you know who that is?"

He shook his head. "No, but I thought it might be important, so I kept it safe."

My heart pounded. Victor was one of Dwight's associates, but he had a professional nine-to-five, and I never would have expected him to be caught up in any kind of illegal or questionable activity. Still, I knew instantly what they were looking for. "Where is it now?"

Erick led me to a small, untouched corner of his closet and pulled out an unsealed envelope. "Here," he said, handing it to me with a shrug.

I carefully opened it and pulled out a single sheet of paper. I skimmed over the words, chilling in their simplicity, then read them aloud: "Give it to me."

"Sis, isn't that the name of your hit single?" he asked, his voice hushed with awe and fear.

"Yes."

"Is Dwight still bothering you?" my brother asked, becoming angry.

"Honestly, he won't leave me alone," I said, now crying.

"What does the title of your song have to do with anything? Does he want money from you or something?"

"I don't know," I said as I reread the note.

That night, as I lay awake in Erick's guestroom, the pieces of the puzzle started to come together. Dwight's associate and Victor's involvement were all connected. The stakes were higher than ever, but protecting my brother was my concern, first and foremost. He couldn't know the true meaning behind the words of the letter, at least not yet.

Chapter 7

KAI JAE

The next day, I went to visit Dwight, my husband, who was serving fourteen years for trying to smuggle drugs on Delta airlines while carrying an illegal weapon. As far as I knew, he had not discovered that I was the one who had set him up. I had to keep up the act of being a supportive wife, or he would have my head. His connections in the streets were still strong, but the streets had been quiet so far.

Dwight eventually found out that over 200 grand was missing from his stash. The D.A. spun a story to the jury about seizing his closet safe and finding over $700,000 in cash. The truth was that Dwight originally had over a million in dirty money. I kept the books, and I'd been carefully concocting an exit plan for a while, setting money aside for my escape. My only mistake was taking an additional $200,000, instead of the original 200 grand stashed away. I got too greedy. The numbers didn't add up even with that, though, so I knew some of Detroit's dirty cops had helped themselves to a few thousand. I was just glad he never knew that $400,000 of the missing money was in my hands, at least not at first.

I denied it when Dwight accused me of taking the money, but after my sudden move to L.A., he figured out the truth. It was suddenly crystal clear to him that I had taken off with a nice chunk of his change, and he was none too happy about it.

After the trial, I retrieved the money, which I'd hidden in my grandmother's old house, under a loose floorboard near the back bedroom. It was a rundown house, but her children still paid the taxes on it. Since I was still in the city, I often checked the property to make sure no squatters had moved in. After packing and making sure my travel plans were lined up, I hit the road and drove straight to California. I scored a nice spot, locked in the deal with MUSIC4LIFE Records, and—boom!—history was made.

To safely put my nest egg away without rousing too much suspicion, I made small cash deposits into my bank account only a few times a month. When the royalty checks for my music started coming in more frequently, I was able to deposit bigger amounts. I was glad for that, because I didn't feel safe with all that cash sitting in my apartment.

Dwight was abusive, but I had him to thank for my street smarts. Because of him, I'd learned how to talk my way in and out of almost anything, even stealing money right out from under his own nose. Sometimes, I did feel guilty for how I played the man. He did hold me down for a while, but I was done living under his terms. My husband was obnoxiously jealous, abusive, controlling, and manipulative.

Dwight was my first love, but things changed during his sophomore year in college at Fayetteville State University, where he was an English major. He started hanging out with the wrong guys, was placed on academic probation, and was eventually kicked out of school. When he returned to Detroit, he quickly climbed the criminal ranks to become one of the biggest drug dealers in the city.

For me, Detroit was a prison of memories and screw-ups, but I had played my own part in that. Dwight was doing time because of me, and I knew it would be over for me if he ever found out. He had trusted me with his money and his life, and I had flipped that trust to see him locked up while I took off with his funds.

Dwight's downfall started with a lie. I told him I had met a big-time dealer from Cuba through one of my gigs. The man I called Alfredo was really Cole, an undercover FBI agent who threatened to pin all sorts of charges on Erick and me if I didn't help him bring Dwight down. I wasn't about to go to prison as any sort of accessory or to let my brother get locked up for anything, so I complied with Agent Cole's demands.

I had learned to be a decent liar, and I'd gained Dwight's trust, so it wasn't too difficult to get him to buy the story I spun about Alfredo needing someone to smuggle fifteen kilos of pink cocaine back to Cuba. "Easy two million," I nonchalantly said, as if it were something as casual as switching the laundry. "He can't go back to Cuba himself, so he just needs someone to fly it back," I fibbed.

Dwight saw dollar signs and was all in. He trusted me completely and never suspected a thing. Blinded by greed and stupid faith in me, he agreed. Under my guidance, he stashed the drugs in a secret compartment in his suitcase, a bag designed to evade TSA scans. Of course, Agent Cole, posing as a TSA agent, knew exactly when to run a supposedly random check on Dwight's carry-on. It was all perfectly orchestrated.

***

As the plane descended into Detroit Metropolitan Wayne County Airport, I felt a mix of relief and dread. The gray skyline of Detroit stretched beneath me, a harsh reminder of the city's unforgiving nature.

I hated the city, but it was over. I arrived at the prison, gave the guard my ID, and waited for them to bring Dwight in. He had lost weight since the last time I'd visited him, his frame gaunt and his eyes hollow. I felt pity for him, albeit not as much as I had for myself when he struck my face with his fists whenever he felt like it.

I put on my best fake smile and watched as the guard walked Dwight in. He greeted me with the same hard look he always had, softened only slightly by seeing me. We made small talk as he sat across from me, but my mind was elsewhere. The guard kept staring at us, to make sure there were no problems with the visit this time. I couldn't blame him, since the last time, we really got into a fight over an Instagram photo he had seen on my page. I had taken it for an industry event, but Dwight was none too happy that I was "doing the most," as he called it.

The small, sterile room echoed with the murmur of other inmates talking with their own visitors. The tiny, metal table between us was a flimsy barrier against the tension that crackled in the air. Dwight's eyes bore into mine; he was searching for something, maybe reassurance or some sort of pathetic control. I had my own life in L.A. now, my music, and my freedom, but every visit reminded me of the lie that had set me free and trapped him.

I took a deep breath, trying to steady my nerves. I had to break the news that it would be my last visit. The divorce papers were ready, lurking in my bag like a ticking bomb. I'd had them drafted months ago, but every time I meant to give them to him before, I had chickened out, terrified of his reaction.

"Dwight…" I started, my voice barely above a whisper.

His eyes narrowed, sensing the gravity of my tone.

"This is my last visit," I blurted.

He leaned back and crossed his arms over his chest. "What are you talking about?"

I reached into my bag and pulled out the envelope, then slid it across the table to him. "These are divorce papers. I've moved on, Dwight. I have a life in L.A., and I can't keep coming back here. It's time to let go."

He didn't touch the papers but just stared at them as if they were some kind of poisonous or foreign object. The silence stretched on, heavy and suffocating.

Finally, he looked up at me, his eyes cold and hard, and said, "You can't leave me."

I swallowed hard, refusing to let him intimidate me. "Yes, Dwight, I can, and I will."

The guard took a step closer, sensing the tension.

Dwight's eyes flickered to the guard, then back to me. "You think you're better than me now, don't you?"

I shook my head. "It's not about being better. It's about being free. I deserve to be happy, and so do you."

He laughed bitterly. "Happy? In here? Bitch, you're delusional. How's Erick, by the way?"

I stood up, feeling a rush of determination. "No, Dwight, not delusional at all. In fact, I finally see things clearly. My brother is fine. Don't think I don't know it was your goons who broke into his apartment and left that nasty note. How clever, using my song title to try to get to me."

"Go live your life, bitch, but don't think for a second that you're free of me! No one leaves me!" he yelled as the guard hauled him back to his cell.

As I walked out of the visiting room, wiping the last of my tears away, the weight lifted off my shoulders. The lie that set me free had kept me trapped in guilt and fear for too long. Now, I was totally liberated from it, ready to embrace my new life and leave the past behind.

The city of Detroit faded into the distance as I boarded my flight back to L.A., the sun setting on one chapter of my life and rising on another.

Chapter 8

JUNIPER

The day I had been dreading and anticipating for weeks finally arrived. If I passed the bar, I would officially be an attorney. Steven, my boss and the owner of Harrison, Matthews, and Associates, was one of my biggest cheerleaders. During my work at his prestigious law firm, he convinced me to return to law school to seek my degree in entertainment law. The firm even covered my tuition. Steven always emphasized the distinction: "An *attorney* is licensed to practice law and represent clients in court, while a *lawyer* might not be licensed to practice. Both complete law school, but I want you to be practicing!" he said. Those wise and encouraging words echoed in my mind as I went through my studies: "All attorneys are lawyers, but not all lawyers are attorneys. If you want your name on the building, you have to be an attorney."

Life was a whirlwind, and I had a lot to balance when it came to raising my Kaylee, working on my education, working, and planning my wedding to Lorenzo, the man who had saved me from DaMarco's toxic grip and showed me I could love again. Recently, I'd learned the disturbing news that DaMarco was still hooking up with my cousin, Alexius. For all I knew, they were just sex buddies, friends with benefits, but I really couldn't care less. He had treated me like shit during our relationship, so if they wanted each other, they deserved each other. Tas, my fiery sister, tended to get more riled up about things. She was ready to throw hands with Alexius, but the future attorney in me held her back.

I tried to shake off the stress as I stepped into the shower and let the hot water stream over my breast and drip down my legs. In a thick lather of Victoria's Secret Amber Romance soap, I washed my entire body and thought about my man. Lorenzo and I had made a promise to each other to wait until marriage to make love. Many times, things had gotten hot and heavy, but we managed to put a stop to it to keep our mutual promise. Shit little did he know that Ms. Rose, my friend from the Adam & Eve sex store, gave me plenty of orgasms, all I would need until Lorenzo could give me the real thing.

"Mommy!"

The sound of Kaylee calling my name outside my bathroom door jerked me back to reality. Instantly, my mind began to race through potential exam questions. Steven had drilled me with countless practice exams, and I'd aced them all. Brian Matthews, his partner, had also been a rock, offering support whenever I needed it.

I toweled off and slipped into my favorite bathrobe, then walked into the kitchen. "What did you need, honey?" I asked my daughter.

Kaylee's naturally curly hair created a wild halo around her face as she munched on cereal, engrossed in her tablet. "Just checkin' on you, Mommy," she said. "You're gonna crush it today, right?" she asked, her eyes sparkling with confidence.

I smiled and kissed her forehead. "I sure hope so, baby girl."

Lorenzo strolled in after dropping Symone off at her grandparents' place. His presence was as calming as ever. He handed me a mug filled with my favorite herbal tea. "Just breathe, June. You've got this."

His reassurance gave me a boost. I dressed in my navy pantsuit, the one that made me feel invincible, then glanced at the clock. "Time to go," I said under my breath. "It's now or never."

The city was alive as I stepped out. I merged onto the 101 freeway while listening to a symphony of honking cars and bustling pedestrians. I navigated through the traffic, my mind alternating between exam strategies and wedding plans.

At the testing center, I quickly found my seat and took a deep breath. The noise of the city faded as I focused on the task ahead. When I began the test, I found a rhythm. My pen flew assuredly across the paper. Steven's advice guided me through, question by question. Hours later, I walked out, the weight of the bar finally lifted from my shoulders. I had done my best. Now, all I could do was wait.

As I made my way back through the urban maze, I called Lorenzo. "All done," I said.

His voice was the anchor I needed. "Come home, babe. No matter what, we're proud of you."

With the bar behind me, I felt a wave of relief wash over me. We were told it could take six weeks for the results to come back, but that was simply fine by me. It gave me the perfect window to focus on the new song I was writing for Kai Jae. She was absolutely killing it in the industry, and her talent was only enhanced by her unstoppable energy and work ethic. Collaborating with her was going to be legendary.

Still, there was something else gnawing at the back of my mind, something I hadn't shared with anyone, not even with Ren. It had all started a few weeks ago when I was at the Ritz-Carlton, catching up with Dr. Blair, my former advisor who just so happened to be my boss's stepdad. He had recently retired and had moved to Florida, but he was back in town to attend the college graduation of his twin daughters, Markayla, and Makenzie. I wanted to see Dr. Blair before he flew back, to thank him for making a real difference in my life in a positive way.

We met in the plush hotel restaurant, the kind of place where the chandeliers sparkled like diamonds and the waiters moved like shadows. I was deep in conversation with Dr. and Mrs. Blair when I saw two familiar faces, Kai Jae and Spex, very close, very together, and walking in like they owned the place. I nearly choked on my drink. They didn't see me, as tucked away in the corner as I was, but I saw everything: the way they laughed, the way their bodies leaned into one another, and the way they spoke without words, conveying messages with their hungry eyes, like they shared some secret language. It wasn't just a casual meet-up; it was more like the opening act for a sex session about to happen.

Spex was a slick, smooth-talking radio announcer who had a reputation for mixing business with pleasure. Kai was on fire, her career skyrocketing. Based on those facts alone, them being together made sense. *But this?* I thought, struggling to process what my eyes beheld. It was a complication I hadn't anticipated. I kept my cool and continued my chat with the Blairs, but my mind was running in other directions. I just couldn't let it go. My thoughts kept drifting back to Kai: her talent, her drive, and now, a twist. I felt like a live wire was buzzing in my brain. If it was meant to be a secret hookup, it could blow up and make a mess of our work. The weight of the whole thing settled on my shoulders, causing me to slump a bit in my seat. I could only hope the Blairs would not notice the change in my demeanor. One thought screamed louder than any: *This is about to get really interesting, and possibly messy.*

By the time I headed home from meeting with my advisor, I felt like everything was closing in on me. The hum of traffic below my house window sounded more oppressive than usual. I tossed my keys on the counter, grabbed my phone, and dialed Nikki. She was my girl, but she was also a seasoned P.I. who'd been deep in the game for years. We had crossed paths while I was helping Steven on a case, and we'd kept each other in the loop ever since. There was no way I could let Lorenzo in on it, at least not yet. For his own sanity and protection, and for the sake of our relationship, I decided he didn't need to know about every twist and turn.

"Hey, Nikki, it's Juniper. How's it going?" I asked when she picked up.

"Juniper! What's good?" she replied, her voice cutting through the city noise like a knife.

"I need some info on the down-low, discreet. It's about Kai Jae, an artist I'm working with, and a radio announcer named Spex."

She paused, creating a silence that told me she was already piecing things together. "Business or personal?" she asked, even though I was sure she already knew the answer.

"Both," I said, playing it close to the chest.

Nikki knew when to press and when to let things unfold of their own volition. "All right. Gimme a bit. I'll see what I can dig up."

As I spilled all the info I had on Kai Jae and Spex, a mix of anticipation and dread twisted in my gut. It wasn't just about the music anymore. Now, it was about navigating the gritty, unpredictable tangle of ambition, secrets, and scandal—a scandal I was damn near in the middle of. There was an uneasiness in my spirit about Kai Jae, an unsettled feeling that while she had a sweet girl persona, she had always been a bit too quiet for my liking.

The next day, a menacing cloud seemed to hang over me. I headed to the studio to work with Lorenzo on the new song for Kai, but my mind was a million miles away, tangled in what Nikki might uncover. Each beat of Kai's track felt like a countdown to some impending revelation. *What if Nikki finds out something explosive? What if this whole thing blows up in our faces?* I questioned, even though I knew I had to stay sharp.

A week later, my phone buzzed, and Nikki's name lit up the screen. I quickly picked up the call. "Hello?" I said, my voice shaky and anxious.

"Got something for you," she said, low and serious. "Meet me at Java Brew Café in an hour." The coffee shop was our go-to for private meetings. It was cozy, crowded, and perfect for blending in.

I grabbed my jacket and headed out, eager and nervous to hear her findings.

When I arrived, Nikki was already there, drinking a coffee, with a manila folder on the table in front of her. She was striking, as always, dressed in a black tank top that showed off her toned arms and fitted jeans that hugged her small waist. Her skin glowed the color of deep chocolate, smooth and radiant under the soft café lighting. Her almond-shaped eyes, framed by long lashes, were sharp and discerning, a deep brown that almost seemed to shimmer. Long, goddess-blonde braids cascaded past her waist, their intricate patterns catching the light with every movement. Her high cheekbones that accentuated her sculpted features, and her full lips were painted soft nude, adding a touch of elegance to her fierce appearance. A small diamond stud adorned her nose, and a gold bracelet glinted on her wrist as she moved.

"Glad you could make it," the gorgeous P.I. said, her eyes meeting mine with an intensity that made it clear it wasn't just a social call. She leaned in and glared at me, sharp and focused. "Juniper, what I found on Kai Jae is… Well, it's big."

"Big? As in…bad?"

"Matter of opinion, I guess," Nikki said. "She's tied up in some heavy shit. Her ex-husband, Dwight, is serving fourteen years in Detroit, at the William Dickerson Detention Center, for drug trafficking. Turns out, she set him up to be arrested. I figure she wanted out of that life, but it wasn't as clean a break as she was hoping for."

The revelation hit me like a freight train. I took a deep breath, and the noise of the clattering cups, steaming espresso machines, and giggling baristas faded into the background. "She set him up?"

Nikki nodded. "Yeah, orchestrated the whole thing. She wanted to break free from his criminal and abusive ties, and the divorce followed soon after. Now, though, it looks like some of his associates aren't happy about how things went down. She's still tangled up in their mess."

It was big, just as she'd said, much bigger than I'd imagined. "So, she's in danger?"

"Potentially, and as for yo' boy Spex, I didn't find much. He's just a damn man whore. My contact told me he be at those alleged crazy Diddy parties. He's clean otherwise though." She leaned back, and a sly grin spread across her face. "They just screwing and shit. A few contacts told me he's into bondage." She giggled, a surprising contrast to her usual no-nonsense demeanor.

I leaned in, intrigued, despite myself. "Bondage, huh? Didn't peg him for the type."

Nikki's grin widened, revealing perfectly white teeth. "You'd be surprised what people are up to behind closed doors, but, yeah, Spex ain't nothing to worry about too much. He's just another player in the game, keeping himself entertained."

I shook my head, trying to process the information. Nikki always had a way of digging up the most unexpected details. It was one of the reasons I relied on her so much. I left the café, paying no mind to the city chaos around me. The stakes had just skyrocketed, and I was right in the thick of it, forced now to navigate a web of deceit and danger. Music would have to take a backdrop. Now, it was about survival in a city that thrived on secrets.

When I got back to the studio, I couldn't shake the feeling of impending doom.

Lorenzo was the first to notice my distraction. "Everything all right, ma?" he asked, looking up from the mixing board.

"Yeah, just a lot on my mind," I replied, not ready to unload the whole truth just yet.

The next few days were a blur. I kept my head down, trying to focus on the music, but the knowledge of Kai's situation weighed heavily on me. I met with her to discuss the track, all the while watching her carefully. She was poised, but there was some fear in her eyes that she couldn't completely hide. "Kai, is everything okay?" I asked, trying to sound casual.

She hesitated before answering, "Yeah, just…a lot going on, ya know?"

I nodded and did not pry, deciding it was not the time to press further. Even so, I knew I had to be prepared. Truth had a way of coming out, and it wasn't just about navigating the music industry anymore. Rather, it was about dealing with the darker underbelly that came along with the industry and the people in it.

A couple of days later, I found myself in the studio, writing. The others had left, so I was alone with my thoughts, and I just couldn't shake the tension. I pulled up the latest track and let the beats wash over me, hoping to drown out my worries. Instead, it only intensified them.

My phone buzzed, pulling me out of my thoughts, but I felt a lump of worry in my throat again when I saw that it was a message from Nikki: "Can you meet me at the spot?"

I stared at the screen, my heart racing, but I eventually found the courage to send a thumbs-up emoji.

The coffee shop was nearly empty when I arrived. Nikki was seated at a corner table, her expression even more serious than before. I walked over and sat down, trying to mask my anxiety.

"Thanks for coming," she said. "I know it's late, but this can't wait." Her voice was low as she leaned over the table and said, "Sis, turns out Kai is in deeper trouble than you know."

I leaned forward, my stomach knotting. "What kind of trouble?"

Nikki glanced around before continuing in a whisper that danced into my ear through the steam of her latte, "My contact told me someone in the music business is Dwight's half-brother. They're pressuring her, fast and hard. I know y'all have a lot of connections, so do you have any idea who this person may be?"

I swallowed hard. "Damn, I don't know all that much about Kai. I just write for her, and Lorenzo has been mainly managing her. She is hot right now, and she's rubbed elbows with a lot of greats in the industry," I said. "I don't know who might want to hurt her though."

"Well, you're gonna want to keep an eye on her. Let me know if anything seems off. Also, if she asks for help, don't hesitate. I've got some plans in motion, but it's going to take time."

I nodded as the weight of her words settled on me. "I'll do whatever I can."

Nikki gave a tight smile. "I know you will. Thanks."

As I left the coffee shop, I felt a mixture of dread and determination. The music industry was a minefield, but I wasn't about to let Kai navigate it alone, not when the stakes were so high.

Back in the studio, I found it even harder to focus. Every beat, every lyric seemed to echo with hidden meanings. I pulled out my notebook and started jotting down everything I knew about Kai's situation, trying to piece together a plan or at least some information that Nikki could use. I couldn't let the darkness win. I had to be ready for whatever came next.

Chapter 9

KAI JAE

Leaving those divorce papers with Dwight was both liberating and nerve-wracking. I knew ending our toxic relationship was the right decision, but Dwight's refusal to accept it added a layer of tension I couldn't shake. Then came the unsettling calls. Each time my phone rang with an unknown number, my heart skipped a beat. The distorted voice on the other end, with warnings like, "Watch your back," sent chills down my spine. It felt like someone was lurking in the shadows, watching my every move, just waiting for the perfect moment to strike. I couldn't escape the feeling of being stalked.

As if that weren't enough, there were Dwight's calls from prison. Despite being behind bars, his anger and bitterness seeped through the line, making my blood run cold. His threats were like daggers aimed straight at my heart. "You'll regret leaving me and stealing my money, bitch," he said, his voice dripping with venom. "I'll make your ass pay."

The truth was, I was the one who had placed the ledgers and spreadsheets on a small thumb drive shaped like an elephant, its trunk designed for USB port insertion. I replaced the hard drive in his laptop, leaving erroneous information for the feds to retrieve during the raid. I knew the names of all his dealers and the locations of all his pickups and drop-offs. I even knew which city officials were indulging on the side. I tried to convince myself that Dwight's words from behind bars were just the desperate cries of a wounded ego, but, deep down, I knew better. I had stolen his money in a desperate bid to secure my future, and he was ready to seek revenge.

Honestly, I had no idea what Dwight was capable of anymore, who he was working with who could do damage on the outside. The break-in at my brother's place only made me feel more vulnerable. The unknown emerged before me like a dark abyss, threatening to swallow me whole. All I could do was hope and pray that the threatening calls would eventually stop, that I could find some kind of peace in the chaotic storm. Until then, I was trapped in a nightmare of my own making, haunted by the ghosts of my past and the shadows of an uncertain future.

My paranoia grew with each passing day. Every creak of the floorboards, every rustle of the wind outside my window, had me stressed. I installed more locks on my doors, cameras in every corner of my apartment, and even a security system that alerted me to the slightest movement. Yet, the feeling of vulnerability lingered.

The thumb drive remained hidden in a secret compartment in my dresser, a silent reminder of the life I had fled and the secrets I still held. I knew it was dangerous to keep it, but it was the only real leverage I still had against Dwight. I often wondered if anyone else knew about it. I feared Dwight had told his associates, and had sent them out to search for it and destroy me.

He usually called on Saturdays or Tuesdays. One particular

Saturday, while I was awaiting his dreaded call, I decided I was not about to live my life afraid anymore. When the unknown number popped up on my caller ID, I quickly accepted the call, but before he could get a word in edgewise, I blurted, "I am not going to run or hide from you or your pussy-ass associates anymore."

There was a brief, stunned silence on the other end before Dwight spoke, his voice dripping with a mix of amusement and menace, "Well, well, well, what do ya know? My bitch grew a backbone. What brought on this sudden burst of courage, Kai?"

I took a deep breath to steady myself and answered, "First off, I'm not nobody's bitch. You must have me confused with your bald-ass mama."

"Ah, shit. Look at Kai, talking back," he said, laughing mockingly.

"I've had enough of living in fear, Dwight. You and your threats don't scare me anymore."

Dwight chuckled, cold and mocking. "Is that so? You think a little boldness over the phone is gonna change anything, bitch?"

"No," I replied firmly. "What's changed is *me*. I'm done being your victim. I won't let you control my life anymore."

"Big words, little girl," he scoffed, "but words don't mean shit without action. What, exactly, do you think you can do to stop me?"

"I've taken steps already," I said, my voice solid. "I've got people looking out for me now. Not only that, but If anything happens to me, there are people who will make sure you and your associates are exposed. So, go ahead. Try me, motherfucker. Everybody in your little ring will be exposed, and the ones who are still walking free will be locked up."

There was another uncomfortable pause, and I could almost hear the gears turning in Dwight's head. "You really think you can threaten me?" he finally said, a hint of anger creeping into his voice.

"It's not a threat, Dwight. It's a mutha-fucking promise. I'm not the same scared girl you used to intimidate."

He laughed again, more forced this time. "We'll see about that, Kai. Let's just see how long your newfound courage lasts."

"It'll last as long as it takes," I shot back. "You don't scare me, Dwight. You're pathetic."

"Fine," he said, his tone dark and frightening. "If that's how you wanna play it, then game on. When the fire starts to burn your ass, remember that *you* started it!"

"Sure, and I'll finish it," I replied, then ended the call before he could say another word.

As soon as I set my phone down, it buzzed again almost immediately. Against my better judgment, I glanced at the screen and saw another unknown number. With a sigh, I picked it up, but this time, I let Dwight speak first.

"You know, Kai," he began, his tone unsettlingly casual, "I heard your new song on the radio the other day. Not bad. You're making quite the name for yourself."

I felt a chill run down my spine, but I forced myself to remain calm. "Glad you like it," I said evenly. "I've worked hard to get where I am."

"Worked hard, huh?" Dwight said. "Funny how you managed to pull that off with everything else going on. Then again, I guess stealing can be inspiring, right?"

"You're not going to intimidate me with your passive-aggressive compliments, Dwight. My music is *mine*. It has nothing to do with you."

"Ah, but that's where you're wrong," he said, his voice dropping to a threatening whisper. "Everything you do, everything you have, has everything to do with me. Remember that too."

"No, Dwight," I said, my voice strong. "I'm done with your black ass. You may have been part of my past, but you have no place in my future."

"We'll see," he replied, the threat implicit in his words. "How long do you think you can keep this up?"

I ended the call again and noticed my hands shaking slightly. I had told him I was turning my back on fear, but it still gnawed at my insides. Despite that, though, I also felt a surge of determination. Dwight knew about my music, but he didn't own it. He didn't own me either. It was my life and my career, point blank, period.

I called Erick right away. "Put everything in storage," I advised. "I'm moving you to an Airbnb in Midtown for a few months, until I get things situated here."

The silence on the other end was very concerning.

"Erick!" I yelled.

"I hear you, sis. Why the sudden change? What's going on?"

"You're asking too many damn questions, Erick. I'm going to Zelle you five K to hire some movers."

"Uh, okay, sis. Whatever you say."

I hung up with Erick and hurried to get ready for my business meeting. Lorenzo had us set up to rendezvous with the people from *The Tamron Hall Show,* and I knew I had to have a clear head before I got there.

Chapter 10

JUNIPER

I hurried out the door to work, making sure to grab the letter Lorenzo received from Shamar Collins's attorney. With Steven away on a business trip for the past few weeks, this was my first chance to see how we could handle the situation. When Ren admitted he had known for a while that Symone wasn't his daughter, I was in disbelief. Things just didn't make any sense. *What else did Erin lie about? Is Lorenzo hiding anything else from me?* I wondered about the man I was going to marry. The whole situation was messed up, and I wanted to get to work early so I could discuss it with Steven. He was already onboard, and he personally knew one of the attorneys at the law firm representing Shamar, so I was sure he could offer us some helpful advice.

As I navigated through the morning traffic, I couldn't shake the feeling that there was more to uncover. I still hadn't shared the details I knew about Kai. At that point, I was more intrigued by how she had set her ex-husband up. With that on my mind, I called my girl Nikki while I was stuck in traffic, hoping she could shed some light on the situation. "Nikki, you won't believe the mess I'm dealing with," I said as soon as she picked up.

"Girl, what now?" Nikki's voice was a mix of curiosity and concern.

I quickly filled her in on the chaos surrounding Symone, Lorenzo, and the bombshell about Shamar Collins.

Nikki listened intently, not interrupting. "That's wild," she said when I finished. "Listen, I got some more tea for you too," she continued, her voice dropping to a conspiratorial whisper. "You remember me telling you about that convict, Dwight, Kai's ex, right?"

"Of course. What about him?"

"Kai Jae allegedly stole over 200 grand from the dude. My sources confirmed it."

My jaw dropped. "Are you serious?"

"Dead…and he wants it back. My contact pulled the court transcript and gave me all the info. Apparently, Dwight still owed some people money from way back before he got busted."

The traffic started to move again, but my mind was racing faster than my car. If Kai had stolen that much from her ex-husband while she was still married to the man, there was no telling what else she was capable of. The grim news added another layer to the already convoluted situation.

"Thanks for the heads-up, Nikki. This is getting crazier by the minute," I said.

"Just be careful, girl. Don't go gettin' caught in the crossfire. I know Kai is one of y'all's artists and hot right now, but this shit ain't worth it. Don't go putting your life at risk over her BS. I've been following her career. Sure, the girl is bad, but more than that, sis, the bitch is confirmed cray,-cray," Nikki warned.

"I'll keep that in mind. Talk to you later."

I hung up and continued my drive, my mind crowded with a web of lies, deceit, and stolen money. By the time I reached the office, my resolve to uncover the truth had never been stronger. I hurried to Steven's office and found him already immersed in paperwork. "Hey, did you get my email?" I asked as I closed the door behind me. I set my car keys and purse on his mahogany desk.

Steven looked up, his expression grim. "Yes, and I was just about to call you. I've been digging into Lorenzo's paternity case. Juniper, it's more complicated than we thought."

I took a seat, my heart pounding. "Go," I said.

Steven leaned forward and lowered his voice. "What if I told you I know Shamar's attorney, Thomas Greene, from law school. He's a frat brother of mine," he said, laughing.

"Don't make me envision you at a D9 party, Steven," I tried to tease, but nothing about the conversation left room for humor.

"Well, Tom has some intriguing connections. Apparently, Erin, Lorenzo's ex, had an affair with Shamar Collins some years ago. Meanwhile, Shamar was engaged to a woman named Laci."

"Damn," I said.

Steven hesitated, his face tensing up. "There's more, Juniper. I don't know how to say this, but…"

"But what? Spit it, Steven."

"Laci is the woman who stabbed Erin," he quietly informed me. "It was a crime of passion, as those detective shows like to call it. She came home one evening to find Erin and Shamar in bed together, in the apartment they once shared, and she tried to burn it down."

The room seemed to spin for a moment. "Damn. Gangster," I said, smiling.

"Juniper, there's more," he said, in an even quieter whisper.

"Again, spit it," I ordered, now more anxious than ever to hear what he had to say.

"Laci is the other woman DaMarco was seeing when you were still dating him."

"Wait, what? The one he wanted to marry?" I asked, totally shocked. "She was involved with DaMarco too?" I whispered, struggling to process it all, the smile now peeled off my face.

Steven nodded. "Yes, but it looks like she had no idea about you. This whole situation is craziness, a nasty knot of lies, and now there's this paternity issue."

I took a deep breath, trying to steady myself. "So, Erin's stabbing wasn't just a random act of violence, right?" I said, piecing it together. "It was connected to all of this. Where is Laci now?" I asked.

"She's been living a private married life, somewhere in California. Her husband is a professor or something. That's all Shamar's attorney had to offer for now. I'm thinking about putting Brian on this case. I'm sorry, J Breeze."

Steven hadn't called me that nickname in a while, and it carried the smile back to my face, in spite of all the ugly that had suddenly invaded my world. "Brian?" I asked, a bit shocked as his words sank in. "You know if this has anything to do with another woman, that man's wife is gonna trip."

I laughed in another effort to lighten the mood, but it was a futile effort. "Everyone knows his missus is notoriously jealous. Her reputation is practically legendary in these legal streets."

"Yeah, I know," Steven replied, a smirk playing at the corner of his mouth. "She's got her radar up for any sign of trouble."

I chuckled, shaking my head. "Well, let's hope this doesn't add fuel to her fire. The last thing we need is another domestic dispute complicating things even more. We don't need a repeat of last time."

I took a moment to reflect on that incident. One of Brian's clients took him and Steven out to dinner to celebrate their courtroom victory. While Steven was in the bathroom, Brian's wife showed up and saw just him sitting at the table with an attractive female. She instantly accused him of cheating. It wasn't until Steven returned to the table was when she realized it was an innocent business outing, but by then, she'd already created quite the scene, practically turning the restaurant into a *Jerry Springer* episode. Fortunately, my boss showed up before she began throwing chairs.

We both laughed now as we reminisced about that day, but in reality, I still sensed the tension hanging heavily in the air. Brian's wife had a way of making her presence felt, and her jealousy was no joke. It was something we all had to navigate carefully in our interactions.

I had learned in my lifetime that relationships were as tricky to manage as any legal case. The dynamics, the emotions, and the stakes all required a careful balancing act. In the world we lived in, the personal was always intertwined with the professional.

"Yes, Brian is well aware of the details, but he's our best bet when it comes to digging deep and dealing with family court. Something about this situation isn't right. Why now? Why is Shamar contacting Lorenzo now? Why'd he wait four years to care that he might have a kid? It's got a bad smell to it." Steven asked.

"Yeah, this just keeps getting crazier and crazier by the minute. Who'd have thought the woman I saved almost four years ago was stabbed by my baby-daddy's other girlfriend? Shit!" I laughed loudly, but there was some pain behind it. "So, what are we going to do about the DNA test for Symone?" I asked, refocusing on the immediate issue.

Steven took his time to answer, leaning back in his chair and exhaling slowly as he gathered his thoughts. The clock on the wall ticked loudly, echoing my impatience.

Finally, he said, "Signing a birth certificate as a non-biological father has legal implications and can lead to paternity fraud. However, since Lorenzo believed Symone was his at birth, he should be okay legally. Now that his belief has been called into question, though, his only option is to take the test," he explained, his voice steady and reassuring.

I nodded, again feeling the burden of it all pressing down on me, threatening to smother me. It wasn't just about legalities; it was about the lives and emotions of people I cared about. Reluctantly, I picked up the phone and dialed Lorenzo's number, my heart pounding in my chest. "Lorenzo," I said when he picked up, my voice calm but firm, "we need to talk about the DNA test." I relayed Steven's advice, urging him to take the test, despite his initial reluctance.

Lorenzo's silence on the other end of the line was so loud. I could almost hear the gears turning in his mind as he processed the information.

"Look, Ren, I know this isn't easy, but it's the right thing to do," I continued, my tone softening. "Steven and I both believe you're going to be fine."

After what felt like an eternity, Lorenzo finally spoke. "All right, fine. I'll do it," he said, his voice heavy with resignation.

I breathed a sigh of relief and hung up the phone. "He's agreed to take the test," I told Steven, with a small smile of triumph tugging at my lips.

"Good," Steven replied as he reached for his phone. "I'll call Tom and get it scheduled."

I watched as Steven made the call to Shamar's attorney, his

expression serious and focused. He was good at what he did, always calm under pressure, always thinking a few steps ahead. It was one of the things I admired most about him.

"Damn, Erin," I muttered to myself as I walked out of Steven's office.

The hallway seemed longer than usual, each step echoing my frustration and relief. It was just one hurdle in a race that seemed to be lengthening every minute, but at least we were moving forward. I had to believe things would work out, even if the path was unclear.

When I got to Lorenzo's place, I found him in the studio he had set up in one of the spare rooms, completely absorbed in listening to some beats. I usually didn't bother him when he was in that mode, because it was his sanctuary, the place where he went to escape and create. That night, though, I had to talk to him and see where his head was. We hadn't really spoken since my call earlier about the DNA test, and the tension had been on my mind all day. I was sure he felt it too.

I stood in the doorway for a moment, watching him bob his head to the rhythm, lost in the music. The studio was a chaotic haven of wires, keyboards, and sound equipment, a testament to his passion. I hated to interrupt his flow, but the conversation was important. I took a deep breath, stepped inside, and gently placed a hand on his shoulder. "Lorenzo," I said softly, just loudly enough to be heard over the music.

He turned around with a look of surprise on his face that was quickly replaced by a guarded expression. "Hey, babe," he replied, pulling off his headphones. "What's up?"

"We need to talk," I said, trying to keep my tone calm and supportive. "The DNA test is scheduled for two weeks from now. I just want to make sure we're on the same page."

He sighed, rubbing his temples, as if trying to ward off a headache. "Yeah, I know. It's just… It's a lot to process."

I moved closer, feeling the need to bridge the physical and emotional distance between us. "I get it, Lorenzo. I really do, but we need to be clear about what this means for all of us. As far as I'm concerned, I'm her other mother, and I'm ready to fight for her if I have to."

He looked at me, his eyes softening a bit. "You've always been there for her, June. I appreciate that more than you know. It's just... I never imagined we'd be in this position."

I nodded, understanding the mix of emotions he was feeling.

"Neither did I, but here we are, and we have to do what's best for Symone. She deserves to know the truth, and so do we."

He took a deep breath and slowly nodded. "You're right. I just need to wrap my head around it."

"We'll get through this," I said, giving his shoulder a reassuring squeeze. "We'll handle it together, for Symone."

Lorenzo managed a small smile, and the tension in the room eased slightly. "Thanks, babe. I needed to hear that."

As I left the studio, I felt a bit more at ease. There was still a long road ahead, but at least we were facing it together. Symone was worth every bit of the fight, and I was ready to do whatever it took to protect her and our family.

Chapter 11

KAI JAE

My stomach grumbled, pulling me out of my thoughts and back to the present. I shuffled into the kitchen, only to find my refrigerator bare, nothing but an empty, echoing space that left me feeling hungrier and more frustrated. Quickly, at the beck and call of my hunger pangs, I opened DoorDash on my phone and settled for a salad, a light and easy option.

Before placing the order, I added a note for the Dasher: "Please ring the doorbell only ONCE." My headache was already throbbing behind my eyes, and the last thing I needed was for anyone to make it worse by pounding on my doorbell like some hyper kid playing a videogame.

While I waited on my order to be delivered, I had time to take a long, soothing shower. I let the warm water wash over me, desperate to erase the lingering stress of my day. As I stood there with my eyes closed, my mind wandered to Dwight and everything that had happened between us. The steamy water seemed to help clear my thoughts, even if just a little.

When I emerged from the shower, I put on my favorite nightshirt, a soft, light pink one with a cute teddy bear on the front. It was cozy and comfortable, the thin fabric a gentle embrace against my skin. I paired it with some black tights that I sometimes wore to the gym. They clung snugly to my legs, the stretchy material giving me a sense of security and comfort as I moved around the house.

The doorbell rang just once, as per my instructions. I took a deep breath and went to answer it with wallet in hand, as I preferred to tip my drivers in person.

When I opened the door, a chill ran down my spine. The delivery stood before me, exhibiting a most unsettling appearance. He was wearing a wrinkled uniform that looked like it had seen better days, and he looked like he hadn't showered in a month. His eyes darted around nervously, and his hands shook as he handed over the bag. He mumbled something I couldn't quite make out, his voice barely above a whisper. His disheveled hair and unshaven face added to the overall sense of unease.

I forced a smile, took the bag from him, and quickly shut the door behind me. I bolted it shut and set the alarm with trembling fingers. My heart pounded in my chest, the brief encounter having left a lingering sense of discomfort in its wake. I tried to shake off the unease as I unwrapped my salad, but the memory of the shifty Dasher stuck with me, making it hard to focus on anything other than the strange and unsettling interaction.

I walked back to the kitchen and took the lid off the salad, ready to drench it in ranch dressing, only to find that my appetite had vanished entirely. The unsavory character on my doorstep had stirred shadows from my past, memories and worries I had worked hard to bury. I sat at the kitchen table with the unopened bag of food before me and let the horrible recollections rise to the surface, uninvited.

Dwight, my ex-husband, was someone I once thought I loved. That was a mistake. In reality, it was really just a veil over fear and desperation. He was dangerously charming and persuasive, an expert at wearing a mask of civility. Beneath that veneer, however, was a monster, a narcissistic bully who thrived on control and manipulation. I still grappled with disbelief that I had allowed myself to be trapped in his web.

In the beginning, it seemed like a fairytale. We were young and infatuated, two crazy kids, and I thought our love was unbreakable. Sadly, the honeymoon phase quickly soured. After we married, Dwight's darker side began to surface in an ominous transformation that soon made me feel as though I were living in a nightmare.

Dwight was deeply entangled in the drug trade, a fact I only discovered after it was far too late. His lust for power and money was insatiable, and his willingness to exploit and manipulate anyone who got in his way was chilling. As his wife, I became an unwitting pawn in his dangerous game.

I remembered the first time he asked me for a questionable favor. We were at home, and he was pacing in the living room. His movements were erratic, like those of a caged lion, his eyes burning with an intensity that made me shiver. The atmosphere was thick with unspoken tension.

"Kai, baby, I need you to do something for me," he said, his voice strained and urgent.

I felt a knot of dread in my stomach, just like the one that swelled in me when I saw the disheveled DoorDash driver just a few minutes earlier. "What is it?" I asked, trying to keep my voice even as my heart raced.

Dwight stopped pacing and turned to face me, his expression grave. "I need you to pick something up for me. It's... It's important."

He didn't elaborate, and the way he avoided my eyes made my skin crawl. The request itself was shrouded in secrecy, and the fear of the unknown annoyed me. I had no idea what he was engaged in, but the threatening tone in his voice told me it was something dangerous, something that could unravel my world even further.

"Where? And what is it?" I asked, my voice trembling slightly.

"Just go to the old warehouse by the docks," Dwight instructed, his gaze piercing me. "I'll give you the details when you get there. Remember, Kai, don't talk to anyone."

The warehouse he mentioned was a place I had only heard whispers about, an abandoned, decrepit building that loomed on the edge of my awareness like a dark specter. The thought of going there filled me with a profound sense of dread, but Dwight's commanding presence left me little choice.

As I sat at the kitchen table now, with the croutons in my neglected salad growing soggy, the memory of that day and the dirty errands Dwight forced me to do thereafter came rushing back. The feeling of being used, of being just a plaything for him to use in his dangerous game, made me shiver. That delivery driver had stirred up old fears, and I couldn't shake the feeling that the past was somehow catching up to me, its shadows stretching into the present.

"There's a guy I need you to meet," Dwight said, his tone casual but the suggestion of danger unmistakable. "He's...important for my business. Just keep him happy, okay?"

Keep him happy? My mind raced with the potential meaning and insinuation. I didn't understand at first, but the look in his eyes told me everything I needed to know, and my blood ran cold. "No, Dwight. I can't do that," I tried to refuse. "Do you think I'm some sort of fucking whore you can just pimp out? I'm your wife!" The words came out with more defiance than I really felt, but I still had some fire left in me, some will to fight back.

He grabbed my arm, his grip like a vise, and his eyes bore into me with chilling intensity. "You *will* do it, Kai, and you'll like it. You don't have a choice. If you don't cooperate and do what the fuck, I tell you to do, this singing shit of yours is over. I know every club owner in this town."

"What does that mean? You don't even support my career. I've got—"

He cut me off with a single look, an expression that made it clear there was no room for negotiation. The finality in that terrifying gaze was enough to freeze me in place. The fire inside me flickered out, replaced by a cold, paralyzing fear. He was dangerous, and while I'd had my suspicions before, in that moment, all those suspicions were confirmed. Tears welled in my eyes as I realized the extent of what was being asked of me, but there was no escaping it. Dwight was not a man to be disobeyed, and any attempt to fight back were futile.

That night, and many nights after, I did as he asked. Each time, I felt like I was losing pieces of myself, fragments of my dignity and self-worth that I would never get back. The more I gave in, the more I felt like I was disappearing into the shadows of his demands, leaving me with a hollow ache that never seemed to fade.

I remembered the guy's name, Jay. The first time I told Dwight how rough Jay was with me, begging him to let me stop, crying out, "I can't take it anymore, Dwight!" my husband's response shocked me.

"Oh, you are going to take it," he said, then smacked my breasts in a harsh, condescending, dehumanizing, and dismissive gesture.

"Dwight," I protested.

He did not care that my eyes were pooling with tears of humiliation, fear, and hurt. "You'll do what and who I say. So, what if some guy wants to fuck you rough? It won't be the first time...or the last." He stood abruptly and began aggressively roaming his hands all over my body. "You're going to take everything he or anyone else gives you, all right?" he whispered into my ear, his fingers trailing down to my center. "Are you sore?" he asked.

I nodded, feeling a wave of helplessness wash over me.

It felt like a contradiction when he smiled, his touch surprisingly gentle as he wiped my tears away. Then, he carried me to the bedroom and used a warm towel to pat me down, trying to make me feel a bit better.

That night, as I lay in bed with my back to Dwight, I felt his arousal pressing against me. The thought of having sex with anyone else was unbearable.

"I want you, Kai, right now," Dwight said, his voice low as he slipped my panties off.

"I don't feel so good," I weakly protested.

"It doesn't matter," he replied.

When I looked into his eyes, I saw that it truly didn't. His pupils were dilated, and he was clearly high off whatever street drug he was selling, not in the mood for bargaining.

He trailed his index finger down my body, ignoring the tremors that followed each touch. He spanked my ass and squeezed, disgusting me. Then, he began to stroke himself, till he eventually finished on my breasts. As soon as he was through, he fell asleep, and I cried into the darkness until dawn.

***

"Where is it?" he shouted, throwing things around the apartment.

"Where is what?" I asked, my voice trembling.

"The money, Kai! Where's the money?"

"I don't know, Dwight. I really don't know," I said, my heart pounding.

He slapped me hard across the face, and I fell to the floor, my cheek burning with pain. "You stupid bitch," he shouted. "I told you to take care of him. What did you do?"

I couldn't speak, paralyzed by fear and pain.

Dwight appeared over me, his eyes storming with hatred and anger, and I knew there was no escape. "I'll show you what happens when you disobey me," he said, dragging me to my feet.

He took me to a cheap motel, the kind of place where no questions were asked. The man who was waiting there was someone I'd never met before. Dwight shoved me into the room with the stranger and locked the door behind me. The man approached me with a leering grin, and I knew what was expected of me.

***

I hugged myself at my counter, trying to shake off the memory. The feeling of helplessness and violation was still so raw, so real. I was trapped in that nightmare for years, unable to see a way out. Dwight controlled every aspect of my life, and used me for his own gain, without a second thought or a shred of compassion or mercy.

One day, though, everything changed. That was the day I decided to stand alongside Agent Cole. Dwight was caught in our snare, and I couldn't have been happier. I wasn't completely free, and the scars he left behind were deep and lasting, but it felt like things were finally coming to an end, at least to an acceptable escape, as I had envisioned.

Now, I turned away from the window and walked back to the couch and collapsed. I didn't even bother to put the salad in the refrigerator. I stared at the door again, to make sure all the locks were in place, and the silence of the apartment was deafening, amplifying my thoughts.

Chapter 12

LORENZO

Finally, we would see the results of the paternity test. On the way to the lab to have the test done, little Symone was just as happy and curious as ever, asking all kinds of questions as the nurse swabbed the insides of our cheeks.

The lab itself was sterile and cold, with white walls and the faint smell of disinfectant hanging in the air. The fluorescent lights buzzed overhead, casting a harsh glare on the tile floor. The waiting area was occupied by uninviting plastic chairs, the kind that forced sitters to shift and fidget like toddlers in church. Juniper sat beside me, her presence a pillar of strength, even though I could see the sadness etched in her features. She was dressed in a simple but elegant purple and yellow dress, her dark hair pulled back in a neat ponytail, and she did her best to keep up a strong front for Symone's sake.

My lady didn't say much, but her eyes spoke volumes. Each time

Symone turned her innocent, inquisitive little face toward us, Juniper mustered a smile, and she gave my hand a gentle squeeze of reassurance. I knew she was just as anxious as I was, but she hid her struggle well. Her sadness was palpable, a heavy cloud that hovered over us, but she held it together and would not let it spill over and worry our little girl.

I already knew what the lab was going to discover, and I dreaded the day when we'd see it on paper. Now, that day had arrived. Three agonizing weeks had passed, each day a relentless reminder of what I already knew deep down: Shamar Collins was Symone's biological father. Hearing it from the judge would make it official, and then the real battle would begin, the fight to keep Symone if Shamar decided to claim custody. The sleepless nights had taken their toll, with nightmares of Erin and the frightening possibility of losing Symone was messing with my mental health.

The drive to the courthouse was tense, the silence only broken by Symone's cheerful chatter from the back seat. When we walked in, my heart pounded with each step, the weight of what was about to happen pressing down on me. As we sat in the courtroom, waiting for the judge to call our case, every second dragging on like an eternity. The official confirmation would soon come, and with it, our lives would change. Honestly, I wasn't sure I was ready to fight, but Juniper was a comforting anchor, and Brian, our lead attorney, was ready to argue our case.

Over the past few weeks, we had learned a lot about Shamar. He lived in Sacramento and worked as a bank manager. He was single and led a modest life, with no criminal record. He seemed to have things in order, but that only added to my anxiety. If he were a drug addict or some kind of loser or criminal, there would be a better chance of me keeping Symone, as she already had an established home with us. Unfortunately, Shamar seemed like one of the good guys, at least on paper.

According to Brian, Shamar had heard about Symone from his ex, Laci. They had met for lunch one day, and during that conversation, she mentioned having stumbled upon a picture of the baby when she and Erin got into a fight. She stabbed Erin that day, but the memory of the photograph had stuck with her even after the skirmish, and she couldn't shake the resemblance.

Curiosity got the better of Shamar when he heard about the child who looked like him. He started digging around and found Erin's Facebook page. From there, it wasn't hard for him to find mine. As he scrolled through my profile, he found more pictures of Symone, and the resemblance was just as undeniable as Laci had said. Every photo he looked at only confirmed Laci's suspicions and triggered his own.

I could only imagine the shock and confusion Shamar must have felt, the slow realization dawning on him with every click. It had to be like putting together a puzzle, every piece too much of a perfect fit to ignore. It didn't take long for him to reach out, starting the chain of events that had led us to those very seats in the courtroom, waiting for the judge to confirm what we all already knew.

I couldn't help but think about how quickly everything had spiraled due to Shamar's determination. The weeks of uncertainty, the sleepless nights, and the fear of what was to come were now coming to a head. The truth was about to be laid bare, and the real battle for Symone's future was just beginning. As I glanced at him across the courtroom, I saw Shamar, dressed impeccably in a perfectly tailored gray-blue suit, complemented by a crisp, white shirt and a tasteful, patterned tie. His calm composed demeanor only added to his aura of stability and reliability.

The courtroom itself was imposing, with high ceilings and dark wood paneling that gave it a solemn, almost intimidating atmosphere. The judge's bench was elevated, commanding respect. Judge Aaron Thompson, an older Black man with a stern but fair expression, presided over the proceedings. His black robes and glasses, perched low on his nose, gave him an air of authority and wisdom.

Finally, the moment arrived. Judge Thompson cleared his throat, and the room fell into an expectant silence. "The results of the DNA test in the case of Symone Ryan's paternity are conclusive," he robotically announced. "The probability of paternity for the child is 99.9 percent in favor of Shamar Collins. Mr. Collins is this child's father."

As he slammed his gavel, it felt like a punch to my gut. I saw Shamar's composed façade waver only slightly, a flicker of emotion in his eyes. I, on the other hand, was a complete wreck. I had a total meltdown, right there in front of everyone. I simply couldn't hold back my tears, overwhelmed by the cruel reality of the situation.

Judge Thompson's voice softened slightly as he continued, "We will reconvene in thirty days to make a final decision regarding custody. In the meantime, I urge both parties to consider the best interests of the child."

The weight of the judge's words settled over the room, the tension almost palpable. The next month would be a grueling test of strength and resolve. Juniper squeezed my hand, a silent promise of support, while Brian gave me a reassuring nod. Despite the fear and uncertainty, I knew we had to stay strong for Symone. The battle was far from over, and we would do everything in our power to keep her safe and with us.

As we exited the courtroom, my mind was a whirlwind of thoughts and emotions. The judge's pronouncement still echoed in my ears, mingling with the murmur of voices and the shuffle of footsteps around us. I clung tightly to Juniper's hand, drawing all the strength I could get from her. Brian walked on my other side, his presence a solid and comforting anchor in a storm of painful uncertainty.

The corridors of the courthouse felt endless, each step taking us farther from the judge's words but not from their impact. Finally, we emerged into the sunlight outside. The brightness was almost blinding after the dimness of the legal halls, but it did little to lift my spirits with such a heavy weight pressing down on my chest.

"We need to talk," Juniper said gently, steering me toward a nearby bench. Her voice was calm, soothing, but I could see the worry in her eyes.

Brian nodded. "Yes, it's important to strategize. We have thirty days, and we need to use every one of them wisely."

I nodded, trying to gather my scattered thoughts. "So, what's our next move?" I asked, my voice trembling. "How do we prove that Symone's is best off with us?"

Juniper squeezed my hand again, her grip firm and reassuring. "We start by gathering every piece of evidence that shows how much Symone means to you, how much you've done for her, and how stable and loving our home is. We'll need statements from friends, family, teachers—anyone who can attest to the bond you share and the healthy and enriching environment you've created for her."

Brian chimed in, "We also need to be prepared for anything Shamar's side might bring up. As they say, know your enemy. We must anticipate their arguments and have our counterarguments ready. It's gonna be tough, but we're in this together."

Their words brought a semblance of order to the chaos in my mind. I took a deep breath, trying to calm the storm of emotions boiling inside me. "Okay," I said, my voice steadier now. "We'll do whatever it takes, for Symone."

The next few days were a hurricane of activity. We gathered documents, spoke to potential witnesses, and met with our lawyer to plan our strategy. Each piece of evidence we collected felt like a very small step in securing Symone's future. Despite our best efforts, the uncertainty remained, a constant undercurrent of fear and doubt.

One evening, after a particularly long and exhausting day, I sat alone in Symone's room. The soft pink walls and the stuffed animals situated neatly on her bed were a stark contrast to the turmoil inside me. I picked up her favorite teddy bear and held it close. It gave me a plastic smile as I let the tears fall. The thought of losing her was unbearable, a pain too deep to fathom, and I wished Erin was there to explain it all.

Just then, I heard a soft knock on the door. Juniper peeked in, her eyes full of concern. "Can I come in?"

I nodded, unable to speak.

She sat beside me and wrapped her arms around me in a comforting embrace. "We're going to get through this," she whispered. "Symone is our daughter in every way that matters. The judge will see that."

I clung to her words, seeking solace. "I just… I can't imagine life without her," I confessed, my voice breaking.

***

The next day, I found myself standing outside the home of Mr. and Mrs. Cravins. My hands were clammy, my heart racing. Sharing the hard truth about Symone's paternity was something I had dreaded for years, but it was a conversation that couldn't be avoided any longer. I took a deep breath and rang the doorbell.

The familiar chime echoed inside, and moments later, Mrs. Cravins opened the door. Her warm smile faltered slightly when she saw the serious expression on my face. "Lorenzo? Honey, come in," she said, stepping aside to let me enter. "What brings you here so early?"

I followed her into the living room, my anxiety growing with each step.

Mr. Cravins was sitting in his favorite armchair, reading the newspaper. He looked up and smiled. "Lorenzo, it's good to see you. Everything okay, son?"

I took a seat on the couch, struggling to find the right words. "Mr.

and Mrs. Cravins, there's something I need to tell you, something about Symone."

Mrs. Cravins sat down beside me, her eyes filled with concern. "What is it, Lorenzo? Is she all right? Oh, please tell me our sweet girl isn't sick again!"

"She's fine," I assured them quickly. "It's just... It's about her paternity." I paused to gather my courage, then finished, "Symone isn't biologically mine."

The room fell silent, the weight of my words hanging in the air.

Mr. Cravins set his newspaper aside, and his expression was one of shock when he asked, "What do you mean, not biologically yours?"

I took a deep breath, the years of secrecy and fear finally surfacing. "I found out a few years ago, to be honest, but I never thought it would come back to haunt me."

Mrs. Cravins looked at me with a mixture of surprise and confusion. "Years ago, you say? Why didn't you tell us sooner?"

"I didn't know how. I didn't want to lose her, and I didn't want to hurt you. I was scared," I admitted, my voice barely above a whisper. "I couldn't bear to part with Symone, and I didn't want you to think any less of me."

Mr. Cravins leaned forward, and, to my surprise, his expression and voice softened. "Lorenzo, you've been a wonderful father to Symone. Biology doesn't change that."

Mrs. Cravins reached out and took my hand, her grip warm and reassuring. "We've seen how much you love her, how well you've taken care of her. That's all that matters to us."

I felt a lump form in my throat, their unexpected support overwhelming me. "I never thought it would come out," I said, my voice breaking. "Now, though, with a custody battle coming up... Well, I just don't know what to do."

Mr. Cravins nodded and offered a thoughtful expression. "That's simple, son. You fight for her, and we'll fight with you. Lorenzo, Symone is our granddaughter, and she belongs with you. We'll do everything we can to help you keep her."

Tears filled my eyes, relief and gratitude washing over me. "Thank you," I whispered, unable to find enough powerful words to express how much their support meant to me.

Mrs. Cravins squeezed my hand, her eyes filled with determination. "Yes, we're in this together, Lorenzo. We all love that little angel, and we won't let her be taken from you."

The next few days passed in a tumult of activity and emotion. I spent countless hours with Brian, gathering even more evidence to demonstrate the positive role I'd played in Symone's life. We collected statements from teachers, neighbors, and family friends, each one a testament to the bond Symone and I shared.

Mr. and Mrs. Cravins, true to their word, became an integral part of our efforts. They reached out to their own network, gathering additional support and character references. Their involvement lent an undeniable weight to our case, their love for Symone evident in every action they took.

One evening, after a particularly tiring day, I sat down with Juniper and Brain in our living room. The coffee table was covered with documents and notes, the fruits of our relentless preparation. The room was quiet, with only the ticking of the clock on the wall for a backdrop.

Juniper broke the silence, her voice soft but determined. "We're making progress, Lorenzo. We're building a strong case here."

Brian nodded. "We just need to stay focused. We can't let fear or doubt creep in."

I sighed. "I know. It's just… Every time I think about the possibility of losing her, it's like a punch to the gut."

"Not gonna happen. We've come too far, and we love her too much to let that happen," Juniper said.

Her words were a balm to my frayed nerves. I squeezed her hand, drawing strength from her conviction. "You're right. We have to stay strong, for Symone."

As the days turned into weeks, our preparations intensified. Symone's grandparents and I spent countless hours rehearsing our statements, making sure every detail was perfect. We knew the upcoming court date would be crucial, and we couldn't afford to make any mistakes when we took our places on the stand.

Finally, the day arrived. We found ourselves back in the imposing courtroom, the high ceilings and dark wood paneling casting a solemn atmosphere over the proceedings. Judge Thompson presided again, his stern but fair expression giving nothing away.

The tension was palpable as we presented our case. Brian was eloquent and thorough, laying out the evidence with precision. Witnesses testified to the loving and stable environment we had provided for Symone, their words painting a vivid picture of the life we had built together.

When it was my turn to speak, I took a deep breath. My heart threatened to pound out of my chair as I climbed up to sit in the witness chair. I looked at Judge Thompson, then at Shamar, who sat across the room wearing an unreadable expression. "Your Honor," I began, my voice steady despite the nerves, "I may not be Symone's biological father, but I am her dad in every way that matters. From the moment I first held her in my arms, I knew I would do anything to protect and care for her. She is my daughter, and I am her father. Our bond is not defined by DNA but by love, commitment, and countless shared moments."

I paused, and my eyes briefly met Symone's. She was sitting with the Cravin's, her wide eyes watching everything with a mixture of curiosity and confusion. The sight of her gave me the strength to continue.

"I found out the truth about her paternity years ago, but it didn't change how I felt about her. I chose to raise her, to love her, and to be the father she needed, and I will continue to do so, no matter what. I ask you to consider what is truly in her best interest. She belongs with the family who has loved and cared for her all her life."

After I finished speaking, the room fell into a hushed silence. Judge Thompson regarded me thoughtfully before turning his attention to Shamar, who was preparing to present his case.

The next hours ticked by at an agonizingly slow pace. We listened as Shamar and his lawyer made their arguments. Attorney Thomas Greene was a tall, imposing man with a sharp jawline and piercing brown eyes that seemed to miss nothing. His tailored black suit and perfectly knotted tie gave him an air of polished professionalism, but there was an edge to him that put me on guard.

"Your Honor," Greene began, his voice smooth and confident, "I must emphasize that while Mr. Ryan may appear to be a dedicated father, his lifestyle tells a different story." He then paused to let his words sink in. Finally, he continued, "Mr. Ryan is a music producer, a profession known for erratic hours and instability. His income fluctuates wildly, and he often attends rap parties that extend into the wee hours of the morning, sometimes attended by—shall we say—unsavory characters. This lifestyle is not conducive to the stable, nurturing environment a childlike Symone needs."

I felt a surge of anger and frustration as he spoke. It was clear that Greene was trying to paint me as an irresponsible, unreliable parent. I glanced at Juniper, who gave me a reassuring nod, reminding me to stay composed.

Greene continued, "Mr. Ryan's frequent absence due to his profession raises serious concerns about his ability to provide consistent care and supervision for Symone. Can we truly say this is the best environment for her?"

His words stung and felt like personal attacks. I wanted to stand up and refute every claim, but I knew I had to trust in Brian and the case we had built.

When it was our turn again, Brian was determined to prove Greene's remarks false. "Your Honor, while it's true that Mr. Ryan is a music producer, it is a narrow-minded notion to suggest that the profession, in any way, precludes him from being an excellent parent. In fact, Mr. Ryan has managed to balance his career with his parental responsibilities remarkably well. He has structured his work around Symone's needs, ensuring that he is always there for her important moments and daily routines, and he provides for her financially as well."

The judge nodded, urging Brian on after a short pause to allow his words to resonate in the courtroom.

"Furthermore," Brian continued, "the presence and support of Mr. and Mrs. Cravins and Mr. Ryan's fiancée, Juniper Alexander provides an additional layer of stability and care for Symone. The child is already bonded with this loving, supportive family that is deeply committed to her wellbeing."

Judge Thompson listened intently, his expression thoughtful and inscrutable. When Brian finished, he called for a recess. We stepped outside, the fresh air a welcome relief from the tension inside. Juniper and Brian stood by my side, their presence a comforting reminder that I wasn't alone in the fight.

As we waited for the judge's decision, Mr. and Mrs. Cravins joined us, their expressions a mix of hope and anxiety.

"No matter what happens, Lorenzo," Mr. Cravins said, "we're proud of you. You've done everything you could for Symone."

Mrs. Cravins nodded, her eyes shining with unshed tears. "We'll get through this together. Symone knows how much she's loved. Love is what's important. I'm sure the judge will see that."

After what felt like an entire era of time, Judge Thompson's clerk called us back into the courtroom. My heart pounded in my chest as we filed back in, each step heavy with anticipation and dread. We took our seats, swallowed up by tension once more. Juniper grabbed my hand, offering silent support, while Brian gave me a reassuring nod.

Judge Thompson took his place on the elevated bench, his expression as stern and unreadable as ever. He cleared his throat, and the room fell into a keen silence. "After hearing all the arguments presented today," the judge began, his voice steady and authoritative, "While I realize all parties are eager to settle the matter, I find that it requires further deliberation. It is not a decision to be made lightly, and I want to ensure that every aspect is considered thoroughly."

I held my breath, my eyes fixed on the judge, hanging on his every word.

"I need one week to review the evidence and testimonies presented. My clerk will notify your attorneys of the date and time for our next session, during which I will deliver my final decision. For the time being," Judge Thompson added, looking directly at me, "Symone is to remain in the care of Lorenzo Ryan. I urge all parties to continue considering the best interests of the child during this interim period."

I exhaled a breath I didn't realize I'd been holding. Relief washed over me, mingled with the ever-present anxiety of the unknown. I glanced at Juniper and Brian, who both looked equally relieved.

As we left the courtroom, the faces of Symone's grandparents were painted with both hope and concern.

Mr. Cravins clapped a hand on my shoulder, his grip firm. "One more week, Lorenzo. We've got this."

Mrs. Cravins nodded, her eyes still filled with determination. "Symone is where she belongs, and we'll make sure it stays that way."

We walked out into the bright afternoon sun, the weight of the courtroom still lingering but tempered by a renewed sense of purpose. The next week would be another grueling test of patience and resolve, but I knew we had to stay strong for my baby girl.

Chapter 13

JUNIPER

It was heart-wrenching to watch Lorenzo worry about Symone's situation. He was constantly torn apart with concern, immersed in heartache, not knowing whether we would be able to keep Symone or if she would be sent to a family she had no relationship with, just because they shared the same blood. Some days, I didn't even know how to approach him. Fortunately, we had only four days to wait before we would hear the judge's final decision.

Symone had become such a vital part of our lives, and the thought of losing her to strangers was unbearable. She was more than just a case to us; she was family. For that reason, the impending decision hung over us like a dark cloud.

I had to do something. I couldn't just sit back and watch everything fall apart. So, I called Nikki and explained everything to her, laying out my plan.

"Let's do this then," she said, agreeing to help without a second thought.

Before we proceeded, I knew I had to tell Steven. When I spoke to him about the plan and the money, his reaction was immediate. "Juniper, this could mess up Lorenzo's case," he said firmly, with deep concern. "We can't risk doing anything that might jeopardize Symone's future. Plus, that money I gave you is meant for Kaylee."

I understood his worry, but desperation pushed me forward. "Steven, I have to try. We can't just sit around and do nothing, waiting for some judge to determine her fate."

Steven shook his head, his frustration evident. "What if Thompson rules in Lorenzo's favor after all, but you've already paid this man? You could be throwing it away for nothing. Not only that, but if you get caught, you'll be barred from legal practice, your license revoked. You could even serve jail time, Juniper."

I met his gaze, my voice steady. "I don't care. It's a chance I'm willing to take. We can't leave Symone's future to chance."

After some tense moments of discussion, Steven reluctantly agreed to let me proceed, as long as I did so with great caution. He understood my determination and trusted my judgment, but the stakes were high, and the risks were real.

Nikki and I worked quickly. First, we contacted Shamar and arranged for him to fly to Los Angeles for a face-to-face meeting. We booked him into a stylish boutique hotel downtown, renowned for its discreet luxury and impeccable service. The lobby was a masterpiece of modern art and classic elegance, with soft lighting that accentuated the opulence of the surroundings. The room we reserved for him, on one of the upper floors, offered panoramic views of the city, a fitting backdrop for our clandestine negotiations.

On the day of the meeting, Nikki and I arrived early, dressed meticulously to convey both professionalism and determination. I wore a sophisticated black dress that exuded confidence, paired with understated jewelry and classic heels. Nikki opted for a white and blue pantsuit that complemented her commanding presence, her braids still dangling down her back.

When we knocked on Shamar's door, it opened to reveal a man who epitomized elegance and refinement. He was at least six feet tall, and his fair skin contrasting sharply with the charcoal gray of his perfectly tailored suit. His demeanor was calm and collected, but I sensed the curiosity in his eyes as he welcomed us into his impeccably appointed suite.

"Thank you for meeting with us, Shamar," I began, my voice firm despite the nerves that boiling within me. I exchanged a meaningful glance with Nikki before I continued, "We have a proposal for you. If you agree to let the paternity case go, we are prepared to offer you fifty grand, in cash."

Shamar's eyebrows lifted slightly, a spark of surprise crossing his features before he composed himself. He nodded slowly, processing our offer with guarded interest. "Go on."

"We'll need you to sign an NDA, a nondisclosure agreement," Nikki added, handing the document to him, along with a pen.

"I work at a bank. I know what it is," Shamar said. Then, without hesitation, he perused the NDA and signed it, the smooth stroke of his pen finalizing our agreement.

Nikki then handed over an envelope containing the agreed-upon sum, meticulously counted out to ensure transparency and trust.

As Shamar took the envelope, his gaze meeting hers.

Nikki leaned in, her voice dropping to a chilling whisper. "Remember, you've never seen us. If this gets out, I know people who will put an end to your life." The threat was frightening, revealing a side of her I didn't know existed.

Shamar didn't flinch. Instead, he simply nodded once. Composed but with a hint of steel in his eyes, he said, "I was never here."

With that declaration as our insurance, we turned and left the room, leaving behind a palpable sense of unease. Nikki's words lingered, a stark reminder of the dangerous world we had just brushed against. The weight of the NDA and its implications settled heavily on my mind as I exchanged a wary glance with her. It wasn't just business as usual; it was a pact sealed in silence and enforced by the shadowy promise of dire consequences.

The aftermath of our secret meeting with Shamar left me feeling both relieved and anxious. The weight of our actions pounced on top of me as I grappled with the implications of what we had done. A $50,000 payout felt like a fortune, but it was a small price to pay if it meant securing Symone's place in our family.

When I returned home, the atmosphere between Lorenzo and me was tense. I sensed his worry, and it was obvious in the expression on his face, despite his efforts to remain composed for Symone's sake.

In the days leading up to the judge's decision, I found myself constantly checking my phone, half-expecting a call or a message that would unravel our carefully crafted plan. The fear of repercussions loomed large, but I pushed those thoughts aside, focusing instead on being there for Symone and supporting Lorenzo through his moments of doubt.

Chapter 14

LORENZO

The day of the final hearing arrived, and we once again found ourselves in the imposing courtroom of Judge Thompson. The clerk led us in, and we took our seats, almost suffocated by the overbearing tension. The judge entered, and the room fell silent after everyone obeyed the bailiff's orders to be seated. I glanced around and noticed a very conspicuous absence. My anxiety heightened when I saw no sign of Shamar, and I had to wonder what to make of him not being present for such an important hearing.

As we waited, Thomas Greene, Shamar's attorney, repeatedly glanced at his phone in frustration. He frantically dialed a number several times, likely Shamar's, then scrunched up his face in disapproval when the calls went straight to voicemail. The murmurs in the courtroom grew louder with each of Mr. Greene's failed attempt to reach his client.

Judge Thompson's expression was increasingly stern as the minutes ticked by. He cleared his throat, and the room fell silent once more. "Counselor where is your client?" he asked Tom Greene, impatience oozing from his tone.

Greene stood, his polished exterior cracking slightly under the pressure. "Your Honor, I've been trying to reach Mr. Collins, but he's not answering. I'm not sure why he hasn't arrived."

The judge's irritation was palpable. He sighed heavily and looked around the courtroom before fixing his gaze back on the befuddled attorney. "Mr. Greene, regardless of your client's absence, we must proceed. His failure to appear does not reflect well on him, but my decision has been made based on the evidence and testimonies presented."

I felt my heart pound as I listened, every muscle in my body tensing with anticipation.

Judge Thompson continued, his voice firm and decisive. "After careful consideration, I have concluded that it is in the best interest of Symone Ryan to remain in the care of Lorenzo Ryan. The stability, love, and support provided by Mr. Ryan, along with the involvement of Mr. and Mrs. Cravins, offer this child the best possible environment for her growth and wellbeing."

A wave of relief washed over me, nearly overwhelming in its intensity. I glanced at Juniper, whose eyes were filled with tears of joy, and Brian gave me a proud, reassuring smile. The Cravin's, sitting behind us, were equally elated, their faces lit with gratitude and relief that mirrored my own.

The judge's gavel slammed down with a finality that echoed through the courtroom. "This court is adjourned. Good luck to you both," he declared.

As we stood to leave, my legs were shaky with a mixture of

emotions, a warming blend of relief, joy, and overwhelming gratitude. I turned to Juniper and Brian and pulled both of them into a tight embrace. "We did it," I whispered, my voice choked with emotion.

"We knew the truth would prevail," Juniper replied, her voice equally emotional.

The Cravin's approached, full of pride and happiness.

"Well done, Lorenzo," Mr. Cravins said, with a congratulatory slap on my back, "and Symone is lucky to have you."

Mrs. Cravins hugged me tightly. "We'll always be here for you and Symone. You're family, and we'll do everything to support you both."

As we walked out of the courtroom, the weight of the past weeks seemed to lift from my shoulders and fly away. The sun was shining brightly, a perfect contrast to the tension and uncertainty that had filled our lives recently. We had fought hard, and our love for Symone had carried us through.

In the days that followed, life settled into a comforting rhythm. Symone's laughter filled our home, her joy a constant reminder of what we had fought for. We celebrated with family and friends, each moment a testament to the strength of our bond and the power of love.

As I tucked my daughter into bed one evening, she looked up at me with her big, innocent eyes and asked, "Daddy, you'll always be with me, right?"

I smiled. "Always, sweetheart. No matter what," I said, and in that moment, surrounded by the love and warmth of our home, I knew we had found our forever.

Juniper had purposely set aside private moments together to reflect on everything we had overcome. Our journey hadn't been easy. Facing uncertainty, navigating legal battles, and confronting the possibility of losing Symone had tested us in ways we had never imagined. Yet, through it all, our love for Symone and our shared determination to give her the best future had carried us forward.

"To family!" Brian toasted as he joined us in celebration, his voice dripping with pride. He lifted his glass even higher and finished, "To love that conquers all!"

We clinked our champagne flutes together, creating a melodious sound that rang out with the promise of hope and resilience. The journey had tested us all, but it had also united us in miraculous, unbreakable ways.

Through it all, we did our best to protect Symone. The little one really didn't even know what was going on. Juniper and I took pleasure in knowing that she was finally safe and secure in our care. Our home became a sanctuary, filled with warmth and laughter, a place where both of our kids could thrive and dream without fear of uncertainty looming overhead.

As for Shamar, his absence from the final hearing remained a mystery. Brian said we were good, since the judge had rendered his final decision, but I still had my questions about where the man was.

Reflecting on everything we had endured, I knew our journey was far from over. Challenges would inevitably arise, but we would always face them with the newfound strength born from our collective experience. Whether she knew it or not, Symone had taught us the true meaning of resilience and love.

A few weeks after the hearing, I awoke and checked my email. To my surprise, Kai Jae had been nominated for a BET Award for Best New Artist. We were already off to a great start, and that was exactly what we needed to keep Kai's momentum going.

I picked up the phone to share the news with her, and she screamed into my ear with excitement. Her reaction made me smile from ear to ear. It was amazing to be part of such a big moment for her.

Chapter 15

JUNIPER

Leaving the studio one evening, I noticed a car following me. I was not sure if it was just my paranoia taking control or if it was really a threat, but my heart raced either way. Not willing to take any chances, I took a few detours before heading home.

Back at the house, I double-checked the locks and settled onto the couch, my mind still aflutter. Between giving Shamar the fifty grand and the info I knew about Kai, I was nervous. I needed to talk to Nikki again, soon. Things seemed to be spiraling out of control, and I needed to know exactly what we were up against.

I did my best to distract myself by thinking of other things. As I sat there, I realized it had been almost four years since I'd last been with someone sexually, and that was Steven. My celibacy journey had its difficult moments. Some days were easier than others, filled with work and music and the comforting dullness of routine. Other days, though, the loneliness and the physical longing hit me like a tidal wave, relentless and insistent. Hornier than I wanted to admit, I made my way to the guest bedroom, my heart pounding violently with a mix of anticipation and shame. I hated that I had to hide that part of myself, and I was sure Lorenzo would never understand.

That bedroom had become a sanctuary of secrets and privacy. I reached into the drawer and felt the familiar contours of my Rose, the one I'd meticulously tucked away, hidden from Lorenzo's prying eyes like my own secret treasure. The drawer barely creaked when I pulled out the toy, its sleek, purple design catching the soft light from the bedside lamp.

The cool silicone felt familiar and reassuring. My mind spun with memories of Steven: his touch, his voice, and the way he made me feel alive and desired. Steven was gone now, and I was left with only the empty echo of what had been.

I closed the drawer softly and sat on the edge of the bed, with the Rose in my lap. The room was silent, save for the distant hum of the passing traffic outside. I took a deep breath, trying to quiet the noise in my head. I pulled my pants and panties off. I was already wet from just thinking about spooning in bed with Lorenzo, just imagining his hardness pressing against my ass. It was not an easy fight to ward off the urge to make love to each other. I leaned back and let the Rose vibrate on my vajayjay, allowing my mind to wander, fantasizing about Lorenzo inside me. Five minutes later, I was breathing hard and feeling my cum drip down my inner thighs.

"So, *this* is what you do when I'm not here?"

I looked up and, to my horror, saw Lorenzo standing by the bedroom door with his penis poking through his pants. I jumped up, ashamed, and froze, my heart frozen. His expression was a mixture of surprise, desire, and something else I couldn't quite place. I scrambled to cover myself, my face flushing with embarrassment. "Lorenzo, I…"

I stuttered, barely above a whisper. "I-I didn't know you were coming. Uh, where are the girls?"

He stepped closer, the look in his eyes intensifying. "Clearly," he said, his voice low and husky, "but don't stop on my account."

I hesitated, unsure of how to respond. The room seemed to shrink around us, the air thick with tension. I still wondered about the children, but I didn't want to ask again.

He took another step forward, his gaze never leaving mine. "You think about me when you're alone," he said, more a statement than a question. "You imagine us together, don't you?"

I nodded, unable to find any suitable words.

He reached out and gently cupped my face in his hand. His touch was electric, sending tremors down my spine. "Show me," he whispered. "Show me how you think of me."

I swallowed hard as his request sank in. Slowly, I let the sheet fall from my grasp, exposing me to him.

His eyes darkened with desire as he took in the sight before him. "Damn, ma," he murmured, trailing his hand down my neck to my breast. He leaned in, close enough that his lips brushed against my ear as he said, "I want to watch you."

I picked up the Rose again, my hand trembling slightly. He stepped back to give me some space, but he never took his eyes off me. I lay back, parted my legs, and turned on the toy. The enticing hum filled the room, and I let out a soft moan as the vibrations hit me.

Lorenzo watched, his breathing growing heavier. His hand moved to his waistband to free his erection from his pants. Seeing how he slowly stroked himself, matching the rhythm of the toy as I moved it inside me, only made me wetter. The sight of him, so turned on and focused on me, only heightened my arousal.

"Faster," he urged, his voice rough with need.

I complied, increasing the speed and pressure, until my body arched up off the bed. The pleasure built quickly, overwhelming, and all-consuming. I came hard, and my body trembled from head to toe as waves of ecstasy crashed over me. I collapsed onto the bed. My breaths came in short, ragged gasps as the last quakes of my orgasm coursed through me.

Lorenzo's eyes were still locked on mine, dark and intense, his desire evident in every inch of his body. He moved toward me, his erection still prominent, but instead of climbing onto the bed, he settled down beside me. His gaze softened as he reached out to kiss my lips. "You're incredible," he whispered, with a tinge of awe and affection. "I can't wait to make love to you on our wedding night."

I smiled, and a warm glow filled me. "I can't either," I replied, my voice still breathless from the intensity of my orgasm. "Right now, though, I just want to be close to you."

He nodded and offered a tender smile before he lay down beside me and pulled me into his arms. I nestled against him, enjoying the steady beat of his heart beneath my cheek. There was something profoundly comforting about the way he held me; I felt invincible there, with him, as if nothing in the world could harm us as long as we were together. We lay in silence for a few moments, just basking in the closeness.

Finally, Lorenzo spoke, his voice thoughtful. "I've been thinking a lot about our future," he said, "about what it means to build a life together."

I looked up at him, curious. "And?" I coaxed.

He sighed softly, his fingers tracing gentle patterns on my back. "I want to make sure we always communicate like this, openly and honestly. I don't ever want to take you for granted or let any misunderstandings come between us."

I nodded, touched by his sincerity. "I feel the same way. We are a team, and we must always face everything together."

Lorenzo smiled, and adorable crinkles formed in the corners of his eyes. "I knew I was right about you from the moment we met. You're my perfect little freak," he said, smiling.

"Whatever, big head. So, does this mean our celibacy vow is broken?" I asked, suddenly serious.

"Hell, naw. I haven't hit that yet, have I?" he asked with a laugh.

We spent the rest of the evening talking and laughing, sharing dreams, and making plans for our future. It was a night filled with love and connection, a reminder of why we had chosen each other. When we finally drifted off to sleep in each other's arms, I felt a deep sense of contentment, a great comfort in the knowledge that we were building something beautiful together.

The next morning, I called Nikki. "We need to meet, today."

"Same place?" she asked.

"Yeah. Noon, okay?"

"Perfect. I'll see you there."

As soon as I got to the spot, I walked over to our normal table and found her already sitting there with her typical latte. I was eager to get straight to the point. "Are we good on Shamar?" I asked.

"Yes. I heard he bought a new condo and is off living his best life. He didn't really want Symone. He just wanted to make bank off the deal."

Even though it was irritating that Symone's biological father had shamelessly used her as a cash cow, I felt a little better after leaving the café. At least I knew he wasn't trying to cause any trouble, and it couldn't have been him following me around. It seemed he'd taken the money and run, and I was fine with that.

I went to my house to pick up some clothes for Kaylee and me. We slept over at Lorenzo's two to three days a week. She loved playing with Symone, and I loved being with both of them.

Unfortunately, as soon as I turned off my house alarm, an unwanted presence approached me from behind.

"June," the sickeningly familiar voice said, startling me.

"Where did you come from, DaMarco, and why are you here?" I sternly demanded.

"Don't pretend like you didn't see me parked on the other side of the street."

"Obviously, I didn't, or I wouldn't be asking your ass," I snapped as he followed me inside my home.

"Someone sent me a picture you posted on Facebook of you, Kaybae, dude, and his daughter. It had a caption on it, something about 'my family,'" he said, with a nasty snarl and an eye-roll.

"Someone, huh? Probably 'cause they messy. Are you tellin' me you brought yo' bitch ass to my house to ask about some bullshit post I made on Facebook? Dude, as you call him, has a name. It's Lorenzo, and he's my fiancé," I snapped back.

"Fiancé? Pssh." DaMarco laughed and made himself comfortable on my living room sofa without being invited to do so. "If it wasn't for me, you wouldn't even have met dude."

"DaMarco, you had another woman on the side while we were dating," I said over my shoulder, as I went into Kaylee's room to gather her things.

"And you were fucking your boss!" he yelled.

I stepped out of Kaylee's room and stared at him. "Fucked, DaMarco. I *fucked* my boss. Remember? I told you how good it was, the best I had at the time. How nice of you to come in here, bringing back sweet memories," I said with a cruel snicker.

DaMarco jumped up from the couch as if to hit me, but he stopped when my door opened, and Kacia and Philly walked in. I had completely forgotten they wanted to talk to me about something. I was glad to see them, especially when DaMarco stormed out of my house pissed off and nearly knocked Philly down.

"What's up with your baby-daddy?" Kacia asked.

"Girl, just his bitch-assness showing. I forgot you were coming over. I just stopped in to get some clothes to take over to Lorenzo's," I said.

"I texted to let you know we were on the way," she said. When she set her purse on the counter, I noticed it was a new Louis Vuitton Carmel bag, priced at an easy $5,000.

"Sorry. Left my phone in the car," I explained.

Kacia followed me back into Kaylee's room while Philly sat where DaMarco had been a few minutes earlier. He was quiet, and I sensed something was going on between the two of them, but I didn't want to pry.

Kacia sat on Kaylee's bed, also quieter than usual.

Finally, I couldn't take it no more, so I asked, "What's up, sis?"

"June, I'm about to ask you something, something quite serious," she said, tearing up.

Crying wasn't really her thing, so I was even more concerned than before. "What is it, Kacia? What's wrong?" I urged as I placed Kaylee's socks in her Princess Tiana backpack.

"Philly and I have been thinking about something for a few weeks. You know I've been having some issues getting pregnant, right?"

"Right."

"Well, I found out I have uterine fibroids. I'm down to my last two viable eggs."

"Oh, no. What are you going to do? Adopt?"

"Well, we are hoping you, um… Maybe you can consider being our surrogate," she nervously spat out. "I know it's asking a lot, but… I just want a baby so bad, June."

I was completely shocked, as that was the last thing I expected anyone to ever ask of me. I heard Philly in the kitchen, digging a bottled water out of the fridge, but I knew he was only doing that to be closer to the bedroom so he could eavesdrop on our conversation. Knowing he was listening, I frowned and answered in only a whisper, "Wait. They don't have to insert Philly's cum in me, do they?"

Kacia continued, ignoring my question, "Sis, I know you're engaged and planning a wedding, so I will understand if you don't wanna do it. I know the timing's not great. Tas just had the twins and is still healing, so we don't want to ask her. It's really a simple procedure. They just need to run some tests to determine when you're ovulating. The lab will inject a single sperm into each of my remaining eggs. So, no, Philly's semen will not be inserted inside you," she said with a sheepish grin. "The eggs are kept in the laboratory for up to six days. The embryos will be monitored to ensure they are growing well. If everything is okay and the fertilization takes, the embryos will be implanted in your womb using a thin catheter."

I was still looking at her in shock when I heard my mouth answer, "Yes, sis. Of course. It'd be an honor. I just have to talk to Lorenzo. We'll have to push the wedding date up, as I don't want to be showing when I walk down the aisle. A sista gots to be snatched," I said, snapping my fingers.

Kacia smiled from ear to ear and called Philly into the room. "She said yes, babe!" Kacia squealed. "June's gonna be our surrogate," she said, and the two of them hugged each other tightly.

I stared at Kacia's hopeful, grateful eyes, and the magnitude of what I'd agreed to began to sink in. It was a huge commitment on my part, but I couldn't say no to my sister.

"Thank you so much, June," Kacia said, tears welling. "You have no idea how much this means to us."

"I'll talk to Lorenzo tonight," I replied, trying to sound more confident than I felt. "We'll make it work."

After they left, I packed up the rest of our things and headed to Lorenzo's. My mind was occupied for the entire drive with a whirlpool of thoughts: Kai's issues, DaMarco's stupidity, and now, being a surrogate for Kacia and Philly. My life was becoming more complicated by the minute.

When I arrived at Lorenzo's place, the familiar sight of his home brought a sense of calm. Symone and Kaylee ran to greet me, their infectious smiles easing some of my tension.

"Daddy Ren's in his study," Kaylee said, bouncing up and down. "He'll be so happy to see you, Mommy!"

I smiled back at her and ruffled her hair as I walked past. I found Lorenzo sitting at his desk, listening to music.

He looked up when I entered, and a warm, welcoming smile spread across his face. "Hey, you," he said, standing to give me a hug and a kiss. "Rough day?"

"You could say that," I replied. I held him in the embrace and gave him a peck on the lips. "We need to talk."

He pulled back, obviously concerned. "I don't like the sound of that. What's going on?"

"DaMarco showed up at my house."

Lorenzo's expression darkened. "What!? What did that nigg… What did he want, babe?" he asked, trying to avoid saying the n-word.

"He's upset about that Facebook post, the one that refers to you, Kaylee, and Symone as my family. You know him. He's just trying to stir up trouble."

Lorenzo sighed and sat back down in front of his computer.

"Um, babe, there's something else." I took a deep breath when he returned his gaze to me. "Kacia and Philly came over today."

"Okay? Is everything all right?" he asked, with genuine concern.

"They asked if I can… Um, they want me to be their surrogate." I said, unsure of how he would react.

Lorenzo's eyes widened. "Oh. Well, what did you say?"

"I told them I'll do it," I said, then paused to study his reaction. "I did tell them I had to talk to you first. We might need to move the wedding date up."

"You should have talked to me first, instead of giving them false hope," he snapped, seemingly angry.

I didn't expect that from him. He knew Kacia and Philly had miscarried twice, and I was sure I would have his support. His tone left me speechless.

Lorenzo stood and walked to the study door, but before he walked out, he turned and said, "Juniper, our wedding night should be our chance to try to conceive our own child. I want to be able to experience that with you first. Didn't you even consider that?"

As Lorenzo walked out, I felt a knot tightening in my chest. It wasn't how I had hoped the conversation would go. I took a deep breath and followed him into the living room, where he was pacing on the carpet again. "Lorenzo, wait," I said, struggling to steady my voice.

He turned to face me, his expression a mix of anger and disappointment. "June, how could you make such a huge decision without talking to me first? This affects both of us, you know."

"I know," I said, trying to stay calm, "but it's my body, Lorenzo, and Kacia is my sister. She's desperate, and I can't just say no to her without at least considering it."

"Your body, yes, but the Bible even says the wife's body does not belong to her alone but also to her husband!" he yelled.

"Yeah, but I'm not your wife yet!" I screamed back.

"We're supposed to be a team. You made a commitment, one that impacts us both, without even asking how I feel about it."

I watched as Lorenzo sat on the couch, rubbing his temples. His frustration was palpable, and I knew the conversation was far from over.

He took a deep breath and tried to explain, "I just wish you had talked to me first. Don't you trust me enough to include me in the decision?" he asked, his voice tinged with deep hurt that cut through me. "Juniper, what if something goes wrong? What if it leaves you unable to have another child, one of our own? Things can happen, you know. We're talking about your health here, too, and about our future kids." His eyes bore into mine, and I could see the genuine fear behind his words.

I took a shaky breath, trying to collect my thoughts. "I guess I didn't look at it like that," I admitted, my voice barely above a whisper. "I was just thinking about Kacia and Philly, about how much this means to them."

"To them? What about us?" Lorenzo's voice was louder now, filled with anger and pain. "What about the family we're supposed to build together, about those plans we made? This isn't just about Kacia and Philly, June. This is about our future too."

"I know," I said, "but I believe we can do both. Lorenzo, we can help them for now and still have our own family. It doesn't have to be one or the other."

Lorenzo stood up and resumed his pacing. "You don't get it, do you? This isn't just a simple favor. This is nine months of our lives, maybe more. There are potential complications to consider. What about emotional stress? Who knows what else? It's not just about being pregnant. It's about the impact on our lives."

I felt tears pricking the corners of my eyes, but I fought them back. "Lorenzo, I understand the risks, but I also understand how important this is to my sister. I can't turn my back on her."

He stopped pacing and turned to look at me, his face a mask of frustration and hurt. "What about me, June? What about turning your back on me? We're supposed to be partners, and you made a huge decision without even consulting me. That's not what partnership is."

"I didn't mean to exclude you," I said, my voice cracking. "I just… I guess she kind of put me on the spot. I've heard all her cries and desperation for a child. They want a baby so badly, and they've tried everything."

Lorenzo shook his head. "I'm trying to understand, but it's hard when it feels like you didn't even consider my feelings. This affects both of us, June. Right now, it feels like you're putting your sister's needs above ours. Now, I may have to wait another nine months to have a baby with you. I'll have to watch you carry another man's child."

I took a step closer to him and cautiously reached out to touch his arm. His words had cut me deeply, especially when I remembered how much he was there for me when I was pregnant with Kaylee. "I'm not trying to put anyone above us. I just want to help someone I love. Can't we find a way to do both?"

He looked down at my hand on his arm, then back up at me, his expression softening just a bit. "I want to support you, June, but this is a lot to take in. We need to think it through together."

"I agree," I said, my voice trembling. "We need to talk about it, really discuss it. Please, Lorenzo, don't shut me out. We can find a way to make it work. I know we can."

He sighed and nodded slowly. "Okay, we'll talk about it. This time, though, we'll do it together, every step of the way."

I felt a glimmer of hope as I nodded. "Together," I echoed, praying we could find a way to navigate this difficult decision without losing each other in the process.

The next morning, I awoke to a text from Nikki: "Need to meet. Urgent."

I found her at Java Brew Café, she was already seated in our usual spot, with a look of intense concentration on her face. "What's up?" I asked, sliding into the chair opposite her. My mind was still on my touchy conversation with Lorenzo the night before. I knew he was still disappointed in me, and he'd turned his back toward me when I climbed into bed, something he seldom ever did.

"Kai has more than money or leverage," Nikki said, leaning in. "She's got a whole ledger full of transaction details for Dwight's entire operation—names, dates, amounts, and everything."

"Damn, Nikki! Why the hell would Kai keep something like that?" I asked.

"Who knows? Insurance, maybe," Nikki replied.

"What did this girl get herself into?" I asked.

"I have no idea, but the main question is, why are *you* getting so wrapped up in this girl and her drama?" Nikki asked before taking a sip of her hot beverage, which smelled vaguely of pumpkin spice.

"I don't know. I guess it's the lawyer in me. I just want to know the truth. When this all started, I mainly wanted to know if she and Spex are into something shady, something that might cause us problems in the music industry. After all the information I have on her, now, though, I don't trust her. She seems dangerous, like someone who is willing to destroy anyone who gets in her way," I said before I slid an envelope across the table to my friend.

Nikki grabbed the envelope and peeked inside to see $2,500 in cash.

We spoke for just a bit longer, then went our separate ways. As we left the café, I knew I was going to eventually have to tell Lorenzo about all I'd discovered, but for the moment, I'd already unloaded enough on him.

Chapter 16

JUNIPER

When Lorenzo came home from the BET Awards, he was acting strange. I could tell something was off, but I didn't want to push him. Instead, I waited, hoping he would open up in his own time.

Even as days passed, Lorenzo's demeanor didn't improve. He avoided talking about the event altogether and shut down any attempts I made to bring it up. It was unlike him, and it worried me. I knew how much he loved the BET Awards, and he had been looking forward to celebrating Kai Jae's success, just like he had celebrated when his own rap group won a few years before. I tried to give him space and exercise patience, but the tension between us grew with each passing day. It was like there was a wall between us, an ever-thickening one I couldn't break through, no matter how hard I tried.

Then, one afternoon while I was at work scrolling through my phone, a message popped up, a picture of Lorenzo, passed out in a hotel bed, in nothing but his boxers. My heart stopped as I stared at the screen, trying to make sense of what my eyes saw. *Who would send me something like this...and why?* I quickly glanced around my office, my mind racing with questions and suspicions.

As the days went by, more messages assaulted me. One said, "Your man was good at pleasing me." More photos followed, each more incriminating than the last. One was of him lying in bed with a woman. Her head was not visible, but everything from her breasts down was. I tried to brush it off, to convince myself that it was just a prank, but the unease lingered, growing with each new image that appeared on my phone. I couldn't shake the feeling that someone was trying to tear us apart, to drive a wedge between us before we got married, but I had no idea who was behind it or why.

As I continued to search for answers, delving deeper into the digital messages that always came from a private number, an unknown caller. I reached out to Nikki, hoping she could shed some light on the mysterious pictures that had been troubling me. With a sense of urgency, I explained the situation, detailing the disturbing nature of the photos and the stress they were putting on me. I did not share any of it with my sisters or Lorenzo. It was only fair that I did my best to get to the bottom of it before I confronted him.

Nikki's response was swift, her determination matching my own. She promised to look into it, to leave no stone unturned in her quest for the truth. As the days passed, her updates grew increasingly bleak. She found it nearly impossible to trace the source of the messages. One thing we did rule out was that Kai Jae's ex-husband, Dwight, was not behind it. In some small way, that was at least some relief.

My frustration and helplessness seemed unending. After two weeks of it eating at me, I felt it was time to bring it up to Lorenzo. When I got home from work, my mind swirled with unanswered questions and growing doubts. Lorenzo and Symone were at my place, and as I stepped through the door, the familiar sights and sounds of home greeted me: the aroma of Lorenzo's cooking and the laughter of Symone and Kaylee, playing in the living room. Beneath the surface, however, tension simmered, threatening to boil over at any moment. With a heavy heart, I ushered the girls to their rooms, because I needed to speak with Lorenzo alone.

Once we were alone, I couldn't hold back any longer. I confronted Lorenzo about the pictures, about the secrets he had been keeping from me. "Lorenzo," I began, my voice trembling with emotion. "We need to talk."

He looked at me in surprise, as if totally caught off guard. "What's wrong, ma? You look upset."

I hesitated for a moment, just long enough to gather my thoughts before plunging into the heart of the matter. "I found something, Lorenzo. I saw photos, pictures of you, from the night of the BET Awards."

His expression shifted, and a shadow passed over his face. "I-I don't know what you're talking about, June. Pictures of what?" he asked.

"Lorenzo, please," I urged, desperation creeping into my voice. "I need to know the damn truth. What happened that night? Don't play with me," I said, as I pulled up one of the photos on my phone and held it up for him to see.

He took the phone from me and scrolled through all the heinous images, then just stared at the floor, as if he could not meet my glare. Then, in a voice barely above a whisper, he finally opened up about the excitement of the awards show, the thrill of being surrounded by industry giants and rising stars.

I knew there was something he wasn't telling me, something he was holding back. "Lorenzo," I pressed, my heart pounding at a loud staccato, "what happened *after* the show? What *aren't* you telling me?"

The brief silence he gave me for an answer seemed so loud. Then, muttering, he confessed, "I-I honestly don't remember much, June. I had a few drinks, maybe too many. I just... I woke up in my hotel room alone, with just my boxers on. I don't even remember getting in bed. I am telling you the truth. Since I don't remember what happened, I guess there's a distinct possibility those pictures are authentic. I just honestly don't remember," he said.

His admission hung in the air, heavy with implication. I felt the color drain from my face as the truth dawned on me. "A distinct possibility?" I echoed, my voice barely a whisper.

Lorenzo still couldn't meet my gaze. Instead, he turned away, unable to face the pain in my eyes.

In that moment, I knew what I had to do. The realization hit me like a freight train, the weight of it crushing my chest. The man I loved, the man I was about to marry, had betrayed me in the worst possible way. "Lorenzo," I said, my voice trembling with emotion as tears flooded my eyes, "you're telling me you got so drunk that you slept with some random bitch," I said. "If that's the case, I just... I can't marry you. Frankly, I can't believe I stayed celibate for damn near three years for you, when your ass clearly couldn't wait until our wedding night."

He turned to me, shock and disbelief written across his face. "June, please, don't say that. I just... You don't understand."

"Understand what? You did the same shit DaMarco did to me!" I yelled.

Having heard our loud argument, the girls came out of their room. Symone shyly stood behind her father, sensing something was wrong, and Kaylee looked at me with tears in her eyes. We never fought in front of them, and my heart broke when I saw their fear and sadness.

Kaylee hugged my legs and asked, "Are you okay, Mommy?" Her facial features favored those of her father.

Symone grabbed Kaylee's hand. "Let's go back in our room so Mommy and Daddy can talk," she said.

We both watched as our brave little ones returned to their room, and we remained silent for a few more minutes. In that time, I developed a terrible headache.

"Just get your shit and go home, Lorenzo," I said, pointing at the door. "I don't want to look at you right now."

"June, please listen. I am so sorry. Please, babe," he pleaded, moving slowly toward me. His eyes were now flooded with tears of his own.

I reached my hands out in front of me, forcing him to stop. I couldn't bear to hear his excuses, not when it felt like my whole world was crumbling around me. My heart felt like two large bricks had dropped on it.

When he saw I was serious, he just turned around in defeat. "I'll just get Symone and our things tomorrow."

As Lorenzo went out the door, I went the opposite way, heading to my bedroom. I wanted to scream, but in order to keep from scaring the girls, I just sat on my floor and cried instead. I bawled like I hadn't for a long time, not since Daddy's death. It broke my heart to see us ripped apart, but my mind was made up. I knew, in that moment, that our love story had come to an end.

Chapter 17

LORENZO

Shit! I thought, cursing in my head. *She still isn't picking up.*

All the flowers, every message, and every voicemail had been rejected, ignored, or neglected. I would have been lying to myself if I said I didn't realize what she was trying to tell me, but I couldn't accept that no answer *was* her answer.

Just pick up your damn phone, I thought as I rang her for the fourteenth time. I already knew she probably wouldn't, but I still felt my heart squeeze as I hoped to hear her voice again. I thought back to the last grin I'd seen on her face, that wide smile when I did something silly. I thought about the last time she licked my forehead, just being cute. *What if I never experience that again?*

The house felt empty without her there, and the silence was deafening. Something in every corner reminded me of her, from the scent of her perfume lingering in the air to her Amber Romance Victoria's Secret shower gel on the tub shelf, the stuff she had to buy off Poshmark because it had been discontinued. The weight of my mistake was unbearable. I knew I had to make things right. The problem was that I didn't know how.

I have to find a way, I desperately told myself, *a way to reach out to her, to apologize, to show her how much she still means to me.* I still couldn't remember who was in bed with me in the photos, and that didn't make it any better.

My first attempt to set things straight was a straightforward one, if not a bit cliché. Knowing Juniper's love for lilies, I ordered the biggest bouquet I could find and paired it with a heartfelt note: "Juniper, I'm so sorry. Please give me a chance to explain. I love you. Lorenzo." I had them delivered to her workplace, hoping the gesture would warm her heart, but days turned into weeks, and no response came. My calls continued to go straight to voicemail, and my messages were left unread.

Desperate, I reached out to my boy, T-Rock. I couldn't bear the thought of losing my soulmate. I needed his advice and support. "Yo, T, where are you?" I asked, trying to keep my voice steady.

"At the studio with Summer, a new client," he replied, turning down the music in the background. "Why? What's up?"

"I need to holla at you when you're done. Can you meet me at 3rd Base LA?" I asked, hoping he could squeeze me into his busy schedule.

"Got you, Lorenzo. I'll see you there."

After wrapping up at the studio, T-Rock met me at the bustling sports bar in the heart of the city. As soon as he walked in, I spotted him from across the room. T-Rock had an unmistakable presence.

His smooth, brown skin gleamed under the dim lighting, and his gold teeth flashed whenever he smiled. He was decked out in gold chains, a pair of Jordans, jeans, and a crisp T-shirt, his well-groomed face framed by a baseball cap that completed his look.

The place was lively, the clamor of conversation and the clinking of glasses filling the air. The walls were lined with televisions, each tuned to a different sporting event. There was a laidback vibe about it, and it boasted comforting décor, with wooden tables and a long bar that stretched the length of the room.

We settled into a booth and were greeted by a cute Black server. Her smile was warm and genuine as she asked, "Hey, there, what can I get you guys?"

"Wings and a couple beers," I said, trying to sound casual.

"You got it," she replied. She quickly jotted the order down, then hurried off to the kitchen.

As we waited, I noticed the excitement around us. The Olympics were on, and the whole bar was buzzing about Simone Biles's recent gold medal win on the vault. It was a thrilling moment, and the atmosphere was electric, but my mind was elsewhere. I had to find a way to fix things with Juniper, and I hoped T had the answers I needed.

While we waited for our wings and beers, I took a deep breath and prepared to open up to my friend about what had gone down. The noise of the bar seemed to fade as I lowered my voice and said, "T, there's something I need to talk you about."

"Shoot," he said.

"Juniper received some text messages with photos of me in, uh...a compromising position, from the night of the BET Awards. I don't even remember being with another woman in my hotel room."

T-Rock's eyes widened slightly, his expression shifting to one of concern. "Damn, bruh, that's fucked up. Want me to talk to your girl for you? Maybe I can clear things up."

"No, T," I said, shaking my head. "I don't think that's a good idea. I gotta handle this myself. I just don't know where to start."

T-Rock nodded in understanding. "All right, so here's what you need to do. First, be totally honest with her, no matter how tough it is. Apologize and explain what happened, even if you don't have all the details. She needs to know you take responsibility."

I listened closely to his advice and nodded, knowing he was right. "What else?"

"Second," he continued, "give her some space to process everything. Don't keep bombarding her with messages and calls. When she's ready, she'll come to you. Sometimes, the best thing you can do is step back and let the emotions settle. Absence makes the heart grow fonder, right?"

I sighed, feeling the weight of his words. "Yeah, that makes sense, I guess. I've been trying to reach out, but it's not working."

"Lastly," T-Rock said, leaning in slightly, "show her you're committed to making things right. Actions speak louder than words, my man. If she sees that you're genuinely working on yourself and that you value your relationship, it'll go a long way."

"Thanks, T," I said, feeling a bit more hopeful. "I really appreciate the advice."

The server returned with our wings and beers, and I tried to focus on the conversation as we watched Simone Biles celebrate her gold medal win on the TV screen. The excitement in the bar was contagious, but my thoughts were still on Juniper. The only gold I cared about winning was the ring I hoped she still put on my finger.

***

The days seemed to blend together as they melted into a full week. Still, there came no word from Juniper. I knew my friend's advice to have some patience and give Juniper some space was solid, but desperation drove me to take more drastic measures.

The days that followed felt like a blur. I went through the motions of daily life, but everything seemed hollow and meaningless without Juniper. In need of a break and a chance to clear my head and lift my spirits, I called Mr. Mac to let him know I would be taking a few weeks off. It wasn't easy, but I needed some space of my own. I wasn't in a musical space like my artists needed me to be.

I also reached out to Maria, our social media specialist, and asked her to handle my Instagram by posting an update to let everyone know I'd be on some downtime and all my clients would be rescheduled. I asked her to turn off comments, as I didn't want my phone blowing up with questions and speculations.

On a whim, I decided a change of scenery would do me some good. Symone had been talking about visiting her grandparents, and I thought it was the perfect time to take a trip to Miami. Lamar, a cousin of mine, had been asking me to visit, and it seemed like just what I needed to shake off the funk I was in.

I headed to the airport with a mix of nervous energy and anticipation. The flight went relatively smoothly, but there was turbulence in my mind. As we approached Miami, the view from the plane was a stunning mix of turquoise waters and a sprawling cityscape. I felt a burst of hope as we landed, like a fresh start was on the horizon.

I grabbed my bags and made my way to the beachfront hotel I had booked. It was a sleek, modern building with floor-to-ceiling windows offering panoramic views of the ocean. The lobby was bright and airy, with white marble floors and contemporary artwork adorning the walls.

I approached the front desk, and a friendly clerk greeted, "Welcome to the Ocean Breeze. How can I assist you today?"

"I have a reservation under Lorenzo Ryan," I said, feeling more relaxed than I had in quite a while.

She quickly found my booking and handed a keycard to me, then offered a warm smile. "You're all set. Your room is on the eighth floor, and it has a beautiful view. Please enjoy your stay, Mr. Ryan!"

I took the elevator eight floors up. When I stepped inside my room, I was greeted by a breathtaking sight. It was spacious and tastefully decorated, with a large bed draped in crisp, white linens and a private balcony that overlooked the beach. The sound of the waves crashing against the shore was soothing, and I felt a sense of calm wash over me.

I unpacked my things and took a moment to appreciate the tranquility of the space, thankfully a stark contrast to the chaos I'd been dealing with back home. As I settled in, I hoped the getaway would give me the clarity I needed and, somehow, help me find a way to make things right with Juniper.

Exhausted from the three-hour time change and the emotional rollercoaster I'd been living through for the past few days, I decided to take a nap. When I awoke, I felt slightly refreshed and ready to explore Miami a bit. I headed down to the hotel bar to grab a bite to eat and unwind with a few beers.

The hotel bar offered a relaxing vibe, with ambient lighting and a view of the ocean through large glass doors. I enjoyed some nachos and sipped on a bottle of cold Corona with lime, enjoying the sensation as my tension slowly melted away.

Just as I was finishing my cold drink and dipping the last of my tortilla chips in the last of the cheese, my cousin arrived to pick me up. Lamar climbed out of his sleek, black Tesla and smiled at me. He was dressed casually but always maintained a sense of style: dark jeans, a crisp dress shirt, and polished Stacy Adams dress shoes. Diamond earrings sparkled in both ears, adding a touch of flair to his look.

Adding to his charm, Lamar was accompanied by two fine babes. The first was light-skinned, with long, curly hair styled in loose waves. Her makeup was on point: smoky eyes and bold lipstick that made her features pop. She wore a fitted black dress with a subtle shimmer, paired with high-heeled sandals that accentuated her graceful movements.

The second female had a darker complexion, her deep brown skin glowing under the streetlights. She donned a sleek up-do and wore a pair of statement earrings, one of which was a small hoop piercing above her eyebrow, adding an edge to her elegant look. Her makeup was equally flawless, with a warm, bronzy palette that highlighted her beautiful features. She wore a vibrant, patterned jumpsuit that hugged her curves, and her confidence was evident in the way she carried herself.

"Lorenzo, meet Jayda and Stephanie," my cousin said. "Hope you don't mind if they join us tonight. "You ready to have some fun?"

"Where are we going?" I asked.

"We're headed to a club in downtown Miami."

I shook the ladies' hands, one after the other, taking in their warm energy and sexy smiles. "Nice to meet you both." I then turned to Lamar. "And, yes, I'm definitely ready for tonight."

We hopped into the Tesla and sped off toward the club. The city lights and neon of Miami sparkled around us, and the anticipation of the night ahead began to lift my spirits. I hoped it would serve as just the distraction I needed and help me find some clarity so I could successfully clean up the mess back home.

As soon as we stepped out of Lamar's Tesla at the club, I could hear and feel the pulsating bass from inside vibrating through the ground. E11EVN was a high-energy hotspot, its neon lights flashing in sync with the beat of the music. The entrance led into a large, open space with a sleek, modern design, including glossy floors, a long bar that ran the length of the room, and a stage where a DJ was spinning tracks.

The crowd was comprised of a lively mix of people, all dressed to impress. A sea of bodies moved rhythmically, their hands in the air as they danced under the vibrant lights. The air was thick with the smell of cologne, and the clinking of glasses added to the high-energy atmosphere.

Jayda and Lamar quickly disappeared into the crowd, leaving me and Stephanie standing near the bar.

The dark-complexioned beauty in the sexy jumpsuit seemed to take an immediate interest in me. Her confidence was captivating, and she flashed a playful smile as she leaned close to me and asked, "So, Lorenzo, how's the night treating you so far?" Her breathy purr of a voice was barely audible above the thumping bass.

"It's been good," I replied, trying to match her energy. "This place is incredible. I needed a change from L.A."

Stephanie nodded, her eyes twinkling with curiosity. "I can imagine. Sometimes, a night out is just what we need. How long are you in town?"

"Just a week," I said, before I took a sip of my drink. "Just long enough to, uh…clear my head. I needed a short break from everything, ya know?"

Stephanie smiled, her lipstick glistening under the lights. "Yeah, I get it. Well, I'm glad you're here. Miami's a great place to unwind."

As we continued talking, the music shifted to Doug E. Fresh & The Get Fresh Crew's "The Show." The upbeat rhythm made it impossible to stay still. I grabbed Stephanie's hand and led her to the dance floor. She laughed, her eyes sparkling as she followed me.

We danced together and had a great time. That, coupled with the hype of the energetic, happy crowd, improved my mood to the best I had experienced in weeks. I couldn't help but laugh as we moved together, the music fading all else away. Stephanie had a great sense of rhythm and was clearly enjoying herself, which only added to the fun.

As we moved to the beat, I began to feel a genuine connection with Stephanie. For the first time in days, I was able to let go of my worries and just enjoy the moment. We danced and laughed, and the night became the much-needed distraction I needed. I was having a great time, and the lively atmosphere of the club, combined with Stephanie's infectious energy, made it easy to forget the chaos that had been haunting me.

As the night carried on, Jayda and Lamar eventually made their way back to where Stephanie and I were still showing off our moves.

Lamar threw me a broad smile and asked, "So, cuz, you having a good time?"

"Hell, yeah, bruh," I replied, trying to sound enthusiastic. Lamar didn't know every detail about my issues with Juniper, but he understood I was having relationship problems and that I needed to get away for a bit.

A short time later, all worn out from dancing, we all headed out of the club. We decided to head back to my hotel and made our way to the beach when we arrived.

The night was warm, and the gentle sound of the waves created a calming backdrop. Jayda and Lamar strolled into the water hand in hand, to enjoy the cool embrace of the ocean. Stephanie and I chose to sit on the sand, where the moonlight cast a soft glow over everything.

While we listened to the lapping waves, Stephanie turned to me wearing a curious expression. "So, Lorenzo, do you have a girlfriend?"

I chuckled softly as a bit of the weight lifted off my shoulders. "It's complicated. My relationship is in a rough patch right now. I'm just trying to figure things out. That's really why I'm here."

Stephanie nodded in understanding. "I get that. Relationships can be really tricky."

"What about you?" I asked, leaning back on my hands. "Are you dating anyone?"

She smiled and shook her head. "It's complicated for me too. I'm just trying to figure things out, you know?"

We both laughed as we found a bit of comfort in our shared struggle.

"So, what do you do for a living?" she asked, shifting her gaze to the stars above.

"I'm a music producer," I said, with a bit of pride.

"Music? Really?"

"Yep. I work with a lot of different artists. One of them is Kai Jae."

Stephanie's eyes lit up. "Kai Jae? I love her! I'm a huge fan. Her songs are so dope. The Shade Room forever posting her."

"That's what's up," I said, genuinely pleased to hear it. "I've been working with her for a while now. She's definitely dope."

Stephanie smiled warmly. "That's really cool. It's always nice to meet someone whose work is something they love."

We spent the next few hours talking about music, our lives, and everything in between. The beach was peaceful, and the conversation flowed easily. For a while, it felt like the weight of my recent struggles was lifting, replaced by the simple pleasure of genuine connection and shared laughter.

Jayda and Lamar eventually made their way back to where Stephanie and I were sitting.

"I'm ready to head back, fam," Lamar said, with a friendly nod. "I'm tired. Maybe tomorrow we can hit up some of the malls and check out a few more beaches."

"I'm good with that," I replied, feeling a bit more relaxed and excited about the plans.

***

The next day, Lamar returned with both women. As plan, we visited the mall and enjoyed a relaxed day of shopping and exploring. I bought

Symone a few new clothes, and Stephanie and I chatted as we browsed the racks and shelves.

Stephanie looked at the blouse I was holding. "So, you have a child, Lorenzo?" she asked.

"Yes, a daughter," I said with a smile and nod. "I think this would look cute on her."

Stephanie looked thoughtful. "That's nice. I don't have any kids yet. Maybe one day."

The day went by quickly, and it was soon time for us to head back. Lamar dropped Jayda off at her apartment, as she mentioned she needed to get some sleep before her twelve-hour shift at Jackson Memorial. "Nice to meet you, Lorenzo," she said with a warm smile.

"Nice to meet you too, Jayda. Take care," I replied, as she climbed out of the Tesla and told us goodbye.

Stephanie turned to me with a hopeful look. "Hey, Lorenzo, maybe I can hang out with you at the beach near your hotel," she suggested.

I smiled. "Sure. Sounds like fun."

Lamar dropped us off at my hotel. I noticed a satisfied expression on his face in the rearview mirror, as if he felt he'd administered just the medicine I needed to pull me out of my slump.

"Don't worry, Lamar. I'll catch an Uber home," Stephanie assured him.

"Sure, you will," he said with a wink, then drove away.

Stephanie and I walked into the hotel together. When we reached my room, I opened the door and stepped aside to let her in. It was still as inviting as before, and I was relieved by how relaxed and at ease we both seemed.

"Make yourself at home," I said, offering her a seat. "I'm gonna grab a drink. Would you like anything?"

Stephanie shook her head. "I'm good for now. Thanks."

I ordered some Crown, then glanced over at her. She was looking out the window, just staring at the beach, calm and content. The day had gone well, as had the evening before, and I was looking forward to spending more time with her.

Stephanie and I settled down on the couch and continued our conversation, laughing and enjoying each other's company. The sun was starting to dip below the horizon, casting a warm, golden glow through the window. The atmosphere was relaxed, and there was an easiness between us that made it simple to talk about just anything.

She really was a beautiful woman, wearing short shorts that highlighted her toned legs and a tank-top that showed off her gold elephant pendant necklace. Her flip-flops revealed perfectly manicured toes, and a small mole on her right shoulder caught the light as she moved. Her silky legs seemed to shimmer under the soft lighting.

"So," I began, trying to keep the mood light, "why is your relationship complicated?"

She laughed softly and shook her pretty head. "You really want to get into that?"

I nodded, intrigued. "Yeah, if you're comfortable sharing. I'm all ears."

Stephanie glanced around the room for a moment, as if searching for the right words. "Well, it's a bit of a mess, to be honest," she finally said. "They're very supportive, but there's also been a lot of back-and-forth. We lead busy lives and have our own priorities. Sometimes, it feels like we're on different pages. It's just challenging to find balance."

As she spoke, I noticed something I hadn't before: there were clear braces on her teeth. They were subtle but gave her a youthful charm I hadn't noticed the night before.

She caught me looking and smiled, a little self-conscious. "Yeah, braces. Just trying to straighten things out, literally and figuratively," she joked.

I grinned, appreciating her openness. "Sounds like you've been through quite a bit. Like you said, relationships are definitely complicated."

Stephanie nodded, her eyes meeting mine. "It's not easy, but I guess that's part of the journey. What about you? What's the real story with you and your complication?"

I sighed, feeling a bit vulnerable. "It's been tough. We've had our share of ups and downs. Right now, we're in a really rough spot. I'm just trying to figure things out and get some clarity."

Stephanie reached out and touched my arm gently. "I'm sorry to hear that. It sounds like you're both dealing with a lot."

We spent the next hour talking about our lives, our struggles, and our hopes for the future. The conversation flowed easily, and I found myself opening up more than I had with anyone in a while. Stephanie was a good listener, and her empathy made me feel understood.

The more we talked, the more I realized how much we had in common, and it was a great comfort to connect with someone who understood the complexities of relationships and life. The night turned out to be a surprising mix of comfort and connection, and, for the first time in days, I felt a bit of hope and relief.

Before I knew it, the clock had struck 8:00, and a small growl came from my belly. The conversation had been so enthralling that we'd literally forgotten to eat dinner. "Hey, want me to order some room service?" I asked, in an effort to silence my stomach and to break the comfortable silence we'd fallen into.

"Sure, that sounds great," she replied, her eyes brightening at the thought.

I picked up the phone and ordered burgers and fries and the glass of white wine that Stephanie requested. I opted for water, as I'd had too much to drink already on the trip. I wanted to stay clear-headed, so I would be able to make the right decisions about how to deal with Juniper. Despite enjoying Stephanie's company, I still longed for my family to be whole again.

Room service arrived promptly, and the waiter set our meal out on the table, then held out his hand for a tip. The delicious aroma filled the room, and my stomach growled again in anticipation. We dug into the food, and the conversation flowed even more easily while Stephanie sipped her white wine.

Right after biting a fry in half and washing it down with a small gulp of wine, Stephanie suddenly grew serious. "Lorenzo, there's something I need to tell you. Please don't judge me or get mad."

I looked at her, curious and a bit apprehensive. "Um, okay, but just to be clear, are you crazy?" I teased with a grin.

She laughed and shook her head. "No, or at least I hope not. It's just… Well, it is a bit complicated."

I raised an eyebrow. "Okay. I'm listening," I said, urging her to continue.

Stephanie took a deep breath and blurted, "The complicated relationship I mentioned earlier is actually with Lamar *and* Jayda. We're, uh…polyamorous."

I stopped eating, my fork suspended about three inches in front of my mouth. The revelation took me by surprise, and for a moment, I could only stare at her, speechless. I did my best to process the new information and asked, "Polyamorous, huh? What, exactly, does that mean?"

Stephanie explained. "Well, it's a consensual, open relationship with more than one partner. It's about having multiple emotional or romantic connections simultaneously. Lamar and Jayda are both a part of it, and I'm involved too."

I struggled to wrap my head around it but did my best not to sound foolish or insulting. "So, you, Lamar, and Jayda are all together? That sounds...intense."

"Yeah, it can be," Stephanie admitted. "It's very complicated, like I said. Lately, Lamar has been spending more time with Jayda. It's been a bit challenging to navigate, but we're all trying to make it work."

"I didn't expect that," I admitted. "It's definitely a lot to take in."

Stephanie nodded, her expression one of understanding. "I know it's not what you're used to hearing. It's different, not the normal, run-of-the-mill relationship, but it's part of my life right now. I just wanted to be honest with you."

I appreciated her honesty, even if the situation was unexpected. "Thanks for telling me, Stephanie. It is a lot to process, but I'm glad you felt you could share it with me."

We continued eating in thoughtful silence, the complexities of our lives hanging in the air between us. Despite the shock, I felt a deeper connection with her because of her openness, her willingness to confide in me about something so personal. She was certainly full of surprises, but in a strange way, being with her helped me understand more about myself and the world around me.

Nevertheless, as I tried to digest everything Stephanie had told me, I couldn't help but feel a bit disoriented. "So, Jayda isn't just Lamar's girl, and you sort of belong to both of them? He didn't bring you along for me, huh?"

Stephanie laughed softly, with a mix of amusement and resignation in her voice. "Kind of, I guess. I mean, Lamar did mention he could tell your heart was somewhere else. I told him I'd give you some space."

I nodded, feeling both relief and confusion. "Yeah, my heart is definitely somewhere else."

We both stood from the table and made our way to the balcony. The night air was cool and refreshing, and the sound of the waves gently licking the shore was like a lullaby. We leaned against the railing, taking in the serene view and the ambiance of the beach.

***

It was almost midnight before we left that balcony. Inside the room, Stephanie lay down next to me on the bed. That left me feeling uneasy, and a mix of emotions swirled inside me. Her presence was comforting, but my thoughts kept drifting back to Juniper and the mess I was trying to untangle. The last thing I needed was to be in bed with yet another woman.

Stephanie seemed to sense my unease. She turned to me, her eyes reflecting understanding and sadness. "I think it's best if I head out," she said softly before she picked up her phone to summon an Uber. Before she left, she leaned in and kissed me gently on the lips. "It was really nice meeting someone like you, Lorenzo. I wish things could have been different. I hope you and your girl work things out."

I watched as she gathered her things and left the room. As the door closed behind her, I felt a pang of regret mixed with the lingering warmth of our brief connection. I appreciated her honesty and her openness with me, but in the end, the night left me with more questions than answers.

As I lay back on the bed, the quiet and loneliness enveloped me. I couldn't shake the feeling that while Stephanie had brought some clarity, I was still lost in my own emotions and uncertainty about the future.

***

At the very least, my week with Lamar in Miami was a refreshing change of pace. As my visit neared its end, we no longer discussed Stephanie or the details; it felt easier to just let some things be. Lamar was a great companion and friend, and we spent our remaining time exploring, relaxing, and enjoying the city.

On our drive to the airport, the car was filled with a comfortable silence, only occasionally broken by light conversation.

"You glad to head back to L.A.?" Lamar asked. "I'm sure you're anxious to see Symone." He glanced over at me as he maneuvered through traffic.

"Yeah," I replied. "It's time to get back to reality. Thanks for everything this week, cuz. It was exactly what I needed."

"No problem," he said with a smile. "Glad I could help. You know, if you ever need a break again, just hit me up. We'll do it all over again."

"I might just take you up on that," I said with a chuckle. "Everyone can use a change of scenery every now and then."

Lamar pulled up to the terminal, and we quickly said our goodbyes and hugged. "Safe travels, Lorenzo. Take care of yourself."

"Will do. Thanks again, Lamar."

After I landed at LAX, I weaved through the airport with a mix of relief and anticipation. I was eager to get back to my life in L.A. but also a bit anxious to face everything waiting for me there. I had pressed a temporary pause on my life, but now it was time to press play again, no matter what I had to face.

To my surprise, I spotted a familiar face in the baggage claim area. Cari was looking right at me, and my heart skipped a beat. She seemed just as surprised to see me as I was to see her. For a moment, everything seemed to fade away, as if only the two of us occupied the bustling travel hub.

Chapter 18

KAI JAE

The lights of Los Angeles twinkled in the distance as the BET Awards wrapped up. The energy inside the venue was electric, and I could hardly believe it when my name was called for New Artist of the Year. My heart pounded with excitement as I stood and walked forward, with my custom black-navy ruched, deep-V gown by LaQuan Smith flowing effortlessly around me. The thigh-high slit revealed just enough to highlight my curves, adding an extra layer of confidence to my step.

As I made my way to the stage, the lights caught the shimmer of my jewelry, custom-made by Isshi, a talented Black jeweler based in New York. Each piece was a testament to his craftsmanship, and the bling added the perfect touch of elegance to my look. My hair, styled in a high ponytail, swung with each step, cascading down to the top of my butt, a flawless creation by Beauty by Kay, who also beat my face to perfection.

Lorenzo, T-Rock, and Mr. Mac were in the audience, beaming with pride. The three of them were my rocks through the ups and downs of my career. Unfortunately, Juniper couldn't make it, as she was buried in preparation work for a significant case her boss had assigned to her. I understood, and I was proud of her for how hard she had worked to achieve her position in the legal field.

As I stood onstage, with hard-earned trophy in hand, I felt an overwhelming surge of gratitude for my team. All had worked tirelessly to make sure I looked and sounded my best, and that unforgettable night was the culmination of all that hard work and dedication.

After the show, the night was still young, the city abuzz with possibility. I glanced over at Lorenzo and found him already on his phone, lining up plans for the night. We wanted to celebrate by hitting the hottest spots in the city and popping bottles with some of the biggest names in the industry.

As we stepped out into the warm night air, I was thrilled by a sense of exhilaration. The streets were alive with music and chatter, the perfect backdrop for a night of celebration. We headed to a sleek rooftop lounge that afforded us panoramic views of the city, the perfect place to toast to our inevitably exciting future. With a flute of bubbly in hand, I looked around at the glamorous faces surrounding me: artists, actors, and influencers, all there to celebrate and unwind. The music pulsed through the speakers, a mix of the latest hits and classic anthems, setting the perfect vibe. Spex was the official DJ, and he knew just what to spin to make the party perfect.

Nearby, a group of musicians gathered around a familiar face, R&B sensation Usher Raymond. His presence brought a certain electrifying energy to the room. To my surprise, I was invited into the conversation. Usher spoke about his ongoing residency in Las Vegas and shared personal stories of the incredible experiences and the unique connection he forged with his audience there. It was as inspiring as it was interesting, and I was flattered to be there to listen.

As the conversation flowed, Usher turned to me with a warm smile. "I've heard great things about your music," he said, his eyes twinkling with genuine interest. "How would you feel about joining me on stage in Vegas? I think our styles complement each other beautifully."

My heart nearly beat out of my chest at the mere thought of performing alongside such an iconic artist. It was beyond thrilling to even be asked. "I'd be honored," I honestly replied, trying to keep my excitement in check.

Usher nodded, and a look of satisfaction crossed his face. "Fantastic! Let's make it happen. We'll be in touch to work out the details."

Hours later, I found myself standing on the balcony of the hotel room wearing nothing but my panties and bra, gazing out over the sprawling urban landscape. The streets below were finally quiet and peaceful, as if all the world was sleeping. I took a deep breath and let the cool morning air fill my lungs.

My head was still buzzing from the celebration, thanks to the champagne and adrenaline that had kept me a bit on edge. I pushed the door open to reenter the room and found Lorenzo, still sprawled out on the bed, his toned body clothed only in boxers. The room was a mess, with empty champagne bottles and gummies scattered about, the evidence of the chaos that had happened hours earlier.

Memories of the events began to flood into my mind as I sobered up. After the rooftop party ended, we retreated to Lorenzo's suite for a final celebratory drink. The management company, always cautious, booked several rooms for us, so as to avoid any risk of drinking and driving. It was a wild night, and as we laughed and recapped the evening, I felt a mischievous impulse.

Lorenzo and I were both ecstatic about Usher's invitation for me to perform with him in Vegas. The thought of sharing the stage with such a legendary artist was surreal. We talked animatedly about the possibilities, brainstorming ideas and envisioning what the experience would be like and what it might mean for our careers.

"Yo, I need to use the bathroom," Lorenzo said.

The immaculate suite exuded an air of modern elegance, with clean linens and minimalist décor. Soft, ambient lighting cast a warm glow over the spacious living area, where plush leather couches beckoned invitingly. Abstract art adorned the walls, adding a pop of color to the otherwise muted palette of grays and creams.

A sleek, marble-topped bar stood in one corner, stocked with an impressive array of top-shelf liquor and sparkling glassware. The room was blessed with subtle touches of luxury, from the velvet throw pillows scattered artfully on the couches to the delicate crystal chandelier dangling from the ceiling.

Floor-to-ceiling windows offered a spectacular view of the skyline, and the twinkling lights cast a mesmerizing glow over the bustling streets below. It was a sanctuary amidst the chaos of the city, a place where we could unwind and revel in the excitement of the night's festivities.

While Lorenzo was in the bathroom, I took the opportunity to drop some liquid gummies into his drink. He shortly returned and continued our conversation, unaware of what was lurking in his glass. It didn't take long before his speech slurred, and his eyelids drooped. He mentioned feeling tired and wanting to lie down. I guided him to the bed, helped him out of his clothes, and snapped a few pictures with my phone to capture his enticing vulnerability.

In a haze of desire and envy for Juniper, who had his heart, I tried to take things further by giving him a hand-job and sucking on the tip of his penis, but his body wouldn't respond. Frustrated, I settled for what little reciprocation I could get and removed my clothes to climb into bed next to him. I snapped some more photos to capture the moment of the two of us together, in an intimate embrace. He didn't comply but didn't deny either, so I didn't feel too bad about it as I aimed my lens at the two of us.

The next morning, when I saw him passed out on the bed, a small bit of guilt began to creep in. I knew I had crossed a line. Lorenzo was a dope manager, but when I spotted him talking to Zara Bloom, the new girl on the scene, I felt I had to do something to protect my place as his top artist. Zara already had a collaboration with Missy Elliott. Not only was that record produced by Timberland, but it had sparked to Number 20 on the Billboards in only a week. Zara was the next buzz, and I couldn't let her have the whole pie. I wanted my piece, too, especially since everyone was always comparing me to her.

Spex had accidentally revealed during one of our sex bondage sessions that MUSIC4LIFE Records had been trying to sign my competition, and Lorenzo had been talking to her about producing a record. I was not about to let that country bumpkin from Memphis steal the spot I had worked so hard for.

The more I thought about Zara, the more determined I became. It was no secret that the girl was talented, but I had put in the work, all those late nights in the studio, all the endless promo tours. Lorenzo was with me through it all, and he had made promises to me that he would focus on my career. He was not supposed to get distracted by the latest rising star, the next wannabe flavor of the week. Sure, Zara was cute, and her voice was angelic, but with all her body enhancements, I was sure that after one twerk and a few ass drops, her fake ass would pop. The pictures I took would serve as a reminder of who really had Lorenzo's loyalty, who he was really in bed with, figuratively and literally.

I carefully gathered my clothes and dressed quietly, so as not to wake him. I stealthily picked up the empty bottles and gummies, in a bid to eliminate all proof of my reckless decisions. All the while, my phone continued to buzz with notifications, with messages of congratulations. Social media was blowing up with mentions of my award, and Spex kept asking for my room number; I knew he wanted sex, but I had other plans.

I stepped out into the hallway, quickly found the elevator, and pushed the button for my floor. At that point, I knew there was no turning back. I had to focus on my career and keep Lorenzo on my side, and I couldn't afford any distractions.

Back in my own room, I sat on the edge of the bed, staring at the cityscape. The events of the night replayed in my mind, a blur of celebration, envy, and regret. I knew taking those naked pictures of Lorenzo was wrong, but the competitive fire within me burned fiercely. Music was a ruthless industry, and I'd learned that staying on top sometimes meant playing dirty.

I opened my phone and reviewed the photos once more. They were my safety net, my way to ensure that Lorenzo remembered where his loyalties lay. With a deep breath, I deleted the most compromising ones but kept a few, just in case. I had won New Artist of the Year, and I intended to keep rising. That pigeon Zara Bloom was not going to derail my career.

The city below was full of opportunity, and I was ready to seize it. "*Carpe diem*," I said to myself as I packed my things and called an Uber to take me to my place before my flight. It was time to move forward and stay ahead in the game. I knew I had the talent, the drive, and the determination to succeed, and I was willing to do whatever it took to maintain my spot at the top.

Chapter 19

JUNIPER

I should have been over the moon about passing the California bar exam with a score of 1890 out of 2,000. Becoming an official attorney was a dream come true. Mama was ecstatic and wanted Lorenzo, the girls, and me to come over and celebrate. Sadly, I hadn't shared the news with them yet. *How can I tell them I had to call off the wedding because of his infidelity?* I wondered, mortified about the situation. It had been two months since I had last spoken to my so-called fiancé. He texted me constantly, begging to talk, but I just couldn't bring myself to face him. Those images of him with another woman were burned into my mind, a betrayal that cut me deeper than I ever thought possible.

In the meantime, life moved on in other ways. The songs I had written for Kai Jae were already recorded, and she was on tour with Mary J. Blige. Sam, her tour manager, had put everything in motion, and her forward momentum was impressive.

Despite my professional success, I felt a hollow ache inside. The city around me, once vibrant, now seemed gray and lifeless. I was sinking deeper into my own misery, isolating myself from everyone who cared about me. Steven, my boss and once my lover, even encouraged me to talk to Lorenzo, but I continued allowing my own stubbornness to get the best of me.

When I walked into the office after the bar, I saw that it was decorated with congratulatory messages and streamers, courtesy of the staff. They clapped and cheered for me, proud of my accomplishments. I tried to portray that I was happy, but I was miserable deep inside. I really only wanted to celebrate my win with Lorenzo, my main supporter.

Mr. Ray, the parking attendant who kept me in the loop of everyone's business, beamed from ear to ear as he told me how proud he was of me. "Finally, you can hang your bar license on the wall with all your other achievements," he said, then shook my hand enthusiastically.

Steven called me to his office, which still looked exactly the same as it had the day he gave me my informal interview. That interview was more like an initiation into a secret world than a formal job discussion, culminating in a wild night that turned Steven from a mere boss to a complicated secret lover. I often smiled at the memory, that interview like no other. Over the past three years, our relationship had evolved for the better.

When he told me he wanted me to stay and work for him, with a promise to leave the past behind, I agreed. True to his word, he never mentioned it again, nor did he mention the $200,000 he had given me as a "baby shower gift," which I considered hush money. The past was the past, and the fact that he sent me to law school and celebrated my accomplishments was nothing short of amazing. He and Britney had broken up the previous year. Since then, he'd been casually dating, insisting he wasn't looking for anything serious.

"Juniper, now that you're an official entertainment attorney, what are your plans in the firm?" he bluntly asked. He had scheduled the meeting with me to go over my new contract and to discuss the services we could provide to our entertainment clients. He also wanted to strategize on how I could make a name for myself in the legal community, given my lack of experience. Although I had worked on cases with Steven, I had always only played a supporting role.

Sitting across his desk from him, the weight of my new title settled comfortably on my shoulders. "Well, Steven, my plan is to build a solid client base and network. To accomplish that, I want to attend industry events, get involved in high-profile cases, and leverage social media to build my personal brand."

He nodded, his gaze thoughtful. "Good. I lined up some introductions for you at next week's entertainment law conference. It's a great opportunity to meet potential clients and mentors. Also, we've got a case I'd like you to take the lead on, a copyright dispute for a major recording artist. It will be your first solo project, if you're up for it."

I felt a rush of excitement and nerves. "Of course I'm up for it," I said. "Thank you, Steven. I won't let you down."

"You've earned it, Juniper," he said. He then looked me straight in the eye and said with sincerity, "Just remember, in this city, your reputation is everything. Keep your head down, work hard, and the rest will follow." He paused for a moment, then leaned forward slightly. "Now, let's talk about your salary. I'm willing to offer you starting pay of $128,000."

"A year?" I asked with a gulp. I didn't mean to sound so amateurish, but I had never really thought about the pay increase before.

He laughed. "Yes, Juniper, a year. You'll still receive bonuses for the cases you bring into the office. Call it a finder's fee. Your medical and dental benefits, paid time off, and two-week vacation, and life policy remains unchanged. Next year, we can revisit your salary and discuss a potential raise, which will be based on your performance."

As I left his office, the celebration was still on, the buzz of it echoing in the halls. My conversation with Steven had left me with a surge of determination. The urban jungle of entertainment law was fierce and competitive, but I was ready to make my mark. I looked around at the bustling office, at my smiling colleagues, and I knew it was just the beginning of my journey. The skyline outside seemed to pulse with the same energy I felt inside, a testament to the endless possibilities that lay ahead.

Later that evening, after most of the office had cleared out, I found myself back at work. Kaylee was with DaMarco, because his parents were in town and wanted to spoil their granddaughter for a few days. I couldn't bear to go home to an empty house, so the office seemed like a better alternative.

I knocked on Steven's office door and peeked inside to see him thumbing through a pile of documents. "Hey," I said, softly. "Mind if I come in?"

He looked up, surprised but not displeased. "Of course not, Juniper. What's on your mind?"

I sat down and took a deep breath. "I've just been thinking about everything."

"Everything? Like what?"

"About how far I've come, how far *we've* come."

Steven nodded and set his pen down on the desk. "Yeah, it's been quite a journey."

"Do you ever regret it?" I asked.

The question hung heavily in the air for a moment before he answered with a question of his own: "Well, if we're speaking of regret, guess who I ran into at the mall last week?"

"Do I really wanna know?"

Steven picked his pen up again and tapped it on his desk. "Hannah," he finally said.

"Hannah!? Oh, Lord. Did you run?" I asked.

"I wish. She looked me straight in my face and called me a flea-infested dog."

We both looked at each other and shared a laugh.

"I see someone is still mad," I said before I picked my purse and keys up to leave.

"Thank you, Juniper," he said, his voice sincere. "Now go home and get some rest. Tomorrow's a new day, and you've got a lot ahead of you."

On the way home, my mind drifted back to Lorenzo's unfaithfulness. The pain cut deep, like a relentless ache that wouldn't let go. I missed Symone terribly and fought the urge to call Lorenzo to ask to see her, but I had to focus on my own healing. If the man I had planned to marry was willing to sleep with random females, calling off the engagement was the only sensible choice.

My phone buzzed constantly with texts and calls from Tas. Out of all my siblings, she'd always been the closest with me. She knew me better than anyone else. I didn't answer her calls and texts because I needed space to process everything. Tas being Tas, though, I knew it would only be a matter of time before she'd showed up at my door.

When I pulled into the driveway, the house appeared larger than usual, its silence amplifying my loneliness. I took a deep breath and walked inside. The familiar scent of lavender greeted me, a smell that once brought comfort but now felt bittersweet.

I headed to the kitchen and put on a pot of coffee, a simple act to ground myself in the comfort of mundane routine. The humming of the percolating machine filled the quiet kitchen as I stared out the window, lost in thought. Memories of Lorenzo flooded back: our laughter, our plans for the future, and all the promises we made. It all felt like a cruel joke now.

The coffee finished brewing, and I poured a cup, then savored the warmth in my hands. I took a slow sip, hoping to steady my racing thoughts. I wandered into the living room and sank into the couch, then pulled a blanket over myself. The weight of the situation pressed down on me, making it hard to breathe. I grabbed my phone and scrolled through the countless messages from Tas, each more concerned than the last. I typed out a quick reply to let her know I was okay, then set the phone aside.

I set my mug down on the coffee table, closed my eyes, and let the tears flow freely as the emotional dam finally broke. It was liberating, in a way, to release all the hurt and anger I had been bottling up. I hugged the blanket more tightly around myself, seeking comfort.

Eventually, the tears subsided, and I felt a strange sense of calm wash over me. I knew it was just the beginning of a long healing process, but acknowledging my pain was a step in the right direction. I got up and headed into the bathroom for a hot shower, in the hopes that the warm water would wash away some of the emotional pain clinging to me.

As the droplets cascaded over me, I let my mind wander to the future. The plans I had thought I could count on had been shaken and shattered. Now, I had to rebuild my life, to focus on my career, and to be the best mother I could be for Kaylee. Lorenzo's betrayal had broken my world, but it hadn't destroyed me. I was stronger than the pain, stronger than the heartbreak.

As I stepped out of the shower, I felt a renewed sense of determination. I dried off and changed into comfortable clothes. Feeling a bit lighter, I picked up my phone again and texted Tas to let her know I was ready to talk when she had time. I had to invite people back into my life, to lean on my loved ones as I navigated that difficult chapter.

The next afternoon, there was a knock on my door. I opened it to find my sister on the other side, holding a red car seat, her face a mix of concern and determination. "Juniper, what's going on?" she asked, her voice cutting through the fog of my depression as she took in my disheveled appearance.

"Where is PJ?" I asked, as I watched her unstrap little Bailey from the seat.

"With his damn daddy. Girl, I needed a break from at least one of the twins," she said, smiling. "Speaking of kids, where's Kaylee?"

I smiled for just a second. "With DaMarco. I needed a Mommy break too." Then, in that instant, I broke down in front of her, and rivers of tears began rolling down my face in heaving sobs. "I-I called off the engagement, Tas. I just can't do it anymore."

Her eyes widened in shock. "What!? Why? What happened?"

I had no choice then but to spill it all: the infidelity, the shattered trust, and the wedding that would never be. Tas listened quietly, her expression shifting from shock to anger to fierce determination.

As I talked, Bailey began to cry. Without missing a beat, Tas picked the baby up and snuggled her against her breast for feeding. It was such a natural, nurturing moment that it grounded me, reminding me of the simple, pure things in life amidst all the chaos.

"Something doesn't add up," she said finally, her voice resolute as Bailey suckled peacefully. "I think Lorenzo was set up. We need to get to the bottom of this."

"Sis, your tits are huge. Can I squeeze them?" I asked, briefly changing the subject.

"Bitch, focus," Tas scolded with a laugh.

"Okay, but set up? Are you sure?"

"I think so," she said.

I wanted to believe her, but the pain was still raw. "I don't know, Tas. It's hard to trust him after everything."

"You're an attorney now, sis. You know how to examine all the evidence, right? Maybe this is just…circumstantial. Think about it. A real bitch wouldn't hide her face if the pictures were real."

Her words sparked a small flame of hope within me. *Maybe she's right,* I thought. *Maybe there is more to the story than I realized.* I went into Kaylee's room to grab a blanket so Tas could lay Bailey down to sleep.

"Let me see those pics, sis. We need to figure this shit out. You said it was the night of the BET Awards, right?"

"Yes."

"Okay…" Tas said, continuing to look at the photos.

We began to dig into the details, analyzing everything with a fine-toothed comb. Tas was relentless, and her belief in Lorenzo's innocence was a true sign of how much she believed in him and in my relationship with him. We pored over the text messages, photos, and everything that could provide any little clue to what had really happened that night.

Slowly, patterns began to emerge. The night of the alleged infidelity was filled with inconsistency. That, too, gave me some hope that maybe things were not what they seemed.

"Look, June. See the corner of this pic? What's that on the bottle?"

I grabbed my MacBook off the kitchen table and Googled "Chem Dawg." I was shocked to learn the product was liquid, recreational gummies. "Sis, how the hell did you see that? It's microscopic. You're freaking Columbo!"

"Girl, you must've forgot who you're talking' to I'm the queen of catching a nigga. You're the attorney. Why am I finding all the evidence?" she teased. "I bet whoever was in the room with him gave those to him, then took the pictures when he was out of it."

"Why though?" I asked.

Tas shrugged. "Blackmail, maybe?" She stood and went into the kitchen, where she dug through Kaylee's snack basket. "What's up with that artist you're both working with. What is it? Kia? Jae Kia or something like that? That chick who won the BET Award," she asked as she returned with a granola bar in hand.

"Kai Jae. Sis, naw. I had her checked out already?"

"You did?"

"Yeah, but it was for some other shit I don't want to get into right now, definitely not Lorenzo related," I said.

As we shifted through the photos on the phone, my skepticism began to crumble. Every image, every clue screamed that it was a setup. My heart ached for Lorenzo; he was fighting to talk to me, to have a chance to prove his innocence, and I just turned my back on him. We looked at the last photo of the unknown woman lying next to him, the one taken from her breasts down.

"Bitch body nice though," Tas acknowledged. "This whole thing is seriously fucked up. I can't believe you didn't give him the benefit of the doubt."

"I know," I admitted, my voice thick with regret. "I was so blinded by anger and suspicion that I didn't see the bigger picture. Honestly, I didn't even try to look. Lorenzo must feel so alone. Tas, what have I done?"

My sister nodded. "We'll figure this out. We'll clear his name."

Determined, I continued sifting through the mess, each photo dragging us closer to the truth. The more we uncovered, the clearer it became that Lorenzo was a victim, not the cheater I had accused him of being. The guilt troubled at me, but it also fueled my resolve to set things right. I refused to stop until we exposed whoever was behind it. I demanded justice for the person who had shattered my trust with the man I loved.

Chapter 20

KAI JAE

"Kai Jae, please delete the pictures."

The upset was obvious in Lorenzo's voice when I finally found the gall to show him what had happened months before. His pleas were raw, his voice cracking with hurt. He was under the impression we had slept together that night, and I couldn't really blame him, considering how those photos looked.

It all came to a head when he mentioned Zara Bloom again. We were in his studio, working on a track for a Tyler Perry movie set to be released in the fall. It was a remarkably huge opportunity for me, a rare chance to see my voice and music featured in a major film. Still, the vibe between us had been off for weeks with some unspoken tension simmering beneath the surface.

When he asked me to listen to a track he was planning to give to

Zara, I lost it, that tension boiled over out of its pressure cooker. All the bitter jealousy and frustration that had been building up inside me exploded. "If you give Zara that fucking track," I yelled, "I'll tell Juniper we had unprotected sex the night of the BET Awards."

Lorenzo paled. "T, give us a minute," he said. After we watched him grab his phone from the mixing board and walk out of the studio, Lorenzo stared at me with suspicion. "What are you talking about, Kai? I don't remember anything like that," he said, looking off to the side.

"Really?" I said, pulling out my phone. "These pictures say different."

His eyes widened when he scrolled through the alleged evidence, especially the photograph of me in bed with him, both of us barely dressed, his unconscious body next to mine. The immediate guilt and shame seemed almost too much for him to bear, but I had to stand my ground. I could not and would not let Zara take what I had worked so hard for, even if it meant causing Lorenzo some pain and embarrassment.

Lorenzo looked at me, his eyes filled with disappointment and disbelief. "So, *you're* the fucking reason Juniper called off the engagement?" he asked, his voice low but laced with anger. "You sent her those pictures? How could you do this to me, Kai?"

A cold wave of guilt washed over me, but I refused to back down. "I did what I had to do," I said, my voice shaking slightly. "This industry is brutal, Lorenzo. I can't risk losing everything."

Lorenzo shook his head, still overcome with deep pain and anger. "You didn't just risk everything, Kai. You destroyed it, ruined our professional relationship, and for what? A fucking track? For someone who hasn't done shit to you but respect your craft? The same woman who begged me to work with you? She is your biggest fan!" he yelled.

His words cut deeply, and, for the first time, I felt the full weight of my actions. In that moment, I realized I'd not only betrayed Lorenzo but also Juniper, who had been nothing but supportive of my career. MUSIC4LIFE Records had worked so hard to make me who I was, but I had stupidly let jealousy and fear drive me to do something I would regret for the rest of my life.

"I-I'm sorry," I whispered in a stutter, with tears welling in my eyes. "I didn't mean to hurt you. I just… I was so scared of being replaced, you know?"

Lorenzo sighed deeply and rubbed his temples, as if trying to soothe a pounding headache. "Sorry isn't going to fix this shit, Kai. Honestly, I don't know if anything can." With that, he turned and walked out of the studio and slammed the door behind him, leaving me alone to bear the heavy burden of my guilt and the harsh reality of what I had done.

A few minutes later, Lorenzo walked back in with T-Rock in tow, his face still etched with anger. "We need to finish this track," he said, his voice tight. "After this contract is up, though, we're done. I can't work with someone I can't trust."

I opened my mouth to protest, but the look in his eyes stopped me. I knew that was the price of my ambition, the cost of playing dirty in an industry that thrived on cutthroat tactics. In the end, I won the battle but lost the war.

T-Rock kept his mouth shut as he just stood by and looked on, dutifully waiting for me to return to the booth.

As we resumed working, the atmosphere was colder than ever. Every note, every beat felt like a step toward our inevitable end. The track came together perfectly, a testament to our combined talents, but it was tainted, a constant reminder of the betrayal and the broken trust between us.

When the session finally ended, Lorenzo packed up his things without a word. As he walked out, I realized I had achieved my goal at the expense of something far more valuable. The industry was definitely dog eat dog, but I had learned the hard way that integrity and trust were worth far more than any track or deal. Lorenzo stormed out, leaving a thick tension in his wake.

My heart pounded at a fever pace as I grabbed my bag and rushed out to my car. My hands shook violently as I fumbled to unlock the door and slide into the driver seat. I needed to talk to someone, to find some clarity. *Spex*, I thought, certain he was the only one who would understand. If anyone knew the ins and outs and ups and downs of the music world, it was him. With trembling fingers, I dialed his number and waited, each ring amplifying my anxiety.

"Yo, pretty, what's good?" Spex answered, his voice casual.

"Nothing, Spex. It's all bad," I blurted, my voice cracking again. "It's really bad. Can we talk?"

His tone immediately shifted. "What happened?"

I took a deep breath and spilled the whole sordid story to him. I confessed to using the photos to manipulate Lorenzo, told him about the horrible confrontation in the studio, and sadly explained Lorenzo's ultimatum when it came to our contract.

There was a long silence on the other end before Spex finally asked, "Kai, are you fucking serious right now?" His voice resonated with something teetering between disbelief and anger. "Lorenzo's my boy. How could you do that shit to them?"

At that point, my frustration boiled over. I was looking for a confidant, not a lecturer. "You think I had a choice?" I argued. "You know this industry is cutthroat, Spex. Zara was about to take everything I worked for!"

He let out a harsh laugh. "So, your solution was to backstab one of the few people who had your back? That's messed up, Kai. You do realize you didn't just hurt Lorenzo, right? You destroyed any trust he had in you, but you messed with Juniper too. What for? A damn track?"

"Loyalty and respect don't pay my fucking bills," I snapped, more tears dripping down my cheeks. "You don't know what it's like to be constantly overlooked, always second best. I had to do something to protect my reputation!"

Spex's voice was cold. "You think Zara would stoop that low? Sure, she's ruthless, but she's not dirty. You didn't protect anything, Kai. You just made enemies, big ones, and you broke Juniper's heart in the process. How could you do that to them?"

"How do you know what Zara is like or how low she'd stoop? Are you fucking her too!?" I yelled.

"Kai, fuck!" he yelled back at me.

I gripped the steering wheel tightly, my anger and regret mixing in a toxic brew. "You think I don't know I messed up? I was desperate, Spex. I needed to protect my career."

"Great, so you went, and fucking wrecked it," he said bluntly. "I'm tellin' you now, Kai, Lorenzo wasn't playin'. If he said he's done with your conniving ass after that contract, he meant it. What are you gonna do next? Where you gonna go? You think anyone in this business is gonna trust you after that? You've burned every bridge."

The reality of his words hit me like a punch to the gut. "What can I do, Spex? How do I fix this?"

"First, you and I, this fucking relationship or whatever the fuck you wanna call it... We're done, fucking finished, and I mean that literally. I don't fuck with bitches who fuck with my people. Second, you better call Ren and Juniper and make this shit right," he said before hanging up in my ear.

My eyes blurred with salty tears as I sat in my car. The consequences of my selfish, foolish, cowardly actions crashed down on me. I had fought so hard to climb to the top, only to find myself standing on the edge of a cliff of despair, staring down into the abyss of my own making.

I started the car and drove into the night, my mind racing to find a way to make amends, to rebuild the trust I had shattered. The road ahead was uncertain, filled with obstacles and challenges, but one thing was clear: I had to face it head-on and find a way to rise from the ashes without losing what was left of my soul.

I wasn't too surprised when Lorenzo canceled his next three sessions with me. It worked out okay for the time being, because I was otherwise occupied anyway. I had to take a flight to Detroit from LAX because Dwight had been calling me relentlessly. My ex's messages were urgent and angry and had escalated to the point of threats that his people on the outside would come for me.

Every little jerk of the plane was just a deeper reminder of the turmoil I had left behind and the confrontation I was flying toward. My mind spun out of control, cruelly replaying every disastrous moment with Lorenzo and the bitter argument with Spex. The turbulence seemed to mirror the chaos in my life, each jolt forcing me to recall the gravity of my situation.

As we descended, the gritty skyline of Detroit came into view, a stark contrast to the sunny glamor of Los Angeles. After we landed, I navigated through the bustling airport and hailed a cab to take me to Detroit Detention Center. My stomach churned with anxiety as the city streets blurred past, each mile carrying me closer to facing Dwight.

The jail was a cold, imposing structure, its gray walls reflecting the bleakness of my situation. After enduring the dehumanizing security checks and making my way through the labyrinth of sterile hallways, I finally reached the visitor area. This time, rather than going through the usual setup with a glass partition and phone, I was escorted into a private room. The door closed behind me with a heavy thud, and I found myself face to face with the man I used to be married to. I sat down across from him, my hands trembling slightly.

Dwight's eyes were hard and unforgiving, and he had locked them on mine the moment I walked in. "Kai," he began, his voice a low growl, "do you have any idea what kind of shit storm you've caused?"

I swallowed hard, struggling to maintain my composure. "Dwight, I know I messed up, but—"

"But nothing!" he interrupted, his face contorted with rage. "You stole from me, Kai. I trusted you, and you fucking betrayed me. Do you know what happens to people in here who find out someone has screwed them over?"

"I had no choice," I claimed, with a tremble in my breath. "I needed the money to keep my career afloat. I was desperate. Besides, have you forgotten all the years you made me fuck other men to pay your debts? What about the times you beat my ass? You owed me, Dwight, and, like I said, I was desperate."

"Desperate?" Dwight sneered. "You think that justifies robbing me blind? I was counting on that money to secure my future once I get out. Now, I ain't got shit!"

"Secure *your* future? What about mine? You think beating on me and turning me into your personal whore was justifiable? Forgivable?" Tears stung my eyes, but I blinked them away. "I'm sorry, Dwight. I really am. I'll find a way to pay you back. I'll make it right."

He laughed bitterly. "Just how do you plan to do that? From what I hear, you managed to fuck up your entire career. Lorenzo's done with you, right? From what I gather and what I've heard, you've burned too many bridges to count, Kai."

My confusion deepened as Dwight's words sank in. "What you hear? How did you find out so quickly?" I asked, my voice tinged with disbelief.

Dwight leaned back in his chair, a grim smile playing at the corners of his lips, the eerie grin I'd seen too many times in my nightmares. "The streets talk, Kai. Word travels fast, especially juicy gossip like this."

The revelation sent a chill down my spine. I had always been cautious, careful to keep my personal and professional lives separate, but somehow, my secrets had leaked into the world with alarming speed. Even behind prison walls, they knew things about me. It was a sobering reminder of just how precarious my position had become.

"But who—" I started, my thoughts swirling with suspicion. "Who would tell you something like that? No one even knows I was married."

Dwight's smirk widened, his eyes glinting with malice as he leaned forward. "You think you can just hand me a pile of fucking divorce papers and walk away, Kai?" he asked, his tone dripping with menace. "You think a simple apology is gonna make everything right?"

I could feel the weight of his words pressing down on me, suffocating any semblance of hope that had managed to linger in my heart. "I didn't know what else to do," I admitted, my voice barely above a whisper. "I'll do whatever it takes to fix this mess, Dwight."

Dwight's laughter echoed off the cold walls of the room, sending shivers down my spine. "Whatever it takes, huh? That's rich, coming from someone who's already proven she's willing to screw over the people who put their trust in her."

His words cut deep, reopening wounds I thought had begun to heal.

Before I could respond, Dwight's expression hardened, his gaze turning steely as he leaned in closer, his voice low and dangerous. "You're lucky I haven't sent my boys to fuck you up…or maybe just fuck…" He stopped and laughed, his breath hot against my cheek. "Don't think for a second, I won't. I've got eyes and ears everywhere, Kai. You will never, ever fully escape me. I know where you live, where you sleep. I got people watching. They'll come for you when you least expect it. Believe me when I say you won't see it comin'."

A chill swept through as the realization sank in that I was truly at his mercy. Dwight was not a man to be trifled with, and his threats were not to be taken lightly. I had crossed a line, and now I would have to pay the price, with no end to the torment in sight.

As I sat there, paralyzed by fear and uncertainty, I knew escape was futile. Dwight was imprisoned by cement and bars for the time being, but I was imprisoned by him and his threats. He had me in his sights, and there was nowhere left to run. All I could do was brace myself for the storm that was surely coming. All I could do was pray that somehow, some way, I would find a way to weather those storms and survive.

Chapter 21

KAI JAE

Everything was falling apart. Spex wouldn't speak to me, and my plumbing was such a disaster that my entire kitchen flooded before I even woke up. On top of that, I was exhausted and nauseous for some reason I could not determine.

I called the apartment manager, hoping for a quick solution. With the ridiculous amount of rent I paid, I expected prompt assistance. "Hello?" I said as soon as Mr. Daise answered.

"Hello?"

In the background, I heard loud noise and someone cursing. "Wow," I muttered.

"What do you need?" he asked, followed by even louder cursing.

"My kitchen is flooded, and I need someone to come look at it."

I heard a mumble that sounded something like, "Bitch," coming from under his breath, but he answered matter-of-factly, "Can't come myself right now, but I'll send somebody."

"Than—" I tried, but before I could finish thanking him, all I could hear was a dial tone.

I sat on the soaked floor of my apartment and broke into a fit of tears. The water from the toilet had overflowed and sent a flood into the kitchen, creating a smelly, wet mess. Once pristine and bright, with my white granite countertops and stainless-steel appliances, my kitchen now looked like something out of a disaster movie or home insurance commercial. Murky water was pooling around the cabinets and seeping into the hardwood floors. The stench of sewage was overwhelming, only worsening my nausea. My beautiful kitchen, my sanctuary, was ruined, and I felt utterly helpless.

Weak bitch, my mind taunted as I wailed on the floor. Longing for escape and a distraction, I began to wonder, *What is Spex doing right now anyway? Does he miss me as much as I miss him? Is he in pain too?*

My phone pinged, and I scrambled to look for his name, only to discover a spam call. Then came another ping, this one indicating a text from the building super: "Got a plumber headed to your place at noon."

It wasn't ideal, but at least it was a plan. The smell was getting worse, though, and I had to get out of there, so I decided a walk was in order.

I walked for about twenty minutes before I had to admit it wasn't helping at all. I turned to go back and felt even more exhausted and drained. As I climbed the stairs to my apartment, a wave of dizziness hit me, so severe that I had to stop and grip the railing for support. The past few days had buried me in a fog of fatigue and unease, and now my head felt like it was spinning out of control. I finally reached my door, struggled with the keys, and collapsed onto the couch inside, trying not to breathe too deeply, so as not to be overtaken by the stench.

Much to my surprise, the plumber was already there, working on the kitchen. I waved weakly and mumbled something incoherent. He finished more quickly than I expected, recited a few instructions I didn't catch, then left.

"Hey, Shaun," I said when my housekeeper picked up the phone. "Do you have time to come over and do an emergency cleaning? I'll give you an extra $200."

"Sure. Be right there."

Shaun was a tall, lean guy with short-cropped hair and a friendly smile. He always wore a neat uniform and had a calm, reassuring presence. When he arrived, he took one look at me and said, "Kai Jae, you really need to see a doctor."

The air conditioner's soft hum gave me a momentary escape from the relentless heat. I closed my eyes, hoping the dizziness would pass, but it only grew worse, joined by a wave of nausea. I could literally feel in my gut that something was wrong. I forced myself to sit up and began to consider the possibilities. *Maybe it's just the heat, or perhaps the stress of recording.* Then, I began to connect the dots—fatigue, dizziness, nausea—and a more alarming thought crept in. *Wait. Isn't my period, like...really late? Oh, no!* Panic began to rise in me. I grabbed my phone with trembling hands and dialed Erick's number.

He answered on the second ring, his voice immediately filled with concern, "Kai? What's going on?"

"I don't feel well," I admitted, my voice trembling.

"What do you mean? Flu or something?" my brother questioned.

"I don't think so. I'm dizzy and super nauseous, and... Well, my period is late."

There was a long pause on the other end of the line before he asked the question, I'd already been asking myself: "You think you should take a pregnancy test?"

"No," I whispered. "I'm scared, Erick. What if... I can't be pregnant! Everything's just starting to go well."

"Calm down, sis. We need to figure this out. Can you get to a pharmacy to buy a test?"

I nodded, even though he couldn't see me. "Yeah, I'll go now."

"Call me as soon as you know something," he urged. "Kai, whatever happens, we'll handle it together. You know that."

"I know," I said. "I'll call you back soon."

His words offered a bit of comfort, but the knot in my stomach only tightened as I grabbed my keys and headed out the door, my mind racing with worst-case scenarios.

The pharmacy was only a few blocks away, but the drive felt endless. Inside the store, I made a beeline for the aisle with the "Family Planning" sign hanging above it. My eyes frantically scanned the shelves, and I grabbed the first pregnancy test I saw, without even bothering to read the details. I just needed an answer, one way or another.

I sensed the cashier giving me a sympathetic look as she rang up my purchase, but I couldn't bring myself to meet her eyes. I just wanted to get out of there and find out if my fears were justified.

By the time I returned to my apartment, I was pleased to see that Shaun had already finished cleaning. The whole place smelled like lemon and fresh cinnamon, a welcome change from the earlier chaos. I locked the door and went straight to the bathroom.

The instructions on the test were simple, but my hands were shaking so badly that it took a few tries to get it right. I set the timer on my phone and sat on the edge of the bathtub, with my heart in my throat. The fresh scent in the apartment was calming, but the knot in my stomach remained. I couldn't stop thinking about what the results of such a test might mean for my future. The wait felt endless, each second ticking by slowly as I stared at my phone, willing the timer to hurry up.

Five minutes had never felt so long. I stared at the plastic gadget, yearning for it to reveal the truth. Finally, the timer went off, and I forced myself to look.

"One line. Not pregnant," I said aloud.

Relief washed over me, but it was quickly replaced by confusion. *If I'm not pregnant, then what's wrong with me?* My period was definitely late, and I felt worse than ever. I needed answers, and I needed them right away.

I called Erick back, my voice a bit steadier than before. "The test was negative, but I still don't feel right. I think I need to see a doctor."

"Okay," he said, his tone reassuring. "Go to the hospital and get checked out. Better safe than sorry."

I sighed, feeling a mix of frustration and determination. "Thanks, Erick. I'll let you know what the doctor says."

"Hang in there, sis," he replied.

I hung up and took a deep breath, trying to steady myself. The clean, fresh scent Shaun had left behind offered some small comfort, and he hadn't left even a smudge or a speck of dust anywhere. I grabbed my keys again and headed out the door, determined to get to the bottom of whatever was going on. The thought of seeing a doctor made me nervous, but I knew it was the right thing to do. As I walked to my car, I couldn't help but hope that it wasn't something serious, but I also knew I had to be prepared for anything.

As usual, the emergency room was buzzing with activity. I checked in at the front desk and explained my symptoms to the receptionist. She nodded sympathetically and handed me a clipboard full of paperwork.

I took a seat in the crowded waiting area and started filling out the forms, my mind dizzied with worry and dismay. Even in the midst of my unknown illness, I couldn't stop thinking about Spex. *Should I tell him what's happening?* Our relationship was already on shaky ground, and I wasn't sure how he'd react if I told him where I was.

After what felt like forever, a nurse called my name and led me to a small examination room, where she took my vital signs. My pulse was racing, and my blood pressure was higher than normal. She jotted down a few notes on my chart, promised a doctor would be in soon, then walked out.

As I sat on the examination table, it was a struggle to calm down. The sterile smell of the room mingled with my anxiety only made me feel more stressed. I hoped the doctor would have some answers and that my condition was something simple and treatable.

At last, the door swung open, and a middle-aged woman walked in. The doctor had a striking presence. Her shoulder-length hair was a blend of blonde and black, styled elegantly. Her makeup was flawless, enhancing her warm, compassionate, kind eyes and radiant smile. Her beautifully manicured nails were short enough to accommodate her work but also polished to perfection, adding a touch of sophistication. "Kai Jae?" she asked, glancing at my chart.

I nodded in response.

"I'm Dr. Lewis. What brings you in today?"

I took a deep breath and tried to steady my voice. "Well, I've been feeling off lately, sort of dizzy, nauseous, feverish. Also, my period is late. I'm worried I might be pregnant."

Dr. Lewis listened attentively, jotted a few more things down, then said, "We'll run a blood test to confirm. It might take a little while for the results to come back, but we'll make sure to get them to you as quickly as we can. When were you last sexually active?" she inquired gently.

I hesitated for a moment before nodding. "About a month ago," I replied.

"All right," she said. "In addition to the pregnancy test, I'd like to rule out any potential STDs, like chlamydia. Given your symptoms, it's important to check for that as well."

I nodded and did my best to absorb all the information.

The nurse returned to draw a couple vials of blood. The procedure was over quickly, but the wait for the results was sure to be a long one or at least to feel that way.

As I sat there, my mind was a whirlwind of what-ifs: *What if I am pregnant? Will I be a single mother? Will Spex want anything to do with the baby...or me?* I did not know how he would respond, but the thought of raising a child alone was scary as hell.

Minutes dragged on, each heavier than the last. I tried to distract myself by scrolling through my phone, but nothing eased the growing panic in my chest.

Eventually, Dr. Lewis returned, with a folder in her hands, and my heart raced as she sat down beside me. "Kai, I have your results," she said. She opened the folder and quickly continued, "First of all, you're not pregnant, and your STD results were negative."

A wave of relief washed over me, so strong that I nearly cried. "Then why is my period late, and why do I feel so terrible?"

Dr. Lewis smiled gently. "Stress can do a number on your body. From what you told me, you've been under a lot of it lately. It's common for the menstrual cycle to be affected, either heavier or delayed or absent altogether. As for the other symptoms, you might be fighting off a virus or simply exhausted. I recommend getting plenty of rest, staying hydrated, and trying to manage your stress level."

I nodded, relieved but still exhausted. "Thank you, Dr. Lewis. I appreciate it," I said.

As I walked out of the clinic, I felt a wave of relief wash over me. I was not going to have a baby, not anytime soon, and that was a huge weight off my shoulders. Still, even with that burden lifted, I had a lot more to sort out: my relationship with Spex, Lorenzo, Juniper, my career, my health, and getting Dwight off my back.

I spent the rest of the day trying to take it easy, doing my best to heed the good doctor's advice. I drank plenty of water, ate a bit of food, and allowed myself to relax for the first time in what felt like ages. By evening, I was feeling a little more like myself, though the fatigue still clung to me.

As I lay on the couch, my phone buzzed with a call from Erick. I answered it eagerly, needing to hear his voice.

"Hey, Kai! Got your text. How are you?"

I took a deep breath and felt tears prick the corners of my eyes. "I'm actually relieved, Erick. I thought I was pregnant, but I'm not. The doctor said I'm just really stressed and tired, and it's made me feel sick."

Erick's voice softened with concern. "Kai, I'm so sorry you're going through all this. I wish I could be there with you."

"Me too," I whispered, wiping away a tear. "It's just been a lot lately—the music, the pressure, everything with Spex."

"Have you talked to him?"

I shook my head but suddenly realized my brother couldn't even see me. "No," I answered.

Erick was quiet for a moment, and I could almost hear him thinking. "Kai, you need to take care of yourself first. As far as I am concerned, Spex can go to hell. Your health is more important than that nigga.

Promise to take some time for yourself, okay?"

I unnecessarily nodded again, feeling a bit more grounded. "Okay, Erick, I promise."

We talked a bit longer, reminiscing about Detroit and catching up. It felt good to connect and be reminded that I wasn't alone in the world. By the time we said our goodbyes, I felt a bit stronger and more ready to face the challenges ahead.

The next morning, I awoke feeling slightly better. The dizziness had eased, though I still felt drained. I decided to continue focusing on self-care and trying to lower my stress levels. Unfortunately, all my efforts to take it easy just didn't work.

One night, the weight of it all became too much. Exhausted, I finally drifted into a restless sleep, only to find myself trapped in a nightmare that felt all too real. In the dream, I was onstage, blinded by the bright lights as I sang to an empty auditorium. The seats, once filled with cheering fans, were now vacant, their silence a cruel mockery. My voice faltered, and the lyrics came out hollow and broken to echo off the empty walls.

My schedule required a listening session with Lorenzo, our first encounter since I had fessed up about sending the messed-up pictures and texts to Juniper. The hurt and pain I heard in his voice from my betrayal were gut-wrenching. Honestly, I was not sure I could ever set things straight. I really hoped he'd cancel the session, as he had with the others recently, but when I didn't get a call from him, I knew it was time to face the music and deal with the fallout of my own actions.

I finally arrived at the studio, but instead of finding Lorenzo, I saw Jamal, an engineer who was a beast at mastering track. "Where's Lorenzo?" I asked when I saw him.

Jamal replied, "I'm not sure. Lorenzo texted and asked me to let you listen to the songs. If you need any changes, just let him know, and you two can work on it together."

The absence of Lorenzo left me feeling a mix of relief and frustration. It was good to move forward, but I was still dealing with the consequences of my actions. I took a deep breath and prepared to listen to my recorded songs, hoping to smooth things over as best as I could.

Listening to each track gave me a little joy. "Everything's cool, Jamal," I said. "We don't need to redo any of the tracks."

After all the hustle and grind, my debut album was finally done. Still, even with the music coming together, I couldn't shake the heavy feeling. It wasn't just about the album; it was about avoiding Lorenzo. The idea of seeing him again and being forced to confront the mess I'd created was tough to handle. I tried to keep my head up, but deep down, I dreaded the moment when I'd have to face the fallout and the hurt, I'd caused. I was glad the tracks were solid, but I knew I couldn't avoid the real talk with Lorenzo forever.

After we wrapped up, Jamal asked, "Hey, I'm starvin'. Wanna go grab a bite to eat with me?"

It had only taken us an hour to go through the full album, so I was down. "Sure. Where?" I said.

Jamal grinned. "Samurai Hibachi Grill LA is only a few blocks away."

"Cool. I've been wanting to check that place out and see the cooks in action," I said, beaming him a smile full of thanks. "Let's do it."

I hopped into my Benz and followed Jamal to the restaurant. When we arrived, I was impressed. The spot had a sleek, modern vibe with dark wood accents and colorful Japanese lanterns hanging from the ceiling. The grill stations in the center of the room were surrounded by a horseshoe of tables, where diners could easily watch the chefs show off their cutting and culinary skills. The air was filled with the sizzle of meat and the aroma of spices that made my mouth water.

Like a true gentleman, Jamal pulled out my chair for me and gave a friendly nod. He rocked a crisp white tee, dark jeans, and a pair of fresh sneakers. His brown complexion was smooth, and his arms were covered in tasteful and interesting tattoos. He had a clean-shaven face and sported stud earrings in both ears. He definitely had a style that worked for him.

I selected beef ribs with chicken, fried rice, and veggies. Jamal ordered the same but skipped the veggies. The chef was all about putting on a show. He started by placing a big jug of oil on the grill, then began his performance, making bunny ears with his hands and flipping the oil around before getting to work. It was pretty entertaining to watch as he expertly cooked our food right in front of us.

In the need to chill out, I ordered frozen margaritas, but Jamal kept it simple with water. We sat back, enjoyed the show, and let the delicious aroma fill the space between us. It was a welcome distraction and a good way to unwind after a heavy day.

The food was absolutely delicious, and I had a great time hanging out with Jamal. When we finished, he covered the bill and walked me to my car.

As we stood by my ride, he asked, "What do you have planned for the rest of the day?"

"Oh, I think I'm going to make one of my crazy cooking shows for my fans on live."

"Wow! Can I watch?" Jamal asked.

I smiled. "Sure. Why not?" I said. "Just follow me."

He hopped in his car and followed my Benz back to my high-rise apartment. When we walked in, he seemed impressed by how clean and organized my place was. As I was pulling ingredients from the fridge, I noticed Jamal just standing there, watching me. My plan was to make some chicken in my air fryer and pretend I didn't know what I was doing, just to get my live audience talking and laughing. That was the whole point of the live cooking shows, to keep things fun and engaging.

After setting everything up, I posted an Instagram story: "Cooking with KJ will start in twenty minutes…" Within seconds, my phone started blowing up with notifications from people asking what I was going to mess up this time.

While I readied things for the live stream, Jamal seemed absorbed in his phone, texting away.

"You good, Jamal?" I asked when I noticed he was oddly silent.

He looked up, as if startled. "Huh? Oh, yeah, just dealing with some last-minute recording issues from a previous artist." Then, out of nowhere, he asked, "So, Kai, are you dating anyone?"

I hesitated. No one knew about Spex or our unconventional relationship, and I wasn't sure how close Jamal and Spex were. After a moment, I answered, "Not really. I'm just focusing on myself right now."

Jamal nodded and didn't push further, but I could tell he was curious. As the countdown to my live stream ticked away, I focused on making the show entertaining while Jamal settled in, obviously still curious about the behind-the-scenes of my life.

Chapter 22

JUNIPER

I finally gave in and invited Lorenzo over so we could talk. He sat on the loveseat and darted his eyes around my house like he hadn't seen it in years, even though it had only been four months. We were alone, because he had dropped Symone off at her grandparents,' and Mama had taken Kaylee to Chuck E. Cheese. My mother still wasn't aware of our breakup, and I hoped that everything would go well enough that night that she would never have to find out.

I ordered some food from The Capital Grille, and it was already plated on the table in the kitchen. The aroma of comfort foods—perfectly cooked steak and creamy mashed potatoes—filled the air, helping to ease some of the tension that hung between us.

"Would you like some wine?" I asked, trying to keep my voice steady.

"Sure," Lorenzo replied as he took a seat at the table.

I filled his glass with some Risata Moscato d'Asti, one of his favorites, then sat down across from him. The city lights flickered through the windows, casting a warm glow over the room. Lorenzo just stared at me, his eyes filled with a storm of longing and pain. It reminded me of the night he came over when I was pregnant with Kaylee. That night, he had graciously allowed me to yell my frustrations about DaMarco before we cried together and discovered that we were in love. I wanted that feeling back, but I needed answers first. I had to hear the truth about the night of the BET Awards, the night someone took naked pictures of him. I had to know the truth, and I needed to get it out of him.

"Lorenzo," I started, my voice trembling slightly, "we need to talk about that night. I need to know exactly what happened."

He took a deep breath, and his eyes never left mine as he sincerely said, "Juniper, I swear I don't remember much. I had a few drinks, and the next thing I knew, I was waking up in my room, half-naked."

I wanted to believe him, but the images of him with that woman were burned into my mind. "How can you be so sure? The pictures don't lie, Lorenzo."

"I know they don't," he said, his voice desperate, "but I'm not lying. You know me, Juniper. You know I'd never willingly hurt you like that."

I looked down at his wine glass at the golden liquid swirling around. "Then who did it? Who would want to set you up?"

Lorenzo sighed. "It was Kai," he said.

The mention of her name sent a chill spiraling through me. I would never have suspected she would stoop that low, and it didn't make any sense. "Kai?" I said, arching a brow at him in confusion. "Why? Why would she do that?"

"Jealousy. Somehow, she heard I wanted to produce a track for Zara

Bloom. I hadn't even mentioned it to her, but she found out somehow. So, when we went back to my hotel room... Well, I believe she drugged me."

"Hmm. I think Spex told her," I said quietly.

"Huh? Spex? What? I mean...how?" he asked, baffled.

"They're sleeping together, Lorenzo," I revealed. "It's been going on for months."

"How do you know that?" Lorenzo asked.

"I saw them together at Ritz-Carlton the day I met the Blairs for dinner. Babe, Kai is not who we think she is. "We need to let her go," I said. I stood up from the table as the anger began to boil inside me.

"I can't believe I didn't see it," he said, casting his eyes to the floor. He then stood and moved closer to me. "Juniper, I'm so sorry. I should have been more careful."

I turned to face him, my eyes burning with unshed tears. "We both should have, but I guess it's a lesson learned. We need to be smart now. Kai is dangerous, and it's clear that she'll do anything to stay number one," I said, even more furious. "Tas asked if I think Kai has anything to do with it, and I told her she didn't."

"Huh? Why?" Lorenzo asked, looking at me in confusion. "Why would you say that?"

"Ren, I've been... I've had Kai investigated."

"Investigated? Why? What's this about, Juniper?" he said, a bit agitated.

"Well, it all started when I saw her with Spex. I asked my girl Nikki to check her out, along with Spex. She didn't find anything on him. He's just a whore, as we pretty much already knew," I said with a laugh.

"What about Kai?" Lorenzo asked sternly, apparently unable to find anything humorous in what I said.

"Her ex-husband is in jail for drug trafficking. His people are after her because she stole a bunch of money from him."

"When did you have time to do all this?" he questioned.

"I don't know. Things were just happening so fast, and the more we found out, the more complicated things became."

"Damn," Lorenzo said.

"Um, baby, there is something else I need to share with you," I said, my voice trembling. I was more nervous than I'd ever been, and I dreaded Lorenzo's reaction. I took a deep breath and tried to still my trembling hands. I had to tell him what I'd done, but I was not sure I was ready to admit it.

Three weeks after calling off the wedding, I made an appointment with Kacia's OBGYN. I'd made a commitment to her, and there was no going back. The memory of that day was still fresh in my mind: lying on the gurney, with my legs held open by the stirrups, feeling both vulnerable and determined. The doctor was very nice and explained each step as she inserted the embryo. Her calm voice was a small comfort amidst my whirlwind of emotions. I remembered the cold sterility of the room, the soft hum of the machines, and the steady rhythm of my heartbeat echoing in my ears. It was a strange mix of fear and excitement. At that point, since I was sure I was no longer going to be Lorenzo's wife, I didn't need his consent to help my sister and brother-in-law have the child they'd always wanted.

Now, as I stood there looking at Lorenzo, I felt a wave of anxiety wash over me. *How will he react? I wondered. Will he understand why I did it?* I had to hope he would see the love and sacrifice behind my decision. "Lorenzo," I slowly continued, my voice barely above a whisper, "I went through with the embryo transfer. I'm pregnant with Kacia and Philly's baby."

There was an unsettling silence as the words hung in the air between us, heavy with uncertainty. Lorenzo's eyes widened, and I saw a mixture of shock and confusion flash across his face. I took a step closer and reached out to touch his hand, but he pulled away, his expression unreadable.

"I know it's a lot to take in," I said, in broken syllables, "but I did it for Kacia and Philly. They can't have a baby on their own, and I want to help them. It felt like the right thing to do…and the right time, because… Well, you know."

Lorenzo's silence was worrisome.

I saw the conflict brewing in his eyes as he struggled to process the shocking news. I felt a lump forming in my throat, and the fear of losing him for good scared me. "I understand if you're angry or hurt," I added, my eyes welling with tears, "but please try to see it from my perspective. I want to give them a chance to have a family, something they desperately want. After our engagement ended, I felt like I had to do it on my own."

He finally spoke, his voice low and filled with emotion. "So, you ended our engagement, refused to talk to me for months, had Kai investigated, and became a surrogate, and I'm supposed to what? Just…understand? This shit is a lot to process. I need some time to think."

I nodded, and tears streamed down my face. "Take all the time you need, Lorenzo. I just need to be honest with you. You deserve that."

The door clicked softly closed as he left. I stood alone in the dimly lit room, just staring at the wine he didn't even bother to drink. The weight of our conversation lingered in the air, mixing with the aroma of the dinner that had grown cold. I sank back into my chair, the reality of what I had done hitting me like a tidal wave. The last few months had been a hurricane of emotions, questions, and difficult decisions, and that moment felt like the eye of a storm.

I stared at the half-empty wine glass, observed my reflection distorted in the golden liquid. *How did it all get so complicated?* My thoughts drifted to Kaylee, and I imagined her happy laughter at Chuck E. Cheese with Mama, the glee of a child blissfully unaware of the chaos unraveling at home. I also missed Symone running up to me and kissing and hugging me.

The buzz of my phone jolted me out of my trance. The ominous message from Nikki read: "We need to talk. Found something new about Kai. Call when you can."

I sighed and rubbed my temples. The investigation had already uncovered so much drama, and now there would be more to deal with. After a deep sigh, I dialed her number, a bit anxious but also hoping for some clarity.

"Juniper, we've opened Pandora's Box," Nikki said, skipping any pleasantries.

"What do you mean?" I asked, my heart sinking.

"It's Kai. She's been making more trips to Detroit."

"Detroit? For what? Is there some amazing pizza joint I don't know about?" I asked, trying to lighten the mood, though I knew it was futile.

Nikki continued, ignoring my attempt at humor, "Looks like she's been visiting Dwight."

"Wait. Her ex, the dealer?"

"Yep."

I felt a chill run down my spine. "Why would she do dumb shit like that? Doesn't she realize what's at stake?"

"That's the thing," Nikki said, her voice edged with frustration. "Kai is playing in Dwight's face, and he's a dangerous man, but she doesn't seem to care. She does whatever the hell she wants, like she's auditioning for Most Reckless Person of the Year."

I slumped in my chair, burdened by the weight of the revelation. We knew Kai and Dwight had a tumultuous past, and I couldn't fathom why she willingly kept talking to him, even just for a visit. "What, specifically, did your contact say?" I probed.

"The good news is that his associates don't seem to be pursuing her anymore. Seems as if she gave Dwight whatever he wanted. Juniper, Kai definitely has street smarts. Ya girl played her cards right over our asses."

"Is that it?" I asked, relieved to finally hear some positive. "She's done with him?"

Nikki hesitated. "Not exactly. I also found out she's got an older brother named Erick."

"Wait, what? Kai never mentioned a brother. Are you sure?"

"Positive," Nikki replied. "He still lives in Detroit, or he did, till recently. Kai moved him to L.A., and he lives with her now."

I blinked, stunned. "So, she's got a brother I never knew about, and she's been visiting her ex in prison. What's next? Is she secretly a superhero too?"

"Maybe she's just trying to keep things interesting," Nikki said, laughing.

I hung up the phone, laughed, and thought to myself, *Who this bitch done paid off?*

Chapter 23

KAI JAE

As the weeks dragged on, I couldn't shake the tension that had settled between me and Lorenzo. The betrayal hung over us like a thick fog, negatively affecting our work and our conversations. Every interaction was tinged with an undercurrent of mistrust. The Tyler Perry track was finished, and it was everything I'd hoped for, a perfect showcase of my voice and talent. Yet, every time I listened to it, I couldn't help but feel a pang of guilt. My sense of accomplishment was tainted by the way I had achieved it.

My phone buzzed incessantly with messages and notifications, congratulations from fans, updates on the movie progress, and news about upcoming gigs. It should have been a moment of triumph, but all I felt was overwhelming emptiness.

I needed to talk to someone, to pour out the turmoil that was eating me up inside. The one person I needed to speak with was Juniper. So, I took a deep breath, gathered my courage, picked up my phone, and dialed her number. My heart pounded as the phone rang, each tone amplifying my anxiety.

When she finally answered, her voice was cold and distant, a stark contrast to the warmth we had once shared. "Hello?" she flatly said.

"Juniper, it's Kai," I began, my voice shaking. "I know I messed up. I'm so sorry for everything. Can we please just talk about it?"

There was a pause before Juniper's voice cut through the silence like a blade. "Kai, I don't want to hear it. You are a selfish bitch."

"Fuck that bitch," I heard in the background.

"Tas, hush!" Juniper scolded.

"I know, and I regret it every single day," I said, desperation creeping into my voice. "Please, just give me a chance to explain, to make it right."

Her response was immediate and brutal: "No, Kai. You've shown me who you really are, and I can't forgive that. Also, just so we're clear, I'm not writing for you anymore. Find someone else to be your muse."

That announcement hit me like a slug to the gut. I tried to respond, but the line went dead before I could utter another word. I just stared at my phone, the emptiness inside me growing. The city outside seemed so alive, so vibrant, but I felt like a ghost in my own life. The buzz of the notifications continued, but they were just background noise to the aching silence left by Juniper's rejection.

I slumped on my couch, the weight of the past weeks pressing down on me. The congratulations and updates that had once seemed so important now felt hollow. I had achieved my dream, but in the process, I had lost something far more valuable.

***

Lorenzo's demeanor toward me remained frosty, colder than the steel of the mixing boards in the recording studio. The contract I signed with MUSIC4LIFE Records had initially seemed like my golden ticket, a promise of fame and fortune in exchange for my talent. Now, though, as the tension simmered between Lorenzo and me, it felt more like a prison sentence, with Mr. Mac as our stern warden, ready to crack the whip if we stepped out of line.

Mr. Mac wasn't the typical music industry bigshot. He didn't care about artistry or passion; all he saw were dollar signs. To him, we were just pieces on a chessboard, and he wasn't about to let his investment go up in smoke because of our trivial squabbles.

So, he summoned us both to his plush office downtown. The man himself sat behind a massive mahogany desk, his imposing figure draped in a tailored suit that screamed power and authority. His sharp features were framed by a perfectly groomed salt-and-pepper beard, and his eyes, sharp and calculating, seemed to bore into our souls as he spoke. The office itself was a monument to his success, with walls adorned with framed platinum records and awards. A grand piano sat in one corner, a testament to his love for music, albeit of the classical variety. The floor-to-ceiling windows offered a sweeping view of the city below, a constant reminder of just how far Mr. Mac had climbed to get to the top.

Lorenzo's frustration boiled over as he attempted to explain to Mr. Mac the root of our discord. "Kai Jae…" he began, his voice tight with barely contained anger. He cleared his throat and continued, "She went behind my back and—"

"I don't give two shits about your personal grievances," Mr. Mac said, cutting him off with a dismissive wave of his hand, his tone icy and final. "Whatever issues you two have, leave them at the door. This album is my investment, and I won't let it go to waste because of your petty drama."

Lorenzo's jaw clenched, and he balled his fists at his sides as he struggled to contain his frustration. He shot me a venomous glare before storming out of the office, leaving the door to slam behind him with a resounding thud.

Alone with Mr. Mac, I felt the weight of his words pressing down on me like the proverbial ton of bricks. It was clear he had no patience regarding our personal problems, no sympathy for the obstacles that stood in our way. All he cared about was results, and if we couldn't deliver, he wouldn't hesitate to cut us loose and find someone who could.

As I left his office, the gravity of the situation hit me like a sucker punch to the gut. If I wanted to salvage the album and save my career, I had no choice but to set aside my differences with Lorenzo and find a way to make it work. Our future depended on it, and I wasn't about to let that slip away because of my lies.

Caught in the grip of paranoia, I kept casting wary glances over my shoulder, Dwight's threats hung over me like a dark cloud. It felt like he was always lurking in the shadows, ready to pounce at any moment. Every stranger in the crowd, every unexpected noise in the night, set my nerves on edge, a constant reminder of the danger I was in.

Not only had Spex stopped talking to me, but he had also blocked me on every platform. It was like a hot knife to my heart, realizing the man I'd shared so much passion with was no longer part of my life. I needed someone to talk to, someone who knew me, someone to confide in, but he was just another person who had blacklisted me for the awful things I'd done.

One day, amidst the suffocating atmosphere, my phone rang, interrupting the silence of my solitude. It was Lorenzo. Despite the apprehension knotting my stomach, I answered, steeling myself for whatever icy words might come my way.

"Kai," he said, his voice curt, devoid of warmth or familiarity, "we've gotta redo two songs on the album. Mr. Mac's not feeling them, and, after hearing them again, neither am I." His words were like a double-edged sword, a glimmer of progress overshadowed by the relentless chill in his tone.

I mustered a response, trying to maintain a façade of composure despite the turmoil brewing within me. "Sure, Lorenzo. Let's meet to go over the details. I'm sure we can make it better."

"Not always," he muttered before he hung up, and I knew he wasn't just talking about the music, "but come on over."

With that, he ended the call, leaving me to wrestle with the bitter aftermath of our conversation. It was a bittersweet victory, knowing the album was nearing completion yet realizing that the distance between us had never been greater. As I prepared to face Lorenzo once more, I braced myself for the inevitable confrontation, unsure if we could ever bridge the gap that had formed between us.

In the studio, the toxic feeling between the two of us seemed to be draped all over the place, like a storm brewing on the horizon. He was already there, and his vibe was frostier than an ice-cold drink on a hot summer day. There were no pleasantries, no warmth, and he just got straight down to business.

"Hey, Lorenzo," I said, in as friendly a voice as I could, but trying to break through his icy exterior was like talking to a stone wall.

He wasted no time in saying, "Just stick to the music, Kai. We've got work to do." His tone was still as sharp as a knife.

I resisted the urge to press him on our strained relationship. It was clear he wasn't in the mood, and I didn't want to push him further away.

As we delved into discussing the songs we were axing, a sense of disappointment washed over me. Our connection used to be strong, but now it felt like we were worlds apart, even in the same room. Even as I did my best to work with the man in front of me, though, another man was on my mind, nagging at me like a persistent itch. I needed answers, even if asking the questions stirred up trouble. "Lorenzo," I proceeded cautiously, "have you heard anything from Spex lately?"

His reaction was swift and cutting. "Why do you even care?" he snapped, suspicion lacing his words.

I stumbled over my response, feeling like I'd stepped on a landmine. "I'm just…curious," I managed to choke out.

The weight of his stare was almost unbearable, and he shut me down with a firm hand. "It's none of your damn business," he declared, putting a stop to all hope of any further discussion on the matter.

I swallowed my pride along with my questions, and the silence between us thickened with even more unspoken tension. It was clear that Lorenzo was not going to budge, and for the sake of my career and my sanity, I wasn't about to push it.

Chapter 24

JUNIPER

I danced around the house, trying to shake off the nerves and excitement of the day ahead, on my way to the shower. The warm water soothed me, and I began to settle down a bit as the steam enveloped the room. I reached for my body wash, but my hand met an empty space where the bottle usually was. It was then that I realized I had left it behind, at Lorenzo's place.

The sudden reminder made my chest tighten with a pain so raw it felt almost unbearable. I just stood there, paralyzed, letting the water cascade over me. The pampering effect of the shower was short-lived. In an instant, tears started to form, and I was soon overcome by an ugly cry, the kind of jerking, loud wailing that only occur when one's heart hurts so much it seems a better option to just rip it out. I sank to the floor of the shower and paid no mind to the water hitting my hair and mixing with my shuddering sobs.

It was the kind of crying that shook me to my core. Each breath felt labored, and the agony cut through every fiber of your being. I let the water continue to run over me, hoping it might drown out the hurt, but it did little to ease the sadness. My sobs were deep, full of pain and frustration, and I feared I might actually break apart, like a fragile vase thrown against a wall.

After what felt like an eternity, I finally managed to pull myself together. I still had to take deep, shuddering breaths, but I ambled to my feet and, on wobbly legs, wrapped myself in a towel. Though my heart still ached, I concentrated on steadying my breathing and tried to focus on the day ahead. I hoped some time spent with Kacia might help me find a bit of joy and distraction amidst the turmoil.

As I worked on pulling myself together, I heard the door creak open. My sister had used her spare key, and she called out for me with that perpetually cheery voice of hers. It was DaMarco's weekend with Kaylee, so we had the whole day to ourselves.

I quickly yelled from the bathroom, "Almost ready!" I tried to sound calm and strong, as I didn't want her to see me in the middle of my breakdown.

I chose an outfit that was both stylish and comfortable. The tight, black jeans perfectly hugged my curves. I paired them with a black V-neck, flattering and casual. For footwear, I opted for silver sandals to add a touch of elegance, and I accessorized with silver jewelry; the simple earrings and delicate necklace complemented the outfit. I hoped Kacia wouldn't notice that I'd removed my engagement ring. It was far too painful a reminder to carry around with me, just a trigger that would drum up the complicated feelings I was doing my best to navigate through.

I pulled my wet hair into a high ponytail and secured it with an elastic band. Next, I applied some light makeup, just a touch of foundation to even out my skin tone, a bit of mascara to brighten my eyes, and soft pink lip gloss to add a bit of color. I wanted to look refreshed and put-together, despite the tears I had shed.

After a final glance in the mirror, I took a deep breath and headed out of the bathroom. When I saw Kacia already settled in the living room, I gave her a hug. "You ready?" I asked, eager to enjoy our girls' day out, hoping it would bring some much-needed distraction and joy.

My sister sensed my energy but didn't say anything at first.

"So, uh... What's on the agenda for today, sis?" I asked, grabbing my purse.

"You already know I have it ready," she finally said, breaking the silence that had me a bit concerned. Her laughter was a welcomed relief.

***

We started our day at a small, cozy café downtown, known for its decadent pastries and aromatic coffee. Kacia and I had spent countless mornings there, laughing over croissants and cappuccinos, but this particular visit felt special.

"One almond croissant and a matcha latte for me," Kacia said, flashing her radiant smile at the barista. She then turned to me, raising an eyebrow. "And for you, Miss Juniper?"

I chuckled. "I'll have a mocha cappuccino and *two* almond croissants. I'm starving."

She giggled. "Eating for two, maybe?" she whispered with a wink.

While we waited for our order, we found a table by the window, where we could watch the world go by. The sun streamed in, casting a warm glow over everything. It was a perfect start to our day.

"So, what's the plan?" I asked again.

Kacia grinned. "Simple. We're gonna eat our way through this city, paint our nails in the most obnoxious colors, then end the day with some epic karaoke. Sound good?"

"Perfect!" I said, my spirits lifting already. "I can use a day like that."

As promised, our next stop was a trendy nail salon, where we were greeted by a chorus of cheerful hellos. The place was bright and airy, filled with the scent of nail polish and the hum of chatter.

"What color are you thinking?" Kacia asked, holding up a bottle of neon pink.

I rolled my eyes playfully. "Something a bit more subtle maybe, like…this," I said, selecting some soft lavender.

"Suit yourself," Kacia said with a grin and a shrug. "I'm going full-on Barbie today."

We settled into our chairs, and the nail technicians got to work. As they buffed and polished, Kacia and I continued our conversation.

"You know," Kacia said, her voice taking on a more serious tone, "I've never properly thanked you for doing this, for carrying my baby. It means more to me than you could ever know."

I waved her off, trying to keep the mood light. "It's no big deal, Kacia. We're sisters. I'd do anything for you."

"It *is* a big deal," Kacia insisted. "You're giving me a chance to be a mom. That's more than a big deal. It's huge."

As the manicurists expertly worked on our nails, I glanced around the salon, admiring its chic décor and vibrant atmosphere. The hum of conversation and occasional laughter created a relaxed, almost festive ambiance.

Kacia's voice brought me back to our conversation. "I know it was a lot to ask, and I'm just so grateful. I've been thinking a lot about how to repay you in some way, but, honestly, sis, nothing I can ever do will ever be enough to truly show how much this means to me."

I smiled softly. "You don't have to repay me, Kacia. Just seeing you happy is the important part. It's enough for me to know I'm able to help you fulfill your dream. This is about family, and that's what matters most."

Kacia looked at me with gratitude and vulnerability. "I always thought it was out of reach for me to be a mom. I've always admired your strength and kindness, but this? This is beyond anything I could have imagined."

We fell into a comfortable silence for a moment, the weight of her humble gratitude hanging in the air. The nail technician carefully applied a final coat of polish, and I couldn't help but feel a deep sense of fulfillment and connection. Moments like those made all my challenges worth it, little gems of happiness here and there that made life worth living.

"Okay, done!" the technician announced, breaking the silence.

Kacia and I admired our freshly painted nails, mine in the soft lavender I'd chosen and hers in the eye-catching neon pink she'd embraced.

"Fabulous! Now, what's next on our list?" I asked, eager to continue our day.

We paid for our manicures and headed out into the bright afternoon. Our excitement was palpable, and, despite my underlying emotions, I felt a renewed sense of joy and anticipation.

We walked into a high-end boutiques, chic and trendy. While I was scoping out the jackets, I spotted an unwelcomed sight. There was Kai Jae, her arms full of the cutest pieces. I had no desire to deal with her or to let her ruin a fun day, so I quickly turned my back and headed for the exit.

"What's going on?" Kacia asked, rushing out behind me. "What happened?"

"Oh, nothing," I fibbed. "I just need to, uh…make a call. "No signal inside," I lied, holding up my phone in a feeble attempt to dodge Kai Jae.

"Juniper!" I heard the woman call out.

Great. She caught up to me, I seethed as I realized I had no choice but to stop.

Kacia followed us out and, with a big smile, began congratulating Kai on her achievements. My sister noticed the twisted expression on my face, and I could tell she was about to ask me about it, but she hesitated when she saw how uncomfortable I was.

Kai Jae tried to engage me in conversation, but my expression warded her off as well, and she just turned and went back inside the boutique.

"What was that about?" Kacia asked as she followed me into another shop, even more expensive than the previous one.

We spent a good hour trying on outfits, laughing hysterically at some of our more outrageous picks. All the while, I tried to put all thoughts of Kai Jae out of my mind.

"Juniper, you have to try this one!" Kacia said, holding up a jaw-dropping emerald, green dress. "On you, it'd be…fire!"

I raised an eyebrow, skeptical but intrigued. "You really think so?"

"Girl, I *know* so. Trust me. You'll slay in this."

I headed into the dressing room with the fancy garment in hand. When I slipped the dress over my head and caught a glimpse of myself in the mirror, I had to admit Kacia was on to something. It fit like it was made for me, clinging to every curve in all the right ways, and the color made my skin pop like nobody's business. I stepped out and performed a little spin to show off the look. "Well? What do you think?" I asked.

Kacia's eyes were like saucers, and her mouth dropped open in a dramatic gasp. "Oh, my God, Juniper! You look like a million bucks! You need to buy that right now."

I laughed and felt a flush rise to my cheeks. "All right, all right. You win. I'll take it."

We continued our shopping spree, and we both picked out some fabulous pieces. It was pure joy to just let go of our worries for a while and soak in the fun of the moment.

As Kacia and I wrapped up our shopping trip, my phone buzzed with a new message. I glanced at it and saw DaMarco's name flashing on the screen. The message said he needed to drop Kaylee off early because he had been summoned to yet another emergency work meeting. His role as a district manager at Dell forced him to travel frequently, and it seemed like his schedule was always changing.

I quickly typed a reply to let him know it was fine. After I sent it, I turned to tell Kacia the bad news.

"No problem, sis. Let me just pay for this stuff, and we'll head home," she said, as understanding as ever.

While Kacia drove me home, the car was filled with the sound of boxes and bags shuffling around behind us and the upbeat music on her playlist, but she turned the tunes down so we could talk a bit more. "So," she began, glancing over at me as we navigated through traffic. "I've been meaning to ask. What's going on with Lorenzo? You haven't mentioned him all day, and you've said nothing more about wedding plans. What's up?"

I felt a stab at her question. Lorenzo and I had been distant, and the wedding seemed like a distant memory now. I didn't want to dive into that mess, especially not on a good day. I took a deep breath and decided to shift the conversation. "Well, all that studying, you know?" I said, trying to sound upbeat. "Hey, I passed the bar exam!"

Kacia's face lit up with excitement. "Oh, my gosh, Juniper, that's amazing! I'm so proud of you!"

I grinned, feeling a rush of relief and accomplishment. "Thanks! It feels incredible to finally put that hurdle behind me. It's like a huge weight off my shoulders."

We talked more about my bar results, and Kacia shared her own updates and plans. The conversation lightened my mood and distracted me from the more pressing issues, like my difficult situation with Lorenzo.

When we arrived at my place, I thanked Kacia for the lovely day and her company. We made plans to catch up again soon, and I watched as she drove away, feeling a mix of gratitude and lingering unease.

A few minutes after Kacia dropped me off, I heard the rumble of DaMarco's truck pulling up in front of my garage. I looked out the window and saw him get out and open the back door of his SUV, to let our Kaylee out of her car seat.

As soon as he unbuckled her, the child leapt out of the vehicle and dashed toward me. "Mommy!" she shouted, her face lighting up.

I scooped her up into a big hug and held her tightly as she wrapped her arms around my neck.

"I missed you so much, Mommy!" Kaylee squealed, her voice filled with joy.

"I missed you too, sweetheart," I said, my heart swelling with love. "How was your day?"

Before she could answer, DaMarco grabbed Kaylee's backpack from the back seat and followed us inside. He flopped onto the couch, looking worn out but relieved. "Man, what a day," he said, rubbing his eyes. "I had to take Kaylee with me to work earlier. We had to deal with a major system crash on about sixty laptops at the main center. It was a mess."

I nodded sympathetically. "Sounds intense. What happened?"

"Well," DaMarco said, leaning back and stretching, "their systems were down for hours. They had to call in the Cavalry."

"Um, you mean…you?" I asked, resisting the urge to roll my eyes.

"Yep," he said. "I had to jump in and troubleshoot. Kaylee was a trooper though. We made it through all that, but now I've gotta head back for another meeting."

"Wow. Sounds like a lot," I said. "I'm glad you got it sorted out."

"Yeah, me too," DaMarco said, then yawned and offered a tired smile. "Sorry I had to cut my weekend short because of these unexpected computer issues."

Kaylee, meanwhile, eagerly interrupted to show me a drawing. "Look, Mommy!" she said, holding up the colorful crayoned rainbow. "I made it at Daddy's work."

"It's beautiful, Kaylee!" I said, admiring her artwork. "I love it."

DaMarco watched us with a grin. "She's been talking nonstop about you. We went to a new park yesterday, and she found the biggest slide. She climbed it like a champ."

Kaylee nodded, her eyes sparkling. "Daddy helped me get all the way to the top, Mommy! I wish you were there to see. It was so much fun!"

"I'm sure it was," I said, giving her a playful nudge. "You're getting so brave."

DaMarco chuckled. "She's got the heart of an adventurer. Anyway, I gotta head out and grab some dinner before my next meeting." Before he walked out the door, he glanced back with a grin. "Oh, by the way, Kaylee mentioned something about not having Symone for a sister anymore. Issues in paradise?" he asked, his tone somewhat mocking, if not a bit hopeful.

I raised an eyebrow, feeling a surge of irritation. "DaMarco, really? Can you just drop Kaylee off without making it your mission to be all up in my business?"

He chuckled, clearly amused. "Hey, I'm just trying to keep up with the soon-to-be newlyweds."

I shook my head, trying to keep my cool. "How foolish of me to think we were having a decent, adult conversation. You can't use dropping our daughter off as an opportunity to spy on Lorenzo and me. We're fine, and it's none of your business. Now, please leave my house."

DaMarco's grin widened, but he held up his hands in mock surrender. "A'ight, a'ight. I'll stay out of it. Just thought I'd ask."

"Appreciate it," I said, sarcastically. "We'll catch up later. Have a good meeting."

As soon as he left, I turned my attention back to Kaylee, ready to enjoy our time together.

Chapter 25

LORENZO

It was heavy, man. *Juniper, my Juniper, is actually pregnant with her sisters' baby.* I didn't want to think about it, but it was stuck in my head, playing on repeat. Every time I reached for my phone, I hesitated. I knew it wasn't right. She had found the courage to share her truth with me, and I'd chosen to smack her with radio silence, to basically ghost her. I knew it wasn't fair.

I stood up and paced the floor. The break from my routine, the trip to visit my cousin, had helped a little. Now, I tried to get back to normal, and I'd even started going on morning runs. It didn't fix anything except improve my cardiac health, but I needed to feel something different.

Symone was with her grandparents, and I was thankful for the alone time to clear my head. I hoped Symone would understand Juniper was gone, and now she couldn't see Kaylee. It wasn't fair to either of them because we couldn't get our issues together.

I plopped down at my table and tried to lose myself in listening to tracks, but my mind kept drifting to Kai Jae. *The nerve of that girl.* She seemed genuine at first, just another talented soul chasing dreams in the industry. Now, she'd assaulted me with betrayal and shattered all trust I had in her. I still couldn't believe it.

As I geared up for the day, getting ready to hit the studio, the doorbell rang. I wasn't expecting anyone, so I headed over to answer it, as paranoid as I was curious. When I opened the door, I was met with a sight that threw me off balance. Her expression was determined but hesitant. It had been a minute since we'd last talked, and things between us were complicated, to say the least.

"Kai Jae," I said, trying to keep my voice even. "What are you doing here?"

She fidgeted, her eyes darting around as if she was searching for something to ground her. "Lorenzo, can we talk? Please?"

I sighed and stepped aside, letting her in. "Make it quick."

She stepped inside and glanced around as if the room held some kind of significance. When she finally faced me, her eyes were full of sincerity. "Lorenzo, I know things have been rough between us, but I came here to apologize…for everything."

I crossed my arms and leaned against the wall, not ready to buy more of her bullshit. "So, what, exactly, are you hoping to apologize for, Kai Jae?"

She sighed, and her shoulders drooped. "I know I messed up. I hurt people I care about, including you, but I want to make things right. I want to fix what's broken between us."

I let out a bitter laugh. "Fix it? After all this time? A little too late for that, don't you think?"

Kai Jae's eyes were pleading as she said, "Lorenzo, I know I can't change the past, but I want to move forward. Can we at least talk it out?"

I shook my head, the old wounds still too raw. "You don't get it, do you? Some things can't be patched up with a quick apology. You can't just stroll back into my life and expect everything to be fine."

Her face fell, and for a moment, I saw a glimmer of real regret. "I understand if you're not ready to forgive me, but I had to try. I need to make things right."

I turned away, my mind spinning with mixed emotions. Part of me wanted to give her a chance, but the bigger part was still too hurt and angry. "Why now, Kai Jae? What's different?"

She hesitated and took a deep breath. "I've been doing a lot of thinking, a lot of soul-searching. Also, I need to find Spex. Do you know where he is?"

My temper flared at the mention of the DJ's name. "You said you came to apologize, but you're really just looking for him! Is that what this is really about?"

She looked down, clearly torn. "I just need to talk to him, Lorenzo. It's important."

The anger and betrayal surged inside me. "Get the fuck outta my house, Kai Jae. I'm not some steppingstone to get to Spex. I won't be used, not by you or anyone else. Also, just so you know, he won't DJ any of your shows. If that's what you're thinking, you've got another thing coming. Besides, you still have to go through me. Unfortunately for both of us, I'm contractually obligated to serve as your manager...for now."

"Please, Lorenzo," she begged, her eyes filled with tears. "I'm desperate."

"I told you to get out," I commanded, my resolution solid.

After a defeated, pathetic nod, and without another word, she turned and walked out.

After she left, I paced the living room, wrestling with a storm of anger and sadness. *The gall of this broad, coming here to get me to talk to Spex. She probably wants him to DJ her listening party.* It only made me more furious to know that was the only reason she was trying to locate him. I was getting very sick of Kai Jae using the people who had only tried to help her, myself included.

After she left, I tried calling Spex to warn him she was on the prowl, but my call went straight to voicemail. I wasn't exactly worried though. Spex had always been unpredictable, and it really was just another notch in his belt.

I decided to send a text, just to keep things in check. There'd be written proof that way, so he couldn't say I didn't try to warn him. If he was avoiding Kai Jae on purpose, he had the right to know she was looking for him. I kept the message as short and straightforward as I could, giving him the details that mattered most: "Spex, Kai Jae stopped by my place, looking for you. Seems pretty desperate. I'm guessing she needs a DJ. I won't sign off on that. Just thought you should know. Call when you get this."

I hit send and leaned back, then stared at the screen. It wasn't really about being concerned for Spex. From a business and personal standpoint, for my own protection, I just needed to manage the situation and make sure he was in the loop. I know it would mess up my money with Kai Jae, but I really didn't give two shits.

My phone buzzed, and I assumed it was Spex getting back to me. Unfortunately, I wasn't that lucky.

"It was so great seeing you again!" Cari texted.

When I ran into her at LAX, we decided to stop by one of the cafés in the terminal to catch up. She told me she had recently moved to Oakland but was in L.A. to visit her boyfriend. It had been a while since we'd last talked, especially after Erin caught us together.

Cari looked better than ever. Her hair flowed down her back, shiny and full. Her spaghetti-strap, yellow top and white pants gave her a fresh, vibrant look. A dainty gold chain hugged her neck, dangling a delicate butterfly pendant just below. Her bright pink lipstick popped, and her yellow flats looked comfortable but cute, perfectly complementing the summery outfit. Her nails were manicured, and her lashes were done nicely.

We sat down with our salads and drinks and chatted about life and changes. I didn't delve into my issues with Juniper. Instead, I showed Cari some photos of the girls. It felt good to share that part of my world with her.

"Look how big they are," she said, pointing to Symone and Kaylee. "They're so cute. Wow, that Symone looks just like her mom." She paused and looked over at me. "Sorry, Ren, but it's true. Anyway, I bet they keep you and Juniper busy," she said with a laugh, completely oblivious to the drama we'd been going through.

I nodded. "Yeah, things have been pretty hectic, but it's all part of the ride."

Cari grinned. "Well, I've been crazy busy myself. Like I said, I moved to Oakland a few years ago. It's different out there, but it's actually kinda great. My new job has its perks, and the city is lively. I'm adjusting well, though I do miss L.A. from time to time."

We spent the rest of the time reminiscing and catching up. It was refreshing to reconnect, and, despite the turmoil I was dealing with, it felt like a moment of normalcy.

I refocused my thoughts back to Kai Jae showing up at my place. I vividly heard my grandmother's voice in my head, so loudly that it was as if she was right there with me: *"Before you decide to cut someone off, think about what you've done. Jesus didn't cut you off, did He?"* Those words hit hard, and I knew Granny was right. My anger was only messing up my work and my peace of mind.

Kai Jae was a star, no matter how I felt about her personally or what had happened between us. I was a businessman in the music industry, and that required me to give her a fair shot and really listen to what she had to say. I picked up my phone and dialed her number. It was time for me to move past my anger. Granny wouldn't get out of my head: *"Forgiveness isn't for the other individual, Ren. It's for you."*

I took a deep breath and waited for her to pick up.

Chapter 26

KAI JAE

I left Lorenzo's place feeling like I'd been hit with a ton of bricks. The rejection stung far more than I'd expected, slicing through my resolve, and leaving me feeling raw and exposed. As soon as I got home, I stumbled through the door and collapsed on the living room floor. The weight of my fractured relationships with Lorenzo, Spex, and Juniper crashed down on me. My strong ambition and drive to succeed had pushed everyone away, and now I was reaping the fallout.

Tears poured out uncontrollably, each sob shaking my body so hard I felt breathless. I hugged my knees to my chest. The cold wooden floor of my apartment was a harsh contrast to the warmth and closeness I'd lost. My mind spun with a cyclone of regret and what-ifs. *How did I let things spiral this badly? Why did I let my drive blind me to the people who truly matter? What the hell is wrong with me?*

The rest of the day was a blur of tears and self-loathing. Nightfall found me exhausted but unable to sleep, my mind stuck on replay, torturing me with my last conversation with Lorenzo. The disappointment in his eyes haunted me.

***

When morning hit, I awoke with swollen eyes and a heavy heart, barely able to drag myself out of bed. I felt like I was running on fumes, but it was a critical day for me. A photoshoot was scheduled for my album cover, and I couldn't afford to look anything less than on point. Wardrobe and makeup were set to roll in, and every detail had to be perfect.

On top of that, I had made plans for Erick to move in, and his room needed prepped. The three bedrooms in my high-rise apartment had been empty for too long, just waiting for him. Juggling all of that while trying to keep it together was a lot, but I had to get it done.

I also had an incredible opportunity to be on the cover of *ESSENCE*, so we had decided to multitask and handle all the photos for the album cover and the magazine in one sitting. Despite all the trouble I'd caused over the last month, the show had to go on. Forest, my stylist, came through with the hottest wears. As soon as he walked in, I knew we were in good hands.

Kelly, Forest's assistant, entered right behind him. She was stunning herself, her deep cocoa-mocha skin glowing in the morning light. Her wavy, black hair was parted in the middle and cascaded elegantly over her shoulders. She wore a brown Gucci sweatsuit that hugged her hips perfectly, and she carried a suitcase brimming with outfits.

As we got to work, Kelly and Forest unveiled a collection of chic, urban outfits that excited me, in spite of the many challenges. There was a pair of sleek, high waisted joggers that fit like a glove, coupled with a cropped, neon-green hoodie that screamed modern edge and attitude.

Next, they offered a soft, oversized, denim jacket with distressed details, the perfect touch for a more laidback, effortless vibe.

The fashion explosion didn't stop there though. Next, Forest pulled out a daring, all-black, leather miniskirt with a high slit. It too was edgy and glamorous. To top it off, there was a sheer, mesh, long-sleeved top with intricate patterns that added a hint of mystery and allure. Each outfit was designed to make a bold statement, and the combinations of textures and styles felt both fresh and juicy.

Kelly and Forest went all out with accessories too. There were chunky gold chains, oversized ear hoops, and statement sneakers that added just the right amount of swagger. With every piece they presented, I felt my confidence building. That feeling was only heightened by the knowledge that the outfits were not just for the shoot; they would also make sure I owned it when I stepped in front of that camera.

We had managed to book the conference room in my apartment for the shoot. The space was perfect: modern and sleek with floor-to-ceiling windows that bathed the room in natural light. The décor was tasteful, with a mix of minimalist furnishings and bold, abstract art pieces that added a touch of sophistication. The long conference table had been cleared off to allow the photographer a place to set up his gear. He was already hard at work when we walked in, meticulously adjusting lights, and arranging backdrops, preparing everything to capture the perfect shot. It felt like everything was falling into place, and I was ready to bring my vision to life.

Just then, Joy, my makeup artist, arrived to beat my face. She walked in with her usual grace, her presence instantly calming. She had an effortless elegance about her, donning a sleek bob and always carrying herself with impeccable style. She pulled out her kit, which was packed with high-end products from Fenty Beauty, NARS, and Urban Decay. Her deft hands worked their magic, blending and sculpting with precision.

She finished off my look with a stunning red matte lipstick, Code Red, from the Tropical Storm Collection. The vibrant, bold color made my lips pop and gave my entire look a fierce, polished finish. As she stepped back to admire her work, I couldn't help but feel a surge of excitement and even pride. Everything was coming together so perfectly, and I was ready to step in front of the camera and own every moment. I was ready to put all their hard work on display and to make everyone proud, including myself.

***

After the shoot wrapped and everyone left, I had to scramble to get things ready for Erick's move. I dashed from store to store, picking up essentials. My first stop was Target, where I grabbed a great comforter set, including soft linens, cozy throws, and plush pillows. I also picked up some high-quality bath towels and washcloths.

Next, I headed to HomeGoods for a few decorative touches. I found some rustic lamps, a stylish area rug, and a few framed prints that would add a personal touch to Erick's new space. I wanted it to feel welcoming and stylish, to be a true reflection of his personality.

While I was out, I called Erick to verify his flight arrival time and make sure everything was still on track. Hearing his voice gave me a bit of reassurance, and I felt a sense of urgency to get everything just right.

When I finally got home, I felt exhausted but determined to set his room up right. I made the bed with fresh linens, neatly arranged the towels in the bathroom, and carefully put all the décor in just the right places. As I stepped back to survey the room, I felt a wave of satisfaction. Despite the chaos of the day, I managed to get everything done, and it looked perfect. Erick would move into a space that was comfortable and thoughtfully designed, and that was exactly what I wanted.

Once everything was done, I sat in my room, flipping through some of the photos, trying to relax after a busy day. Erick's flight would not arrive for a few hours, so I tried to enjoy the calmness. That was suddenly interrupted, though, when the doorbell rang unexpectedly, catching me off guard.

When I answered the door, I saw someone I certainly did not expect, especially after how things had gone down when I had shown up at his place the day before. My heart skipped a beat at the sight of him. Never would I have imagined him to be on my doorstep, not after the way he had reacted to my attempted apology.

"Hey," I said, trying to sound nonchalant but failing miserably. "What are you doing here?"

"I'd like to talk, if you don't mind. I called, but you didn't answer," Lorenzo replied.

I hesitated for a moment but finally allowed him to come inside.

As he walked in, he took a quick glance around my apartment. "Nice place," he said, scanning my modern décor and stylish furnishings and nodding in approval.

I also nodded, feeling a bit awkward. "Thanks. Do you want to sit?"

He took a seat in one of my chairs, looking slightly more relaxed but still serious. "I need to be honest with you, Kai," Lorenzo began. "I'm not totally over what you did to me and Juniper. That whole thing was messed up, and it really screwed with me mentally, emotionally, and spiritually. It tore Juniper and me apart."

I felt a lump in my throat. I'd been dreading the conversation but knew it was necessary. "Lorenzo, I am truly sorry for what happened. I know I did wrong, and I can't even begin to imagine how much it hurt you."

He nodded, still looking pained. "I appreciate that you're apologizing now, but that doesn't change how I felt or what I went through. I may lose my fiancée altogether because of this BS."

"I understand," I said. I paused for a moment, trying to find the right words. "I've been reflecting a lot on my actions, and I realize how thoughtless and selfish I was. I took those pictures without considering the consequences, and I deeply regret it. I was so caught up in what might happen if you produce a hotter song for Zara Bloom. I was worried she might be…your exclusive."

Lorenzo's gaze softened slightly. "Exclusive? Kai, I'd never abandon you for another artist. I don't work like that. Like I said, I appreciate the apology, but it's gonna take time for me to get past this. The damage wasn't just emotional. It affected a lot of aspects of my life, and it hurt the woman I love as well."

"I get it," I said quietly. "I don't expect things to be okay overnight. I just want you to know I'm genuinely sorry. I want to make amends in any way I can."

He took a deep breath and looked at me with a mix of frustration and resignation. "I hope you're telling the truth about working on yourself. That's all I can really ask for."

"I am," I assured him. "I'm trying to learn and grow from this experience, from this…mistake. I know it won't fix everything, and I can't erase the past, but it's a start."

Lorenzo stood up, looking a bit more at ease but still conflicted. "Well, I guess that's all I need to hear for now. Thanks for being honest with me."

"Thank you for coming by and giving me a chance to apologize," I said as he headed for the door. "I hope things get better for both of us, Lorenzo, and for Juniper. I miss her too."

He gave a small nod before adding, "By the way, how did the shoot go?"

"Great," I replied. "We should get the final photos in a few weeks. Maria already has a few up on my Instagram and Facebook fan pages."

Lorenzo smiled faintly. "That's good to hear."

I glanced at my watch, then back at Lorenzo. "I actually have to run an errand now, but it was good to see you."

"Yeah, same here," he said. Then, after one last nod, he left.

As the door closed behind him, I took a deep breath and tried to let out the lingering sadness and let relief wash over me. It was a tough conversation, but I hoped it was a step toward healing, for both of us.

Chapter 27

JUNIPER

I lay in bed, staring at the ceiling, the weight of my depression pressing down on me like a heavy blanket. The three-carat, princess-cut diamond engagement ring I had once worn with pride now sat in its box in a drawer, a painful reminder of what I had lost. My heart ached every time I thought of Lorenzo. Our split had shattered me in ways I never imagined possible. Seeing him at the studio was even harder, when we had to redo two of Kai's tracks. Her second single, "Freak Like Me" had made it to Number 4 on the Billboard 100. She constantly apologized and even invited me out for dinner. I told her I'd think about it, but in actuality, my mind was not yet where I needed it to be. I wasn't ready to even consider forgiveness, let alone an awkward dinner.

My hand rested on my stomach, a faint glimmer of hope amidst the darkness. I was now eight weeks pregnant with Kacia and Philly's baby.

Carrying that precious gift for them felt like the only thing that I had left to give me a sense of purpose in the midst of my sorrow. All I had was that and taking care of my own little girl.

Suddenly, a sharp pain shot through my abdomen, jerking me abruptly out of my tainted daydreams. I winced and clutched my belly, but the cramps grew more intense with each passing second. Panic surged through me as I swung my legs over the side of the bed and stood. With my whole body caught in brutal waves of trembles, I stumbled toward the bathroom, each step agonizing. As soon as I reached the toilet, I felt a rush of warmth between my legs. I looked down and saw blood, bright and terrifying. My heart pounded in my chest, each beat echoing a primal fear that left me gasping for breath. My hands were slick with sweat as I fumbled for my phone, my fingers shaking uncontrollably. I dialed 911, barely able to press the buttons as panic swirled around me. When the operator answered, I struggled to form coherent words. "Please…help…me," I managed to choke out, my voice shaky and barely audible. "I'm eight weeks pregnant and…bleeding."

The dispatcher's cool and collected voice on the other end was a small anchor in the storm of my fear. "Stay calm," she urged gently. "I need you to tell me exactly what's happening."

I took another jittery breath and did my best to steady myself by holding on to the toilet tank with one hand. "I was lying in bed, and I felt a sharp pain, and then… There's so much blood! I-I don't know what's happening. I'm scared. I'm only eight weeks along!"

The minutes that followed were a blur of panic and pain. The paramedics arrived quickly, their faces calm and professional as they lifted me onto a stretcher. The ambulance ride to the hospital felt like it took forever. The sirens blared terrifyingly in my ears as the EMTs stared down at me, and machines beeped around me, only intensifying my fear.

As soon as we arrived at the hospital, I was rushed into an examination room. The doctors and nurses moved swiftly around my gurney, their faces serious as they examined me. I clung to the hope that everything was still okay, that the baby and I were both still safe and healthy.

Kacia arrived soon after, her face pale with worry. She rushed to my side and took my hand in hers. "Juniper, what happened?" she asked, her voice trembling.

"I-I don't know, s-sis," I whispered, tears streaming down my face. "I just... I started bleeding, and—"

Before I could utter another word, the doctor entered the room. He pulled down his mask to speak to us, revealing a grave expression, the look of a man with bad news to deliver. "I'm sorry," he said softly. "It was a miscarriage."

A miscarriage? The word hit me like a physical blow, and I felt my world crumble around me. I had failed Kacia and Philly. The one thing I had hoped would bring some light into my life had been ripped away.

Kacia's grip on my hand tightened, but instead of the comfort I expected, I saw anger in her eyes. "How could you let this happen?" she demanded, her voice quivering with fury.

I stared at her, shocked. "Kacia, I didn't... This was out of my control. I did everything the doctors told me to. I just... I wanted the baby as much as you did."

"You were supposed to take care of yourself!" she snapped, pulling her hand away. "You know how important this was to us, but you just carelessly let it slip away. How could you!?"

Her words cut deep, and I felt a fresh wave of grief and guilt wash over me. "I did everything I could," I whispered, my voice breaking. "I wanted to give you and Philly this baby. I didn't want this to happen."

Tears streamed down Kacia's face, but her anger didn't decrease. "We trusted you, Juniper. Now, we... Because of you, we have nothing. That was my last chance!"

The pain in her voice was unbearable, and I felt my own tears mix with hers. "I'm so sorry," I said with a heaving sob. "I didn't mean to hurt you. I was trying to help."

The tension in the room was suffocating, the weight of our mutual grief and anger hanging heavily between us. Kacia turned away, her shoulders shaking with silent sobs. I wanted to reach out to her, to comfort my sister, but I knew nothing I could say or do would make it right.

As the doctors and nurses continued their work, I just lay there, feeling utterly broken. The loss of the baby was a devastating blow for all of us, but losing Kacia's trust and support felt like the final nail in my own coffin. I had lost Lorenzo, and now I had lost the one thing that had given me hope.

As I lay in the hospital bed, surrounded by the sounds of beeping machines and hushed voices, I felt the full weight of my hopelessness. The future seemed bleak, and I couldn't see a way out of the darkness that enveloped me. The cold sterility of the room mirrored the emptiness I felt inside. The rhythmic beeping of the machines seemed to mock the chaos swirling in my mind. I couldn't stop replaying Kacia's words; her accusations pierced me like a dagger. I had failed my sister and her husband. More than that, though, I had failed the tiny life I'd been trusted to safely carry inside me.

A while later, a nurse came in to check on me, her expression compassionate but detached. She spoke softly, explaining what I should expect in the next few hours, but her words barely registered. My thoughts were consumed by the image of Lorenzo, with painful recollections of the way he used to look at me with such love and trust. I wondered if he would ever forgive me for the choices I had made, for all the pain I had caused. Now, with the baby gone, I didn't even have anything to show for it.

The hours dragged on, and each minute felt like eons. Kacia had left the room, unable to bear being in my presence any longer. I felt abandoned, adrift in a sea of my own guilt and sorrow. I wished for Lorenzo's arms around me, his soothing voice to tell me that everything would be all right, but my rock was gone, and I was left to face the horrible nightmare alone.

At some point, Kacia returned, her face red and puffy from crying. She stood at the foot of my bed, her eyes filled with anger and grief. "You need to understand," she said, her voice strained, "this was our chance, mine, and Philly's. Whenever you bring the girls around, it brings so much joy. Then, Tas had the twins, and I knew a child is what I need, what Philly needs."

"I know," I whispered, my voice hoarse. "I wanted to give you that, Kacia. I really did. I did everything I could to take care of myself, to protect the baby, but sometimes… In life, there are things that just happen, things we can't control."

Kacia shook her head, and more tears streamed down her face. "You don't understand, Juniper. This isn't just about the baby. It's about trust. You were supposed to be there for us, to follow through on your promise. Now, we have nothing."

Her words stung, but I knew she was speaking from a place of deep pain. "I'm so sorry, Kacia," I said, my own tears flowing freely. "I never meant to hurt you or Philly. I want to help, to be there for you in all the ways you need me. I couldn't stop this from happening."

She turned away, her shoulders still shaking with sobs. "I don't know if I can ever forgive you," she said quietly, keeping her back to me.

I reached out to comfort her, but she pulled away, her body tense.

As she walked out of the room again, I felt a crushing sense of loneliness. The bond we had shared, the sisterly trust and love, seemed shattered beyond repair.

The rest of the night passed in a haze. Nurses came and went, checking my vitals, offering hollow words of comfort from strangers, and pumping me with medications that left me feeling woozy and tired. I drifted in and out of sleep, haunted by dreams of what could have been. The future I had envisioned for Kacia and Philly, a future filled with laughter and love, had been cruelly snatched away.

As the morning light filtered through the hospital window, I awoke, still feeling utterly drained, both physically and emotionally. My eyes were swollen from crying, my heart heavy with sorrow and guilt. I hadn't slept much, for nightmarish dreams of the events of the previous day had invaded my slumber. The hospital staff was kind and tried to console me, but they could do little to ease the pain. Thankfully, it was DaMarco's weekend to look after Kaylee, because I could not bear to think of her witnessing any of it.

Suddenly, there was a knock at the door. I looked up, expecting another nurse or doctor or maybe the nice, elderly lady who came in daily to sweep the floor and take out the dirty laundry. Instead, it was Kacia and Philly. I blinked in surprise, my heart racing. Kacia had been so angry the last time we spoke that I didn't expect her to come back, especially not with Philly.

My sister cautiously approached my bed, her expression still revealing sadness and regret. "Juniper," she began, her voice trembling, "I'm so sorry for how I treated you yesterday. I was in shock and hurt, and I lashed out at you. I know that wasn't fair."

My eyes swam with tears again, but these were tears of relief. "Kacia, you have every right to be upset," I said softly. "I understand why you feel this way. I might have reacted the same way."

Philly stepped forward and placed a comforting hand on Kacia's shoulder. "We've had time to talk and think," he said, his voice kind. "We know that this wasn't your fault, Juniper. It was an unfortunate incident, something beyond our control."

Kacia nodded. "I can't blame you for what happened," she tearfully admitted. "It was just... It's hard to process, but I know you did your best. I'm sorry for the hateful things I said, sis."

I reached out and took her hand, then squeezed it tightly. "Thank you," I whispered, my voice breaking. "I really am so sorry for your loss. I wanted so badly to give you and Philly a baby."

Kacia's grip tightened around my hand, and for the first time since the miscarriage, I felt a glimmer of hope. *Maybe, just maybe, we can find a way to heal together.*

Philly looked at me with compassion. "We're here to take you home, Juniper," he said.

As I struggled to sit up, the door opened again, and my heart skipped a beat. Lorenzo's eyes were filled with concern, his expression tender. He crossed the room in a few quick strides and enveloped me in a warm embrace. I clung to him and felt the steady beat of his heart against mine.

"I called him," Kacia said. "I hope that was okay."

"I'm so sorry, Juniper," Lorenzo murmured, his voice thick with emotion. "I heard what happened. I came as soon as I could."

I buried my face in his chest, overwhelmed by a rush of emotions. "I was afraid you were gone," I whispered. "I thought I'd lost you forever."

He pulled back slightly, cupping my face in his hands. "I never stopped loving you," he said softly. "I was hurt, but I can't let you go, not after everything we've been through."

I looked into his eyes and saw only deep love and forgiveness. "Lorenzo, I—"

"Shh," he interrupted, then pressed a gentle kiss on my forehead.

As Lorenzo held me, I felt a sense of peace wash over me. Despite the pain and loss, there was hope, embodied in the man I suddenly realized I still loved. In that moment, I felt naked without my engagement ring, and I hoped he wouldn't notice my bare finger.

Kacia and Philly walked us to the car, and Lorenzo pushed me in the wheelchair. Relief washed over me once again, but it was tinged with sadness for the little one we'd lost. Their presence was a balm to my wounded soul, but their words of apology echoed in my mind, stirring a whirlwind of emotions.

Before we parted ways, Kacia pulled me into a tight hug, her voice soft and filled with regret. "Juniper," she said, a bit hesitant, "I know you've had a lot to juggle, studying for your bar, taking on new cases, writing for other artists, planning a wedding, being a mom. Then, on top of all that, I asked you to be a surrogate."

"Kacia, I-I appreciate your honesty," I managed, my voice trembling with emotion, "but, sis, please stop apologizing. You were just trying to fulfill your dream to have a family. I wanted to help. I really did."

She pulled back slightly and looked at me, searching for understanding in my eyes. "I know, Juniper, and I'll always be grateful for your willingness to try."

Lorenzo opened the car door for me, like the considerate, loving gentleman I remembered him to be. As he helped me into the seat, I felt a warmth in my heart that I hadn't experienced for a long time. We drove away from the hospital, leaving behind the pain and sorrow and looking ahead to a future filled with love, healing, and new beginnings.

Lorenzo glanced over at me, his eyes filled with tenderness. "I love you, Juniper," he said softly, "and we'll get through this together."

"Together," I parroted. I reached out and took his hand, feeling the strength of his love and support. "I love you, too, babe."

Chapter 28

KAI JAE

I was a bundle of nerves and excitement when I attended the Black Women in the Music Industry conference. The event was held in New York, the city that never slept, the Big Apple where dreams were either made or shattered. Walking into the grand hall of The Plaza Hotel, I was immediately struck by the sheer opulence. The chandeliers sparkled like a thousand tiny stars, casting a warm, golden glow over the room. The walls were adorned with rich, intricate tapestries, and the floors were covered with plush, deep red carpet that added a touch of regal elegance to the space.

Upon checking in, each woman was greeted with a beautiful gift, a luxurious, personalized welcome package. Mine included a sleek, leather-bound journal embossed with my initials, a set of artisanal chocolates, and a bottle of exquisite perfume. It was a small but thoughtful gesture that made me feel incredibly valued and honored to be part of the event.

As I navigated through the crowd, I spotted Oprah Winfrey, her presence as commanding and warm as ever. Nearby, Cardi B laughed with a group of other well-known artists, her infectious energy illuminating everything around her. LeToya Luckett was deep in conversation with another attendee, her poise and elegance shining through. They were women I had admired for years, and I could not believe I was fortunate enough to stand shoulder to shoulder with them.

My personal highlight of the night was when I was called to the stage to receive an award for the quickest rise to the top by a female artist. The applause was deafening as I made my way to the podium, the red carpet under my feet only adding to the sense of grandeur. As I stood there, looking out at a sea of inspiring faces, I felt a surge of pride and gratitude.

"Thank you," I began, my voice steady despite the emotions and nerves swirling inside me. "This award isn't just for me. It's for every Black woman who has fought to make her voice heard in this industry. We are powerful. We are resilient. We are…unstoppable," I said, unleashing another round of flattering applause. It was an odd sensation to see and hear the people I so admired were now admiring me.

The rest of the evening was a blur of congratulations, photos, and networking. It was everything I had dreamt it would be, a night to celebrate not only my success but the collective achievements of so many incredible women.

As the event wound down, I slipped out to the front of the building, clutching my coveted award in my hand. The New York night air was cool against my skin as I waited for my ride. When my limousine finally pulled up, I exhaled a sigh of relief and slid into the back seat, eager to reflect on the happenings of the evening. Nevertheless, the moment I sat down and took a peek at the driver, a chill ran down my spine.

The stranger behind the wheel looked back at me in the rearview mirror, his eyes cold and calculating.

My heart pounded in my chest as realization dawned. "Where's Tony?" I asked, my voice shaking as I questioned the whereabouts of my regular driver.

The person in the driver seat smirked, the kind of smirk that made my blood run cold. "Change of plans, Kai. Sit tight," he said, in a gruff voice.

Panic gripped me as the limo sped away from the venue. I fumbled for my phone, but the driver's unending glare stopped me.

"Don't even think about it," he dared.

He drove through the bustling streets of New York, until the familiar cityscape quickly gave way to more desolate areas. My mind raced, desperate to figure out my next move, but my body would not comply with any of its suggestions. The fear completely paralyzed me, especially when the limo pulled up in front of an abandoned wreck of a warehouse on the outskirts of the city.

"Get out," the driver ordered, this time turning to face me.

Trembling but too afraid to refuse, I stepped out of the car, still clutching my award like a lifeline. As we walked into the dimly lit warehouse, shadows danced menacingly on the walls. One of the silhouettes looked sickly familiar, and my heart sank when I saw only one chair, the back turned toward me, with a thin wisp of cigar smoke rising from it.

"Kai Jae," he greeted as the chair swiveled around. "Nice to see you again."

The mysterious driver left me there with the unknown man, and my mind went into overdrive, my eyes darting every direction, searching for a way out of this nightmare. My evening of triumph had dissolved into a harrowing ordeal, and I had no idea how to get out of it. There was only one certainty: *I will not go down without a fight.*

Suddenly, I heard footsteps echoing through the warehouse. Each step sent a wave of dread through me, and my heart dropped when I saw a familiar face emerging from the shadows, with a twisted smile playing on his lips.

"Surprised to see me?" he asked, his voice dripping with mockery.

My mind reeled as I tried to make sense of his presence. "Spex? What are *you* doing here?" I managed to stutter.

Spex's smile widened in an eerie way, with the look of some spooky Jack-o-lantern. "It's really pretty simple, Kai. See, Dwight is my half-brother. I've always lived in California with my mother, but I spent the summers in Detroit, with him and our father. Dwight called me and told me about everything you did to him."

The realization felt like a piano falling on my head. "You set me up," I whispered, the betrayal cutting deep.

He nodded, satisfaction gleaming in his eyes. "Yes, and our plan worked even better than we imagined. I know Lorenzo well. When he said MUSIC4LIFE signed you, it made things real easy. Why do you think Lorenzo was so surprised when I showed up at the studio unannounced?"

The horrible revelation settled over me, the suffocating realization that I had been a pawn in their game all along. No matter how hard I tried, I could think of no escape. Like a torrent through a broken dam, tears burst out of my eyes, smearing my perfect makeup all over my face in a way that would have sickened Joy to no end.

"Spex, we made love," I said. "I was always…willing. I did things that I know you enjoyed," I said, hoping he still had some heartstrings to strum.

Spex hesitated, then grinned that hellish smile again. "No, Kai, we did not make love. We fucked, and then there was that stunt about Monique." He laughed. "That was just a tactic for me to end things to get my plan in motion. She's not pregnant, but you getting all mad about it really turned me on. I figured one last fuck wouldn't hurt," he shamelessly confessed, his words chilling and colder by the minute.

"Spex, I—"

He held his hand up to silence me, and his eyes bore into mine, cold and calculating. "John, leave us," he commanded.

John, the driver, nodded and exited the warehouse. After we were alone, the silence was thick, the air heavy with tension.

"Spex, what are you going to do to me?" My voice trembled as I spoke. "I have the money. I can repay Dwight now. I've got royalty checks, ticket sales from the tour… Oh, and those endorsement check from Prada will be coming in soon. That's $300,000 right there, Spex. Lorenzo didn't want me doing endorsements. He thinks it's trashy, but he still got me a few deals, one with Prada and one with Tropical Storm Collections makeup. It was just finalized."

Spex laughed again and punctuated it with a condescending eye-roll. "Lorenzo knows how to make money. Trashy or not, getting those deals for you is all about business. It all lines his pockets. You're still just a whore, Kai, letting men use you for money. "Don't get it twisted," Spex said. He leaned in, throwing another smile devoid of warmth. "Here's what's gonna happen now. You will pay Dwight back the $200,000 you stole, every last cent."

Only $200,000, half of what I really took? I thought, laughing in my head. "I can get the money," I said, my voice crying in pleas. "I will pay him back. I always meant to anyway. I just needed time to get my life straight, my career on track."

Spex's smile widened, the way a hungry tiger would bare its teeth. "Good. You will open an account in Dwight's name—no tricks and no games. If you do that, maybe—just maybe—we'll let you walk out of here still breathing."

My heart pounded. "So, if I don't?"

Spex's expression hardened, his eyes turning to ice. "You don't wanna find out."

I nodded and swallowed the lump in my throat. "Okay. I'll do it."

Spex's eyes glinted with satisfaction. "We're still watching you, Kai. We have been, every step of the way. One wrong move, and it's over for you. Understand?"

"Yes," I whispered, feeling the weight of his words like a chain around my neck. The room seemed to close in on me, the walls pressing down as Spex signaled for his thug of a driver to come back in.

"Take her to the bank," Spex ordered as he threw a folder toward the man, full of Dwight's financials. He then turned back to me and added, his voice dripping with toxic venom, "Don't even think about telling anyone who I really am, how I'm connected. If you run, we *will* find you."

"Why do I need to set up a bank here in New York?" I asked nervously.

"That's on a need-to-know basis, and you don't," he spat. "When you get there, ask for Victor. He'll facilitate things, and he's expecting you."

After a nod from Spex, John grabbed my arm and led me out of the warehouse. His grip was firm, a silent reminder of the control they had over me. As he maneuvered the limousine to the bank, my mind churned with a mix of fear, anger, and desperation. *How did I let myself get into this situation? How could I have been so blind?*

At the bank, I moved through the motions in a daze. Victor was already prepared, so it all went easily. He didn't say much, and he seemed as nervous as I was, which only made me more anxious.

All the while, John watched me closely, his eyes never leaving me as I completed the wire transfer transaction. When it was done, he nodded at Victor, wearing a look of grim satisfaction. "We good?" he asked the banker.

"Yes. It went through," Victor assured him.

"Good. Let's go," he said before he grabbed my arm to lead me back to the car.

The ride back to the warehouse was silent, the weight of what I'd done hanging heavy in the air. When we arrived, Spex was waiting, his eyes gleaming with triumph.

"It's done," I said, my voice barely more than a whisper.

Spex looked at John, who nodded, then turned his attention back to me. "Good," he said, with smug satisfaction. "Now, get the fuck outta here. Your real driver is on his way. Also, Kai, if you see me DJing, I expect you to dance and wave like everything's normal. You're right. I did care for you, but my brother comes first. You've got a brother, right? You should understand that."

I blindly stumbled out of the warehouse, my heart pounding, and my mind reeling. The world outside seemed harsher and colder as I tried to process it all. I had been betrayed, used, and manipulated. Now, I was left to pick up the pieces of my shattered life.

When Tony, my real limo driver, pulled up, I hurried into the car. He sped back to the hotel, where I checked out of my room, then took me to the airport, where I caught the next redeye back to Los Angeles. I needed the comfort of home, even if nothing felt that comfortable anymore.

Chapter 29

JUNIPER

Losing the baby was devastating. Mama took Kaylee and Symone for a few days so I could get some much-needed rest. Lorenzo stayed with me, and his presence made things a little better. I was physically healed, but emotionally and mentally, it was rough. Kacia said she was okay, but I couldn't shake the guilt of my own stresses causing me to lose her baby. Tas was really the only one who knew about my temporary split with Lorenzo, and, if not for her, I wouldn't have even realized my fiancé had been set up.

Lorenzo walked into the room, holding a salad from McAllister and a small lemonade with fresh lemon slices floating in it. He always knew just what I liked and how to make me smile. I thanked him and set the box on my nightstand. We hadn't officially talked about our issues, but I was thankful he'd wandered back into my life to comfort me after the loss.

Love should not be this complicated, I thought, watching as he began to walk out of the room. "Ren…" I said, desperate to clear the air, so we could have the fresh start we both deserved.

"Yeah?" he replied, turning to face me.

"We need to talk."

He sat on the bed beside me, his face showing concern. He obviously also recognized that we had to address our problems if we were going to move forward with the marriage.

I grabbed my salad from the nightstand, added some honey mustard dressing, then shook the box to mix it all up.

Lorenzo stared expectantly at me, waiting for me to say something. Fortunately, he realized I was waiting for him to speak first, so he did. "June," he said, strong and confident, "I love you more than words can say. You take care of Symone like she's your own, and that means the world to me. Also, you're not just smart. You're brilliant. That heart of yours too! It's made of gold. You've been there for me through everything. I need you to know just how much that means to me, and I'll be damned if I'm going to lose this, lose us. You pour so much into everyone around you, into everything you do. I'm grateful every day to have you in my life, and I won't give up on that."

I listened to Lorenzo spill out his heart, and I felt a warm surge of happiness to know he really was part of my life again. It felt like a missing piece of my puzzle was put back in place, like a weight had been lifted. The miscarriage had left me feeling as if I had to drag myself through a fog of grief, but hearing how much he still loved me and knowing how much I meant to him was exactly what I needed to remind me that we could get through anything and everything together.

After we finished talking, Lorenzo looked at me with a serious expression. "Babe, I need you to talk to Kai Jae," he said.

I felt my blood pressure rising, and I snapped, "What!? No,

Lorenzo. I'm done with Kai Jae. I can't deal with any more of the drama."

Lorenzo took a deep breath. "Yeah, she said you saw her at the store and left real quick. Look, Juniper, you have to forgive her, just as we have needed to forgive each other. Holding on to that anger won't help. It'll only harm you in the long run, more than it has already. It's not worth it."

As I gawked at him in disbelief, the frustration continued to boil within me, but I also understood where my man was coming from. "You're right," I finally admitted. "I'll give Kai Jae a call. I need to work through it, no matter how hard it is. I have to let it go."

Lorenzo nodded, his eyes softening. "I know it's not easy, but we're in this together. We need to face everything head-on if we're gonna move forward."

I took a deep breath and sighed. "Plus, Kai's bringing in good money with my songs. Baby needs a brand-new Birkin," I teased, then laughed and gave Lorenzo a quick kiss. It felt good to find a bit of humor amidst the heaviness. "You know, we might as well make the best of it. We've got enough on our plates without holding on to all this other stuff."

Chapter 30

KAI JAE

Months later, onstage to receive my Grammy for Best Female Artist of the Year, I looked out at the audience. There, among so many talented individuals, I saw Erick, Lorenzo, Juniper, and Jamal, all smiling proudly. Jamal and I had grown relatively close since spending the day together—not in a sexual way but in a cool friendship kind of way. In that moment, I realized I had truly earned my place in the industry. The two people I had once deceived were the ones who always had my back. I was especially appreciative of Juniper, so grateful we had finally sat down and had an adult conversation.

A few weeks prior, she called and invited me to dinner. We decided on Crossroads Kitchen. The L.A. restaurant was sexy and inviting, with a modern but warm atmosphere. It was elegant, featuring rich wooden accents and plush seating that made us feel both sophisticated and comfortable.

Juniper was already there when I arrived, and she looked absolutely stunning. I wore a sleek, midnight blue dress with a subtle shimmer that caught the light beautifully. My jewelry was minimal but gorgeous, a pair of diamond stud earrings and a delicate bracelet. Juniper was equally chic in a flowing, emerald green dress that complemented her effortlessly. Her accessories were understated but refined, and her strappy heels matched her clutch.

We settled into our seats for an exquisite meal. We opted for the truffle risotto cakes as an appetizer, perfectly crispy on the outside and creamy on the inside. Our main course was a delectable assortment of plant-based dishes: grilled portabella mushrooms with a balsamic reduction, creamy cashew cheese ravioli, and a refreshing heirloom tomato salad. The flavors were exceptional, every bite a reminder of how much thought and care went into the preparation. To accompany our meal, we enjoyed a bottle of a rich, full-bodied Cabernet Sauvignon, at the suggestion of the sommelier. The wine offered deep notes of dark berries and a hint of oak, the perfect accompaniment for the dishes we selected.

"You chose a beautiful place," Juniper said, looking around. "How did you find it?"

"Kelly, one of my stylists, told me about it. She's got great taste."

Juniper took a deep breath, ready to let it all out. "I need to be honest with you," she said, getting right down to business. "I didn't appreciate those pictures. It really hurt me. My sister was ready to beat your ass."

"I'm really sorry, Juniper. It wasn't…intentional. I was just a fool, too paranoid about my career. I learned my lesson the hard way, and I promise it won't happen again," I said, trying to convey how genuinely sorry I was. I was a bit uneasy about the thought of her sister attacking me, but I tried to ignore the threat. I hesitated for a moment, then decided it was time to be more honest. "My ex used to…" Then, I quickly reconsidered sharing too many personal details. "Someone used to make me do things I never wanted to do," I said. "Maybe that's why I always relentlessly go after what *I* want, without letting anything or anyone stand in my way."

Juniper listened intently, saying nothing but just nodding as she took occasional sips of wine.

"For a long time, all I knew was survival mode," I added. "I had to cut and run from my past life, and I had to keep pushing, keep fighting just to get through each day."

The silence that followed was heavy, but I saw a flicker of understanding in Juniper's eyes. It was not easy, but acknowledging our personal struggles with one another was a long-needed release.

"I'm sorry for the way things went down," I said, regretful but relieved. "I'm working on being better, and I hope we can move past it."

Juniper nodded again, her expression softening. "I appreciate you saying that. We all have our battles, and it's good to know we can talk about them."

The evening continued with a renewed sense of connection, and despite the challenges, it felt good to make some progress at repairing the bridges I'd burned.

Now, as I walked off the stage with my Grammy in hand, a typhoon of emotions overtook me. I made my way to Juniper and pulled her into a tight hug. "Thank you," I whispered, tears brimming in my eyes. "Thank you for everything."

Juniper pulled back slightly, her eyes shining with pride. "You did it, Kai. You really did it!"

I smiled through my tears. "I couldn't have done it without you and Lorenzo," I said gratefully, smiling.

Juniper shook her head gently. "Don't ever sell yourself short, Kai.

You've always had the talent, the drive. You just needed to believe in yourself."

Erick's eyes welled with tears of admiration as well. "She's right, sis," he said, "and I'm so proud of you!" His voice was choked with emotion.

Jamal also pulled me into a brotherly embrace, making the extra love feel even more appreciative.

Having my brother with me was a huge relief all its own. For one thing, I could keep an eye on him and make sure he was safe. For another, he had always been more than just a big brother to me. He was my rock, my confidant. After what happened to me in New York, I needed him by my side more than ever. We worked out a deal for him to work as my personal assistant, but he was more than that. He was my support system, and he ensured that I remained grounded in the whirlwind of craziness that was the music industry.

We'd been through so much together, from our tough childhood in foster care to navigating our respective paths as adults. Now, as we both pursued our dreams in the City of Angels, I felt blessed to have him with me every step of the way. Our bond was unbreakable, and with Erick here with me, I knew we could conquer whatever challenges came our way and put our tumultuous past behind us.

As Erick walked away to talk to other artists, I took another deep, cleansing breath and looked at Juniper. "I've got something I have to say," I began, my voice wavering.

"What is it?" she asked, placing a hand gently on my shoulder in concern.

"I'm sorry, Juniper. I'm really, really sorry for sending those pictures."

Juniper's expression softened, and she gave my hand a reassuring squeeze. "Kai, I know. We've already talked about this, and I've forgiven you. Let it go, girl! Just enjoy that Grammy!"

I felt a weight lift off my shoulders. "Thank you, Juniper. That means more to me than you'll ever know."

Juniper smiled warmly. "We're family, Kai. Family forgives and stands by each other. Now, let's go celebrate your amazing achievement."

As we made our way to the after-party, Lorenzo joined us and wrapped an arm around each of our shoulders. "I knew you could do it, Kai," he said, grinning. "This is just the beginning."

I laughed, feeling lighter than I had in a long time. "You're right. It can only go up from here!"

"Man, check Erick out. Your brother is having the time of his life," Juniper said, pointing to where he was talking and laughing with Zara Bloom. I was surprised that seeing him with her didn't bother me one bit.

The room was a glittering display of wealth and success, filled with industry elites dressed to the nines. Crystal chandeliers cast a warm glow over the opulent ballroom, their light reflecting off the sequined gowns and polished shoes. Soft music played in the background, setting a sophisticated tone for the evening. Waiters glided gracefully through the crowd, balancing trays of champagne flutes and delicate hors d'oeuvres.

Lorenzo and Juniper wanted to mingle with other guests, so I stood by a grand marble pillar, feeling a bit lost amidst the sea of faces. Erick was gone by then, having taken an Uber back to the apartment because he was tired.

Suddenly, Spex walked in and cut through the crowd like a shark through water. His suit, perfectly tailored, highlighted his broad shoulders and slim waist, the dark fabric complemented by a black satin bowtie. The silver cufflinks on his sleeves caught the light, glinting as he raised his glass to me.

My heart skipped a beat when I saw him, and fear gripped me. We hadn't spoken since I discovered he was Dwight's half-brother, and he forced me to open that bank account. At his request, I had kept my distance, but the wounds were still fresh. Seeing him there, looking every bit the sophisticated gentleman, stirred a confusing mix of emotions within me. I started to walk away, hoping to avoid a confrontation, but his voice stopped me in my tracks.

"Kai!" he called out, strong and clear over the murmur of the crowd.

I turned to face him, my pulse quickening. "Spex," I acknowledged, my tone guarded.

"You look stunning, as always," he said, with a hint of a grin on his face. "Congratulations on the Grammy. 'Bout time they realized you deserve it."

I stared at him, trying to gauge his sincerity. *Is this another setup? Is he just trying to get in my pants again? Did Dwight send him with more demands?* Still, even as uncertainty and humility swirled within me, I managed a calm, "Appreciate it. It's been a wild ride, but moments like these make it all worth it."

Spex nodded and lost his half-smile, and his expression turned thoughtful. "I remember when you were just starting out, hustling to get your music heard. Look at you now."

I chuckled as memories of those early days flooded back. "Yeah, those were the days, but I wouldn't trade this for anything."

"Neither would I," he said, again raising his glass.

We clinked, and the sound was crisp and clear amid the background chatter.

"So, what's next for you?" he asked.

"Oh, I've got a few projects lined up," I said. I nonchalantly glanced at Zara Bloom. "We'll be working on a collaboration this fall. It's gonna be epic."

Spex raised an eyebrow, clearly impressed. "With Zara Bloom? That's more than epic. That's...major. You two are gonna kill it."

"Thanks, Spex," I replied with a grin. "I'm really excited about it. Honestly, it was my brother who made it happen. What about you though? What's on the horizon for the famous DJ?"

Spex took a deep breath and met my gaze with his. "Your brother? I thought that guy was your date. That's why I waited to come over till he left," he said, smiling mischievously.

I chuckled and shook my head. "No, but Erick is my right-hand man, always looking out for me."

"Actually, Kai, I need to talk to you about something else, something I should have told you a long time ago." He looked down at his glass and swirled the liquid around. "I need to apologize to you."

"For what?" I asked, wondering which hurt he was going to be sorry for, since there were so many to choose from.

"For forcing you to find out the way you did about Dwight being my half-brother," he admitted, his voice tinged with regret. "I was afraid for you. When my brother first asked me to run that game on you, I was all in, but once I got to know you, once we got close, I started to catch feelings for you. I convinced him to let you off with just paying him back, to call off the dogs. When you complied and opened that bank account, he promised he was done with you. I don't mean to shatter your night or ruin this great moment, but I think you should know."

"Know what?" I asked, intrigued but uncertain.

"Dwight won't ever bother you again, Kai."

"So, he's keeping his promise? Good."

"No, it's not that. He's…. gone. My brother was killed in a prison raid," Spex said, hanging his head. "Even high-security penitentiaries are vulnerable to riots. A group of inmates, somehow armed and seriously desperate, erupted the place into chaos. Dwight was caught in the middle of it all. He recently joined a gang inside for protection, but he's never been good at choosing friends. During the raid, rival gang members targeted him. In the confusion and darkness, without the protection of the guards or the people who had promised to look out for him, he was cornered and stabbed multiple times. His life ended in a brutal, senseless act of violence," Spex said, clearly holding back his tears. "He was cremated, and Dad and I each took some of his ashes. Dwight wasn't the best brother, and I know he was awful to you, but I loved him."

I took a deep breath and wasn't sure how to feel. Tears came from the tragedy of it all, and they began to roll down my cheeks. Since we were divorced, the prison was no longer at liberty to communicate with me, so I had no idea. Although the news saddened me, I also I felt an unexpected sense of peace.

"I'm sorry for any pain he caused you, Kai," Spex sincerely said. "I wasn't aware of how terrible Dwight was to you during your marriage. Ken, one of his associates, told me about the real reason you left him. My brother lied to me for many years. As for that money, you'll get it back. The account you opened in New York will be closed, and every dime will be wired back to you. Victor is already on it."

The room seemed to fall away as I processed his words. The sounds of the party faded into the background, leaving just the two of us standing there. I looked at Spex and took in his somber expression, and I felt instantly lighter. "Thank you, Spex," I said, my voice trembling. "Thank you for everything."

He reached out and gently wiped a tear from my cheek, his touch warm and comforting. "You deserve to be happy, Kai, more than anyone I know."

I nodded and enjoyed a newfound sense of closure and possibility. "I think I'm finally starting to believe that."

As we stood there, with the noise and glamor of the party returning around us, I realized that it really was a new beginning, just as Lorenzo had said. My atrocious and painful past was behind me, and the future was filled with promise and potential. For the first time in a long while, I was ready to embrace it.

"Kai," Spex said softly, his hand still resting gently on my cheek, "would you like to get outta here? Maybe we can find a quiet place to talk some more."

I nodded, feeling a mixture of relief and anticipation. "Yeah, I'd like that."

We made our way through the crowd, exchanging polite smiles and nods with acquaintances, but my mind was focused on Spex and the conversation we were about to have. The grand ballroom gave way to quieter corridors, the opulence of the party fading into the background as we reached the elevators. We rode up in silence, the tension between us palpable yet strangely comforting.

When we arrived at Spex's room, he opened the door and gestured for me to enter first. The suite was elegantly furnished, and a large bed dominated the center, flanked by modern lamps and a small, dark wood desk. The balcony overlooked the city, and the lights from all the buildings twinkled like a quilt of stars against the night sky.

"Make yourself comfortable," Spex encouraged as he closed the door behind us.

"Odd, my room looks nothing like this one," I said with a grin.

He walked over to the mini-bar and poured a drink for each of us, then handed a glass to me before taking a seat on the edge of the bed.

I took a sip and let the smooth liquid warm me and calm my nerves. "It's strange," I began, "being here with you after everything that's happened. I wasn't sure we'd ever get to this point."

Spex nodded, his gaze intense yet tender. "I know. I've made many mistakes, Kai, but I never stopped caring about you. I hate how I treated you in New York, all those nasty things I said to you. I want to make things right, if you'll let me."

I looked down at my glass and let his words sink in. "It's not going to be easy," I admitted. "We've got a lot of history between us, and not all of it is good."

"I understand," Spex said quietly. "I don't expect forgiveness right away. I'm not even asking yet. I just want a chance to prove that I know I was wrong. Still, even in the midst of all that, I tried to look out for you. I know it doesn't seem like it, but I did," he said, sitting close to me.

I took a deep breath and met his eyes with mine. "I think I'm willing to give that a chance," I said softly, "but it has to be on my terms. No more secrets, no more lies."

"Agreed," he replied, his voice steady and sincere. "No more secrets, no more lies."

We sat in silence for a moment, the seriousness of our conversation hanging in the air. Then, slowly, I moved closer to him on the bed.

He turned to face me and reached his hand out to gently grasp mine. "I missed you, Kai," he whispered, his voice breaking slightly. "I missed you every day we were apart."

I squeezed his hand and enjoyed the warmth of his skin against mine. "I missed you, too, Spex, even more than I realized."

He leaned in and brushed his lips against mine in a passionate kiss. It was soft and tender, filled with all the unspoken emotions we'd both been carrying around for far too long. "May I?" he asked before his hands gently caressed the fabric of my dress, the stunning Grammy creation by Kevan Hall, designed specifically for me.

The dress was a masterpiece, a floor-length gown of deep emerald silk that shimmered with every movement. It had a plunging neckline and delicate, hand-embroidered floral details that cascaded down to the hem. The back was low, revealing just enough to be tantalizing but still elegant. My shoes were silver stilettos, with delicate straps that wrapped around my ankles, sparkling under the lights.

My hair was styled in soft, loose waves that framed my face and cascaded down my back, each strand carefully set to give a natural yet glamorous look. My makeup was flawless: smoky eyes that highlighted the intensity of my gaze, a hint of blush to accentuate my cheekbones, and a bold, red lipstick that matched the confidence I felt that night.

The look in my eyes told him I wanted that moment, that togetherness, as badly as he did. Spex carefully separated me from my designer outfit, his fingers reverently unzipping the gown and letting it slide off my shoulders to fall in an emerald puddle of silk around my stiletto-clad feet. He removed everything, leaving me completely naked and exposed in front of him. I'd endured a full body wax the day before, and my skin was still glowing from my Natural Body & Hair Butter CoCo Mango from Shae Butter Like Whoe, a Black-owned company out of Fort Washington, Maryland.

"You're so beautiful," he said as he coaxed me to lie down on the California king. His voice seemed filled with awe as he took in the sight of me, as if he'd never seen me naked before.

"Thank you," I replied, smiling softly.

My heart raced as Spex locked his eyes on mine. He gently lifted my feet, pedicured, and painted with white polish, and sweetly licked each toe, his tongue sending shivers of pleasure through my body. His touch was tender but electrifying as he caressed my legs and thighs, every movement heightening my anticipation. I yearned for him, and my body trembled with excitement as I eagerly awaited the orgasm I so desperately needed.

His hands slid up to my inner thighs, and he gently parted my legs. I moaned softly as he moved closer to my vajayjay. When his lips finally met my sweetness, I arched my back and moaned more loudly, surrendering to his pleasures. The way he swirled his tongue around my clitoris was pure magic, each flick sending shocks of ecstasy through me.

Spex's kisses trailed up my stomach, his lips leaving a burning path of desire. He moved to my neck and nipped gently at my skin, then returned his mouth to mine again. His kisses were hungry and deep, filled with passion, exploring me. Despite him being fully clothed, I could feel his erection pressing against my leg, hard and insistent, demanding release from its fabric prison.

After emitting a deep, guttural moan of his own, he finally stood and began undressing. He removed the cufflinks from his designer shirt and placed them carefully on the nightstand beside the clock, which now showed midnight. I watched, captivated, as he slowly unbuttoned his shirt and revealed his toned chest and muscular arms. His pants and boxers followed, until he stood before me in all his natural manliness, completely exposed.

Unable to resist, I reached out and traced the contours of his body, basking in the heat of his skin. He leaned in again and captured my lips in a fervent kiss while his hands explored my curves. The intensity of his touch made my skin tingle, every nerve ending alive with desire.

Spex gently laid me back on the bed, and his body hovered over mine. The anticipation was almost unbearable as he positioned himself between my legs, his eyes never leaving mine. I could see the love and lust swirling in his gaze, mirroring my own emotions.

He entered me slowly and filled me completely, and I gasped at the sensation. We moved together in perfect harmony, our bodies entwined, lost in the rhythm of our passion. Each thrust urged us closer to the edge, the world around us fading away as we focused solely on each other.

My moans grew louder, mingling with his groans of pleasure. The intensity becoming stronger and stronger.

"Let's cum together," Spex said, moving in perfect unison with me and letting out moans that mimicked my own.

"Let me know when you're ready," I said.

Spex remained silent for a moment, concentrating as his body continued to enthrall mine. Then, finally, he grunted and said, "I'm about to cum, Kai."

With a final, powerful thrust, we climaxed together, our bodies trembling in unison. The release was overwhelming, waves of pleasure crashing over us, leaving us breathless and weak.

Spex collapsed beside me and pulled me into his arms. Wrapped in each other, we lay there, reveling in the afterglow of our unexpected lovemaking. As I rested my head on his chest, listening to the steady beat of his heart, I knew that moment would be etched in my happy memories forever.

The next morning, sunlight filtered through the curtains, gently waking us from our rest. I stretched and felt a delicious soreness in my muscles, a reminder of our passionate night.

Spex smiled at me, his eyes still heavy with sleep but filled with warmth. "Good morning," he whispered, brushing a strand of hair from my face.

"Morning," I replied, then leaned in for a soft kiss. "Shall we go grab some breakfast?"

He nodded.

I slipped out of bed and gathered my clothes that were scattered across the floor. "I'll get ready in my own room," I said. "Can you meet me in the lobby in an hour?"

"Sounds perfect," he replied, and he gave me a lingering kiss before I left.

As I made my way to my room, I texted Erick to tell him I would be home soon. The events of the night replayed in my mind, leaving me with a sense of disbelief and joy. After a quick shower, I chose a simple but elegant sundress and pulled my hair into a loose ponytail. I only applied a touch of makeup, and I was quickly ready to face the day.

When I met Spex in the lobby, he looked effortlessly handsome in a casual button-down and jeans. He smiled warmly when he saw me, and he held my hand as we walked to a nearby café. The quaint, little place boasted outdoor seating and a charming atmosphere, perfect for a quiet breakfast.

We found a cozy table in the corner and chatted about everything and nothing, just enjoying each other's company as we awaited our food. The connection we had reignited the night before seemed even stronger in the daylight.

When my pancakes and Spex's omelet arrived, I felt a presence nearby. Looking up, I saw Lorenzo standing at the entrance of the café. His eyes widened in surprise when he spotted us, and he was clearly taken aback by our unexpected pairing.

"Kai, Spex," Lorenzo greeted after he made his way to our table, his voice tinged with curiosity. "I didn't expect to see you two together this morning."

Spex and I exchanged a quick glance before smiling at Lorenzo.

"Good morning, Lorenzo," I said, trying to sound casual. "We just decided to grab some breakfast together."

Lorenzo looked from me to Spex, and a knowing smile slowly spread across his face. "Well, it's nice to see you both. I guess last night was…eventful, huh?"

I felt a blush creep up my cheeks, but Spex just chuckled. "You could say that," he replied, giving my hand a reassuring squeeze under the table.

Lorenzo laughed and shook his head. "Well, enjoy your breakfast," he said before he walked away.

Spex looked at me, his eyes filled with affection. "I guess the cat's out of the bag now," he said with a grin.

I laughed, feeling lighter than I had in a long time. "I guess so, but I don't mind. For the first time in a long time, I'm happy, Spex. I'm really, really happy."

He leaned in and kissed me, his lips soft and warm against mine. "Me, too, Kai. Me too."

We ate our breakfast, savoring the food and the company. While I munched on pancakes, I pulled out my phone and logged into Instagram. Notifications flooded my screen, and I scrolled through the many pictures and articles about my Grammy win. My heart swelled with pride and gratitude when I saw the overwhelming support from fans and friends. I was even more surprised when I saw that The Shade Room had posted about me, highlighting my achievement and the stunning Kevan Hall dress I wore.

"Look at this, Spex," I said, showing him my phone. "Even TMZ posted about my win."

"That's amazing, Kai," he said, his eyes shining with pride. "You deserve all the recognition and then some."

I hesitated for a moment, then looked up at him, with a question in my eyes. "Is it okay if I post a picture of us together? I wanna share this moment with everyone."

Spex smiled, nodding without hesitation. "Of course! I'd love that."

I scrolled through the photos we had taken that morning and finally settled on one of me planting a kiss on his cheek. In the photo, we both looked so happy and content, a perfect representation of how I felt.

I typed out a caption: "To the future...♥," excited and nervous to share our happiness with the world. Within minutes, the post garnered countless likes and comments, and I felt a rush of joy.

Spex reached across the table and took my hand again. "Here's to the future," he said softly, echoing my words.

I looked into his eyes and felt an overwhelming sense of love and hope. "To the future," I chorused, squeezing his hand.

Chapter 31

JUNIPER

Finally, the big day had arrived, and I was more than ready to walk down the aisle to marry the man I truly loved. We had planned a small, intimate ceremony and invited only family and a few close friends.

"You good, lil sis?" Dalvin asked with a proud smile, adjusting his tie as he prepared to escort me.

I nodded, feeling the weight of the moment and the love that surrounded me.

Kacia, Tas, and Nikki stood by my side, each in stunning dresses that complemented the soft palette of the ceremony: Kacia in lavender, Tas in delicate sage Green, and Nikki in lovely blush pink that matched the roses that adorned the church.

On the groom's side, T-Roc, and Lorenzo's cousin Lamar, who had flown up from Miami, stood proudly alongside him. T-Roc, known for his impeccable style, was dressed in a classic black tuxedo, tailored to perfection. His crisp, white shirt and black bowtie added a touch of elegance, perfectly complementing the solemnity and joy of the occasion. His confident demeanor and warm smile reflected his genuine happiness for us.

The church, decorated in hues of ivory and soft pastels, resembled a scene from a storybook. Delicate drapes cascaded down the aisles, intertwining with twinkling fairy lights that cast a warm, ethereal glow over the sanctuary. Floral arrangements prettied up every pew, exuding a fragrance that mingled with the sweet notes of anticipation.

Among the guests were Mr. and Mrs. Cravins, who I'd grown to love and respect. Their smiles were luminous beacons of encouragement from the front row. Symone and Kaylee, our adorable flower girls, added a touch of innocence and playfulness as they skipped down the aisle, scattering petals with infectious delight and sweet giggles.

Mr. Ray and his beautiful wife smiled effortlessly. Dr. and Mrs. Blair had flown in from Florida, and they radiated warmth and affection from their seats, their presence a testament to the bonds of friendship that spanned distances. Spex, Kai Jae, Mr. Mac, Steven, two beautiful females who accompanied Lamar, Brian Matthew, and the office crew were all there to celebrate the occasion.

My mother sat in the front of the church with the twins, a picture of love and support, her eyes glistening with tears of joy and pride. Her smile, bright and solid, mirrored the emotions that welled within her as she watched me prepare to embark on the journey of marriage. She clutched a delicate handkerchief, embroidered with my initials, a keepsake from her own wedding day that now bore witness to this momentous occasion.

My wedding dress was a masterpiece of lace and satin, adorned with intricate floral patterns that cascaded down the bodice and onto the flowing train. Each stitch spoke of love and dedication, a reflection of the journey that had led me to this sacred moment. My hair, in a stylish twist, donned a pearl-studded comb that caught the light and shimmered like stardust in the gentle glow of the church chandeliers and candles.

Pearl earrings, a gift from my mother, dangled delicately from my ears, their luster echoing the love and tradition that had been passed down through generations. A matching necklace rested against my throat, a symbol of continuity and the enduring bond of family.

As I walked down the aisle, accompanied by the soft strains of a cello and piano playing Pachelbel's "Canon in D Major," I felt the collective heartbeat of those who had shaped my life. The aisle seemed to stretch into eternity, each step carrying me closer to the man who stood at the altar, his eyes filled with love and anticipation. The air was charged with emotion, and union of joy, hope, and the promise of a future woven together.

In that sacred space, surrounded by loved ones and bathed in the gentle glow of emotional love and physical light, I felt a profound sense of gratitude and serenity. The tears that flowed down my mother's cheeks mirrored the emotions that coursed through my own heart, a mixture of sadness at leaving one chapter behind and overwhelming joy at embracing the next.

As I reached the end of the aisle, Dalvin gave a gentle kiss on my cheek before placing my hand in the waiting embrace of Lorenzo. Together, we turned to face our loved ones, the echoes of vows spoken and promises made resonating in the hallowed space.

In that moment, amidst the fragrance of flowers and the soft hum of whispered blessings, I knew that day would forever be the happiest day of my life. I wished Daddy was there to witness it, but even his absence could not sadden me on such a happy occasion. It was a day of beginnings, of endings, and of the enduring love that would guide us through the chapters yet to unfold.

As the pastor announced, "Ladies and Gentlemen, I now pronounce to you, Lorenzo and Juniper Ryan," everyone in the church clapped and cheered, and we kissed for the first time as husband and wife.

LOVE, LIES 𝄞 MUSIC 3:

The Bridge!

COMING FALL 2025

Chapter 1

LACI

So much had happened in the last five years of my life. Bilal, aka Dr. Jacobs, and I had produced a son, Bilal Jacobs Jr., or BJ for short. When I was released from prison, he took me to the courthouse and immediately married me. I refused to let him go again, and I definitely would not run back into the arms of DaMarco, the man who did nothing but lie to me while we were together. He ended up living with another woman, the one who pushed out his baby girl.

Even though I had more skeletons than a graveyard, I still didn't appreciate the way things ended. DaMarco was the man Bilal drank Hennessey with, the one he played bones with. He was also the brother of his best friend, Javier, who had moved back to Los Angeles from Atlanta and was now working at Harrison, Matthews, Ryan, and Associates. That was the very same law firm where Juniper, DaMarco's baby-mother, worked. She managed to score Javier an interview, and he accepted an offer he could not refuse.

Bilal and I often talked about how he needed to give him all the info on me, but he was not looking forward to that. He had no idea he had married his brother's ex, a woman he knew long before meeting DaMarco. I was the person he fell in love with back when I was one of his graduate biology students at Fresno State. The only info he had shared with Javier was that his soulmate had returned. Tracy, an employee I had fired, was the person I had to lean on to administer my daily medication while I was locked up, and dealing with her was definitely a slap in my face.

I maintained an extremely low profile on social media for that reason alone, and Bilal refused to even go online unless it was for school. I was on my second pregnancy, six months along, expecting a girl this time. We planned to name her Zoey Marie Jacobs. I was much happier than before, and I was doing everything possible to prevent myself from returning to my devious ways.

I had yet to tell him that Shamar, my ex-fiancé, had discovered my profile on LinkedIn. He had moved to Sacramento a year prior, thanks to a job transfer, and he had been messaging me, asking me to meet him for coffee. I didn't respond and just ignored him, hoping he'd eventually get the message. I ended our engagement when I found him in bed with Erin, the woman I stabbed during a tussle. She later died in a car accident. Still, part of me wanted to hear what he had to say. I was curious about what he'd been up to over the years. I wondered if he ever married or had kids.

As I settled into my role at the University of Northern Californía, teaching biology to eager students, I found a sense of fulfillment I hadn't known before. Bilal's support opened doors for me, and I embraced the opportunity to be effective in the lives of young minds. Teaching became my passion, a way to channel my experiences and knowledge into something positive. The classroom became my sanctuary, a place where I could inspire and empower students to pursue their dreams, just as I had when I was younger, but I did not want to see any of them drive down the bumpy road I had.

Nevertheless, even amidst the joy of my professional accomplishments, the specter of Shamar's messages continued to haunt me. Despite my best efforts to ignore him, his persistent attempts to reconnect stirred up old wounds and doubts. Dr. Mable, the trusted therapist I had Teams visits with twice a month, provided a safe space for me to explore those conflicting emotions. Her guidance was invaluable as I grappled with the past and sought to forge a brighter future for myself and my family. She constantly reminded me of all I had gone through, especially with Shamar and DaMarco, so I wouldn't put myself through that kind of trauma ever again.

Meanwhile, preparations for Zoey's arrival filled our home with excitement and anticipation. Bilal and I eagerly awaited the arrival of our daughter, her impending birth a symbol of hope and renewal. Even with that joyous anticipation, though, a sense of unease lingered. Shamar's messages cast a shadow over our happiness, always reminders of the tangled web of relationships and betrayals that had shaped my past.

As I navigated the complexities of my personal and professional life, I leaned on Bilal for strength and support. His unwavering love and devotion remained an anchor in my many storms, guiding me through the darkest moments with grace and compassion. Together, we faced the challenges of the present and the uncertainties of the future, united in our determination to build a life filled with love, forgiveness, and hope. As we waited for little Zoey to come into our lives, I knew we could face all trials together, hand in hand, no matter what they were. I was ready to embrace whatever the future held, and I hoped it would be a good future.

"Hey, babe, why are you staring at me again? This is spooky," I asked, laughing.

"No reason. I just love looking at you," Bilal said, adjusting the pillow under his head.

"You do, huh?" I said before I attempted to get up to make breakfast.

He pulled me back down and started killing me softly with kisses. He knew the spots that instantly turned me on. He had always had that effect on me, ever since that day we had sex in his home on his reclining chair when I was his student. I really loved the man. Even when I was with other people, I thought of Bilal as the one who had stolen my heart, and he was always there for me, always by my side.

He kissed my round belly and opened my legs. The wetness of his tongue had my clitoris hard and, as always, within two minutes, he had me breathing hard and squirting on his face.

"Okay, you can now resume your morning," he finally said, with a naughty chuckle.

I got up to go take a shower but grabbed my phone. I needed to email my students the Zoom link for the class that would start in two hours.

I didn't unfriend Sean on Facebook, but we hadn't really communicated since that awful day, even after his horrible confession. I was sad to read about him passing away from COVID. That news hit me hard. Seeing all the RIP posts on his page really messed me up. As I looked at his profile, I was tangled up in a knot of anger, sadness, and regret. He had screwed up with me, big time, but part of me had always hoped we could sort things out. Once COVID took him, that chance was gone forever.

Tears found their way to my eyes as I remembered the good times we had, before everything went to hell. Despite the mess, there were moments I treasured, moments that made me wish things could've been different. As I reflected on Sean's life, I made a silent promise to myself to live each day with purpose and gratitude. His passing was a harsh reminder of how fragile life could be, of how important it was to make the most of every moment. So, despite the hurt and the loss, I vowed to keep moving forward, to cherish the people I still had in my life, and to never take anything for granted.

After my shower, in the misty bathroom, I tied my hair up into a high ponytail. Shane had convinced me to do the big chop right before everything shut down, and now I was grappling with the challenge of maintaining it as the salons remained closed or seldom open.

As I headed into the kitchen, I was accompanied by the cheerful sounds of BJ playing with his firetruck. He was growing up so fast, already 3 years old and brimming with personality. Bilal and I often debated about his hair, a blend of my complexion and his father's Asian features, and it had already grown past his shoulders.

I began to cook, and my thoughts drifted to my mom. I never would have thought she would be such an amazing grandmother, especially after everything she'd been through. Her time in jail had changed her for the better, and now she was busy planning Zoey's baby shower. It touched my heart that she chose to honor my late grandmother by suggesting Marie to be our baby's middle name. Despite the challenges we faced, moments like that reminded me of the beauty and joy that filled our lives. With BJ's laughter echoing through the house and the anticipation of Zoey's arrival, I couldn't help but feel grateful for the love and support of my family.

Chapter 2

SPEX

I stared at the red, lacy set on display in the store window. *Damn, that would look so good on Kai Jae,* I thought. She looked delicious in red, and I would have a lot of fun peeling it off of her. I felt the corner of my lips curving into a smile as I fantasized about it.

Just as I was about to get out of the car to go in and buy it for my lady, my phone rang. "Who is it now?" I mumbled.

"Hey, baby," answered a voice I thought I'd put behind me.

"Summer?" I said, in such a shocked tone that I didn't even recognize my own voice. A lot of people claimed their ex was crazy, but in her case, it was beyond true. Summer was next-level nuts.

"Yes, Spex. So, you're some kind of hotshot now, huh?"

"What do you want?" I asked, shaking my head. She was always trying to cause trouble, but I refused to even entertain any of her lunatic antics again. Before she could even answer my question, I ended the call.

I met Summer before I even became a celebrity DJ. She always had a smile on her face, and she seemed harmless. In time, I came to learn that it was just a deceiving mask she wore.

In her own way, and not necessarily in a good one, she was unforgettable. I remembered her all too well. Her hair always dyed in the most startling shade of red, usually styled in long cornrows or Senegalese twist, even as she complained that weaves hurt and made her uncomfortable. She always wore red lipstick, which was why I nicknamed her Red while we were dating, cliché as that was.

Needing to get Summer out of my head, I eagerly picked up my phone when Kai Jae called. "Hey, baby," I said, breaking into an immediate smile.

Her voice was a bit raspy, as if she'd just woken up from a deep sleep.

"You okay? Napping?" I asked.

"Yes. I just wanted to hear your voice, and I wanna see you. Erick went to Detroit for the weekend. I'm all alone," she said, in a pouty way that made me want her even more.

"Tonight, sweetness. I promise."

"You better keep your promise," she said.

"Count on it."

I threw my car in drive and headed to the lounge where I was supposed to meet Jahi, a guy who kept hitting me up on Instagram. He claimed he needed to talk to me about something important, but I was sure he just wanted me to sample his music, like all the other cats out there hoping for a foot in the door.

I reached the lounge within thirty minutes and found him already waiting. I could tell it was him by the hawk tattoo on his arm, the same one I'd seen on his page. "What's up, brother?" I asked. I had adjusted my Snap Back to keep people from recognizing me. Since my girl's post, the ladies had been throwing pussy at me left and right.

"Hello. Would you like anything?" he asked, polite and gentle.

I declined, then said, "What about you, Jahi? What can I do for you?"

He smiled and held up a USB drive, his hand trembling ever so slightly. "Oh, it *is* you!" he said, squinting at me. "I've got a track I've been working on for months. I think it could be something special. I'm hoping you'll give it a listen. If you like it, maybe you can play it in one of your sets. Maybe you can even let Kai Jae hear it."

I leaned back and studied him for a moment. It wasn't the first time someone had approached me about beats for Kai. The music industry was tough, and everyone was looking for a big break. "All right, Jahi. Tell me about the track. For starters, what's it called?"

"'Eternal Echoes,'" he said, with a hint of pride in his voice. "It's a mix of electronic and ambient sounds, something unique. I think it'll really resonate with Kai's voice."

I nodded slowly. "Sounds interesting."

Jahi plugged the USB drive into his laptop and pulled up the track.

"So, 'Eternal Echoes,'" I said, leaning forward. "What inspired you to create this piece?"

Jahi's eyes sparkled as he explained, "It started as a way to process some things I was going through, you know, just life difficulties. Music has always been my escape, my way of making sense of the world. I wanted to create something to capture that feeling, that sense of searching for meaning and finding beauty in the chaos."

At least he's passionate, I thought. I listened intently, then said, "I can relate to that. Music has a way of speaking to the soul, doesn't it?"

He smiled, a bit more relaxed. "Exactly. I've been experimenting with different sounds, trying to find the right blend. 'Eternal Echoes' will take Kai Jae's sound to a new level. I mean, if she's willing to give it a chance."

I leaned back for a moment and considered his words. "All right, Jahi. Let's hear it."

When he played the track, I could not believe my ears. It began with a haunting melody, a mix of electronic beats that slowly built into a powerful, emotional crescendo. As the music played, I closed my eyes and let the sound wash over me.

When the track ended, I opened my eyes to find its creator watching me anxiously, awaiting my reaction. I took a moment to gather my thoughts before announcing, "You've got something here, Jahi. The track is well produced, and I feel the emotion behind it. It's definitely a banger."

The young man's face lit up with a mix of relief and excitement. "Really? You think it has potential?"

"I do," I said, nodding. "but you have to understand that getting a track to Kai Jae isn't easy. Yes, she's my girl, but she has to feel it herself, and it still has to be approved by her management company."

"I get that," Jahi said quickly. "I don't expect any guarantees. I just wanted you to listen, to see if you think it's worth a shot."

I appreciated his honesty. "Tell ya what, kid. I'll take the USB and give it a few more listens. If I'm sure it's a good fit, I'll have Kai listen to it. Ultimately, it will be up to her and her team."

Jahi nodded, and a wide grin spread across his face. "That's more than I could even ask! Thank you, Spex. Really, it means a lot. I'm flattered."

I tucked the USB in my jacket pocket and extended my hand. "Keep pushing, Jahi. If you want something in life, you've gotta get out there and take it."

"I will, sir!"

As I stood to leave, my phone lit up with a text from Kai Jae.

"I need to get back," I told Jahi, but I quickly added, "We'll talk again soon."

He waved goodbye as I ignored another call from Summer. Before I even reached my car, I blocked her number and all her social media accounts. I contemplated stopping at the store I'd visited earlier to buy that sexy negligee for Kai, but the constant calls from Summer—from Red, as I knew her—had soured me on the idea and made me change my mind.

As I drove, memories of Summer crept, uninvited, into my mind. Summer was a walking nightmare, a force of nature that swept me off my feet and left chaos in her wake. I remembered our intense arguments, the jealousy, and the constant drama that seemed to follow her everywhere. There were moments of passion, of course, but they were often overshadowed by her volatile temper and unpredictable behavior.

One night stood out in particular. At a party, Summer had too much to drink. She accused me of flirting with another woman, even though I'd spoken to no one else all evening. The argument escalated quickly, and she ended up throwing a drink in my face in front of everyone. It was embarrassing, and it took everything in me to remain calm while she fell on the floor and cried.

Another time, she went through my phone while I was asleep, convinced I was hiding something from her. She found a message from a female colleague about a project we were working on and blew it completely out of proportion. The shouting match that followed was one of the worst we'd ever had.

Then, there was an incident involving my car, which she borrowed one afternoon without asking. When she returned, there was a huge dent in the side. She insisted it wasn't her fault and claimed someone must have hit it while it was parked, but her story didn't add up. I couldn't shake the feeling that she wasn't being entirely honest. The repair costs were steep, and I wasn't DJ Spex at the time, so I didn't have money to throw at unexpected problems like that. She also constantly threatened self-harm if I ever left. When I couldn't deal with her anymore, I kicked her ass to the curb.

As I pulled into the driveway, I shook my head, trying to dispel the unpleasant memories of the bullet I'd dodged. I was with Kai Jae now, and things were different. She was kind, supportive, and drama-free. More than that, she was sane and encouraging, not to mention talented. She understood my hectic schedule because hers was just as crazy, and neither of us never made the other feel guilty about our working hours. That was a stark contrast to the constant emotional rollercoaster I had ridden with Summer.

I parked the car and headed inside, feeling a sense of relief as I walked through the door. Kai Jae was in the kitchen, preparing a late dinner. She looked up and smiled when I entered, her warm, brown eyes filled with genuine happiness to see me.

"Hey, babe. How was your day?" she asked as she walked over to kiss me softly.

She was wearing booty shorts and a white tank-top. Her skin was soft and shiny. I grabbed her ass as I kissed her back. She giggled immediately, and I knew what that meant.

Without another word, I carried her from the foyer to her bedroom and laid her down on her neatly made bed. She watched me, her eyes not straying a second as I gently peeled the skimpy clothes off her body. She moaned as the chilly air hit her vagina. I spread her legs and arms as wide as I could and handcuffed her to the headboard. She looked up at me, thrusting her hips upward.

"You wet for me, sweetness?" I asked.

She nodded.

I used my fingers to part her vagina lips, loving how quickly my fingers got coated with her juices. "All this for me, baby?" I asked.

She continued to moan as I lifted my fingers to my mouth and sucked her off of them one by one. She kept her eyes on me the entire time.

I crouched down and gave her clit a slow, torturous lick, pulling a loud gasp out of her. I thrusted my tongue slowly into her vagina and used my thumb to gently flick her clit, and she moaned even more loudly, wriggling on the bed with pleasure.

"Oh, Spex," Kai Jae purred, struggling to get my name out.

I didn't stop until I felt her legs shaking. Then, I suddenly stood. She whimpered at the loss of contact. I parted her lips with my finger once more and thrusted with no hesitation. Kai Jae screamed. I worked my fingers inside of her while I heard the sound of her vagina squishing around.

"You are so fucking wet for me. Are you gonna cum all over my fingers," I asked, excited.

"Spex!"

I kept thrusting my fingers in and out of her and squeezing her boobs. I pulled at her nipples, loving how they hardened into little pebbles the moment I touched them. I was so painfully hard, my erection straining against my pants. I pulled them off and lined my dick up with her pussy. She bit her lips and tried to look at me, so I rubbed it on her wet clit to make her shiver. I continued doing that, coating the head of my dick with her wetness. Then, just as I was about to slam into her, my phone rang.

I ignored the call and gently pushed into her anyway. I kissed her as I repeatedly pounded into her. "Take it all," I said as my thrusts became harder, our moans louder and louder.

My phone kept ringing, but we were both too loud for either of us to really hear it, our bodies tangled in a sweaty mess.

After a while, I heard Kai Jae mumble, "You should get that. It might be important."

I shook my head and held her hips, desperate to keep her in place while I made love to her. She was wet, tight, and feeling exceptionally good.

"Check it, Spex," she said again.

I sighed in frustration, almost ready to climax and explode inside her, but her nagging for me to pick up my call stole the sensation away.

"Who is it?" Kai Jae asked.

"Unknown number," I answered, then showed her the screen.

I tried to send the call to voicemail, but it rang again.

This time, more frustrated then ever I answered it. "Yes?" I said, pissed at the caller and at Kai Jae for making me answer it.

"Why did you block me, Spex?" Summer said in my ear.

"Spex, who is it?" Kai asked.

Oh, I am fucked, I thought, *so very fucked, right in the middle of fucking. Nice.*

Chapter 3

KAI JAE

"Red?" Spex said into his phone.

I had never seen him look so panicked. "Red?" I asked. "Who's Red?" I tried to stand up, my thighs still trembling from our interrupted passion. I had to set my sexual frustration aside for a bit.

"It was Summer," he said, after he abruptly ended the call.

"Summer? Huh? Am I supposed to know who the fuck this Summer is? I thought you said Red."

"Uh, we used to date?" he said with a weird shrug, putting the final nail in my arousal.

"Is that a question or statement? Dude," I said, wondering why I felt so annoyed.

"Summer—er, Red and I used to date, but it ended a long time ago. I promise."

"Then why is this Red Summer calling you now?"

"I don't know. She's trouble, and I want nothing to do with her. That's why I hung up," he said.

"M-hmmm." I mumbled something unintelligible under my breath and started to put my clothes back on.

"Are you leaving?" Spex had the audacity to ask.

"I am."

"Where are you going, Kai?"

"Away from you," I sassed. I then hurried out of the bedroom and left, slamming the front door behind me, bothered by the call from his ex.

In an effort to cool off, I took a walk around the block, but it didn't help much. *Why does he call her Red? I thought. He still has the nerve to use her nickname? What the...* I tried not to think of all the worst-case scenarios, but it was totally driving me nuts.

I quickened my pace, eager to return and resolve the tension between us. Spex and I had a good thing going, and I wasn't about to let some ghosted troublemaker from his past ruin that. The city lights flickered around me, and I took a deep breath, trying to let go of my anger and hurt. By the time I reached the apartment, I felt a bit more composed, ready to face whatever conversation awaited me. I only hoped Spex would be honest with me, as we'd both promised to do. "No more secrets, no more lies," I whispered, remembering the oath we'd taken.

I pushed open the door and was surprised to be greeted by a warm, inviting aroma.

Spex was in the kitchen, moving around with a sense of purpose, trying to finish the meal I had started earlier. He glanced up as I entered, with a tentative smile on his face. "Hey, Kai Jae," he said softly. "I'm making dinner, pasta carbonara."

I couldn't help but smile, despite everything. "You didn't have to," I said, my voice gentler than I intended. "Besides, that's some white people shit."

"I know, but I wanted to," he said as he set a plate down. "I also want to apologize for earlier."

I walked over to the island and sat on one of the stools. "It wasn't your fault, Spex. It was just... Well, hearing you speak to another woman just threw me."

He nodded in understanding. "I get it, but I want to explain. Summer is... Well, the nicest way I know to put it is that she's complicated. Our relationship was a rollercoaster, to say the least."

The bacon-scented steam rose from the plate in delicate swirls. I took a bite, savoring the familiar comfort of the dish. "Tell me about her," I said, after a moment. "I want to understand, Spex."

Spex sighed and sat down across from me, his expression thoughtful. "We were together for about two years. It was intense from the start. She was passionate but also unpredictable. We had great times, but the bad times were really bad." He paused to gather his thoughts, then continued, "Summer's the jealous type, often without reason. One night, she accused me of flirting with another woman at a party, even though I didn't, she threw a drink in my face in front of everyone. It was humiliating."

I winced, imagining the scene. "That sounds awful."

"It was," he said, "but that wasn't the worst of it. She went through my phone once while I was asleep, convinced I was hiding something. She found a message from a female colleague and blew it out of proportion. The argument that followed was one of the worst we ever had."

I reached out and took his hand, desiring to offer some comfort. "That must have been really tough for you."

"It was," he admitted, "but I stupidly stayed with her."

"Why?"

"Because I thought things would get better. Sadly, they didn't. The final straw was when she borrowed my car without asking and returned it with a huge dent. She claimed it wasn't her fault, but I knew she wasn't being honest."

"Ah," I said.

"Get this. Red, er…Summer got angry when I told her I wanted to break it off, so, to pay me back, she openly had sex with one of our mutual friends. She even sent me a video of it, just to get at me."

I resisted the urge to ask if it really made him angry or if he was kind of turned on by it, because I wasn't so sure if I'd like the answer I would get. I put that thought out of my head and asked, in as understanding a tone as I could muster, "Why do you think she called tonight?"

Spex shrugged. "I have no idea. We haven't spoken in years. Maybe she's feeling nostalgic. Of course, with her, I wouldn't be surprised to find out she just wants to stir things up. Either way, it's long over between us. I'm with you now, Kai Jae. You are more than enough for me, babe, way more than I deserve."

I squeezed his hand. "I'm sorry I got so upset. It just caught me off guard."

"I get it," he said, his eyes sincere. "I would have felt the same way if the roles were reversed, but I promise that Summer is far in the past. I'm focused on us now."

I leaned across the table and kissed him, a gentle promise of forgiveness and understanding. "Thank you for explaining," I said. "It helps to know the whole story."

We finished the delicious dinner, and the tension slowly melted away. Afterward, we curled up on the couch and talked about lighter things, till I began to believe Summer wasn't such a big deal after all.

***

The next morning, I opened my eyes and bolted upright in bed, invigorated with a sense of purpose. I had an appointment with Jamal, and Lorenzo had booked me with a few new music producers to work with on my sophomore album. Jamal had sent us the beat, and Juniper and I had co-written a song for it. We planned to do the track and send it to Missy Elliot to see if she would collaborate with me. I was excited about it and eager to see what we could create together.

After a quick breakfast with Spex, I got dressed and headed out, feeling optimistic about the day ahead. When I arrived at Jamal's studio, the place was a hive of activity, alive and oozing with creativity, with artists and producers working in every corner.

Jamal was in the control room, adjusting levels on a mixing board. "Hey, Kai Jae," my friend said, looking up with a smile. "Glad you made it. Ready to lay down some tracks?"

"You know it," I replied, feeling a familiar rush of excitement. Music was my passion, and working with Jamal always brought out the best in me.

We spent the next hour going over the beat, vocal production, and melodies. Jamal was a genius, the best at what he did, and I knew we'd craft something special together. The synergy between us was palpable, each idea sparking another, ultimately creating a sound that felt both fresh and familiar.

Just as we were about to record a rough demo, the door to the studio opened. A woman whooshed in with long, red goddess locks that cascaded down her back. She was about five-two, with an hourglass figure that instantly had all the males in the studio ogling her. Her bright red lipstick was as striking as her confident, almost confrontational demeanor. "Hey, Jamal," she said, her voice cutting through all the commotion in the room. "Got that beat ready for me yet?"

Jamal was momentarily flustered before he finally stuttered, "Uh, s-sorry, Summer. I didn't realize you'd be here today."

Summer? The Summer? My heart sank as I realized who she was, the self-proclaimed artist formerly known as Red, the woman who had called Spex the night before, throwing a wrench into our evening. I watched as she sashayed over, her eyes scanning the room until they landed on me.

"And who do we have here?" she asked, a smirk playing on her lips. She then walked up to me and, without warning, stuck her red nails out at me and began toying with my weave. "Tell me, when did Spex start settling for fake bitches like you?" Look at this janky-ass weave." She laughed in a most sinister way. "Oh, well. You know what they say. When all else fails, lower your expectations. I guess Spex had to do that after he lost me."

Spex had warned me that she was crazy, but I was the one who felt like a psycho. Somehow, I resisted the urge to smack her. I could feel the anger boiling inside me, but I forced myself to stay calm. "I'm Kai Jae," I said evenly, "but I think you already know that. Who might you be?"

She laughed again, a sound that grated on my nerves. "Oh, you don't know? I'm Summer. Spex's ex, the one who clearly knows how to get under his skin…and yours."

Jamal stepped in to try to defuse the tension. "Summer, let's keep it professional, okay? We're all here to work."

"Of course," Summer said, keeping her poisonous glare on me, her tone dripping with sarcasm. Finally, she turned to Jamal. "So, about that beat…"

Jamal hesitated and glanced at me. "Summer, the beat was sent to Kai Jae first. We're in the middle of working on it."

"Well, *I* paid for it," Summer said, crossing her arms. "Therefore, it's mine, Jamal?"

"She's right," Jamal said, wearing a pained expression. "Summer paid for this beat up front. I'm sorry, but I have to honor that. I'll get with Lorenzo and let him know she's here for what she paid for."

I felt like I had been punched in the gut. All my excitement about the project evaporated in an instant. I didn't trust the words that might come out of my mouth, so I just nodded and began to gather my things. When I felt up to it, I blurted, "It's fine. I'll find another beat."

Summer smirked as I walked past her, but I refused to give her the satisfaction of a reaction. I drove home, gripping the steering wheel tightly, my mind racing with anger and frustration. Not only had she interrupted my intimate moments with Spex, but now, she had also interfered with my work. I was most passionate about my lover and my music, and it felt like this ex of Spex's was trying to blow that all up, to sabotage me at every turn.

When I got home, I found Spex in the living room, listening to music and jotting down notes. He looked up as I walked in, and he immediately sensed something was wrong. Obviously, he had no idea the witch was back in town.

"Baby, what happened?" he asked, concern etched on his face.

"Summer happened," I replied as I angrily threw my bag onto the couch. "She showed up at Jamal's studio and claimed the beat we were working on. Apparently, she paid for it, so Jamal had to give it to her. Why didn't you tell me she's a singer?" I asked, irritated.

Spex frowned, stood, and walked over to me. "She's really starting to piss me off," he said, his voice low and dangerous. "I'm sorry, Kai Jae. I had no idea she'd pull something like this. She's not a singer, not in any way, shape or form. She's nothing more than a wannabe rapper."

"It's not your fault," I said, though my anger was still simmering, "but it does feel like she's trying to undermine me in every way possible. You were right about her being jealous. I'm sure the only reason she's making a comeback in our world is because she saw that Instagram post of the two of us, from Grammy night. We both agreed not to share too much on social media. Summer or Red or whoever this bitch wannabe is... She's the reason I should have kept it all private," I said, frustrated. "I never should have posted that picture."

"Let's sit down and talk about this," Spex suggested, guiding me to the couch. "We need to figure out a way to deal with her."

"We? Oh, we French now. *Oui-oui,* my ass! Spex, she's your problem, and you better put Miss Little Red Riding Hood Bitch on a leash, or I'm gonna beat her ass. I'm from D-town. Don't let all the awards fool you."

"Baby, please," Spex said, looking at me with some level of surprise, since I seldom allowed him to see the Detroit in me.

"I need a nap," I said, "and I'd like it very much if I am not interrupted."

As soon as I lay down, Spex's phone started buzzing continuously. Each notification felt like a jab, a reminder of the tension Summer had hurled into our lives. I turned over in bed, trying to block out the noise, but it was relentless. Finally, I heard Spex get up and head into the shower. The sound of running water running offered a momentary reprieve from the buzzing phone, but the notifications continued their relentless assault.

With a sigh, I got up and walked into the living room, determined to silence the thing. As I approached, the screen lit up with a new message. My heart sank when I literally saw "Red." *I thought he said he blocked her.* Without thinking, I picked up the phone and unlocked it, only to find that Summer's messages filled the screen, a series of increasingly insistent requests:

"Red: Hey, Spex, we need to talk."

"Red: Can we meet up tonight?"

"Red: It's important. I promise I won't take much of your time."

"Red: Just one meeting. Please?"

My hands began to tremble. *What does she want? Why is she so desperate to meet with him?* The rational part of me knew to put the phone down and wait for Spex to come out of the shower, but my emotions and doubts wouldn't allow it. When another message came through, I couldn't help but read it: "Red: I know you're with her, but we have unfinished business. Just one last conversation. That's all I'm asking."

The anger I had felt earlier came rushing back, more intense than before. *Unfinished business? What could possibly be so important that she needs to interfere with our lives again?* I took a deep breath, trying to calm myself, but the fury was too much. I quickly dropped the phone.

I heard the water stop, and a moment later, Spex emerged from the bathroom with a towel wrapped.

"Going somewhere?" I asked, feigning innocence.

"Yeah, I need to meet Jahi. He wants to speak to me about that track," Spex said, and all promises of no secrets between us just flew out the window.

Damn you, Spex. You just lied to me...again.

ACKNOWLEDGMENTS

This sequel has been a joyous journey, and I am deeply grateful to everyone who has followed me from the beginning. Your support has been instrumental in shaping who I am today. This past year has been a whirlwind, full of lessons about family, friendship, heartache, and the importance of prioritizing my mental health. Learning to let go of relationships and friendships that did not bring balance to my life has allowed me to focus and concentrate on what truly matters. Through it all, God has guided me, showing me what truly matters and granting me a sense of peace. I am thankful for the imagination He has blessed me with, allowing me to bring this story to life.

A special thank you to my other half, Marquis, for always believing in me and supporting me through every late-night writing session (even when I'm keeping you awake with the lamp on at midnight, writing). Your unwavering support and invaluable advice have been crucial in helping me achieve this next chapter, and I truly love you.

To my boys, thank you for growing into the incredible men you are. Even though you might not be reading my books, your presence and growth mean the world to me.

I want to thank my mom and my beautiful family, who are spread out all over. You all absolutely mean the world to me. Your love and support have been the foundation of my journey and strength.

I also want to extend my heartfelt gratitude to my team: Thank you to my editor, Autumn Cooley, for always refining my work with precision and care; to my beta reader, Shalonda "Shay" Cravins, for your insightful feedback; and to my cover designer, Kasper Harris of Gifft Grafix, for creating a cover that captures the essence of this story. Your contributions have been invaluable.

A special shoutout to the amazing actress Arischa Conner-Frierson. Your advice, friendship, and the joy you bring through our daily video calls have been a beacon of light in my life. You never fail to brighten my days.

To my best friend, Keesha Rainey, thank you for being a sounding board for my ideas and troubles without judgment. Your support means the world to me.

I also want to thank my friend Melodie Lewis for being the sweetest person alive and a constant beacon of light, and my dear soror and friend Valerie Baston for your love and friendship.

But most importantly, to all my Midnight Storm fans! Without you all, I would not be who I am today. Thank you again for reading my stories and for your unwavering support.

There are many more people I wish I could thank individually. If I've missed anyone, please accept my sincere apologies, and know that your impact has not gone unnoticed.

Thank you all for being a part of this incredible journey, and Welcome To The Storm!

ABOUT THE AUTHOR

Kebra Moore, known by her pen name Midnight Storm, is an acclaimed American novelist hailing from Beaufort, South Carolina. A proud alumna of Claflin University in Orangeburg, South Carolina, she now resides in Texas. Moore is a #1 best-selling Amazon author, celebrated for her works such as Love, Lies & Music and Short Tropical Storm Stories. She is also the co-founder of the "Tropical Storm Collection" lip line and MOKEB LLC. Additionally, she owns Welcome To The Storm Publishing, through which she continues to expand her literary and entrepreneurial reach.

Moore's passion for storytelling began when she wrote short stories for her spouse during his deployment in Iraq. Her husband's encouragement inspired her to continue developing her craft, and over the years, she honed her talent, eventually creating her first full-length novel.

Kebra describes her novels as "sensual, romantic comedies that feature multicultural characters unafraid to release their inhibitions and discover love in its purest form." Alongside her writing, she is passionate about singing, reading, and composing music, enriching her creative spirit.

A dedicated member of Delta Sigma Theta Sorority, Incorporated, Moore is also a published author featured in Delta Authors Directory Volume 10. Beyond her literary achievements, she is a philanthropist and disability activist, committed to making a positive impact. As a devoted wife of over 24 years and mother of two sons, Kebra's journey in writing is just beginning, with many more captivating stories and endeavors to come. Stay tuned for the next chapter in her inspiring career!

Made in the USA
Middletown, DE
02 November 2024